FORTUNE'S BRIDES BOOK THREE

Never Envy an Earl

REGINA SCOTT

To those without home or country,
that you may find welcome and rest, and to
the Lord, who offers us all a home

CHAPTER ONE

Surrey, England, April 1812

How far did she have to go to be safe?

Yvette de Maupassant peered out the window of the coach her friend Sir Harold Orwell had loaned her and saw nothing but wilderness. Well, perhaps wilderness was too strong a word for the sweeping fields and patches of woods, bright with the glory of spring. But after spending the last ten years stealing secrets from Napoleon and his sycophants and traveling among the French elite, the Surrey countryside seemed as foreign as Africa.

"And you had no one in London you could trust?" she asked her companion.

Meredith Thorn smiled from her side of the coach. She would have been at home among French society. Her lustrous black hair was properly confined under a broad-brimmed velvet hat of a lavender that matched her eyes. The ostrich plume that curled down one cheek had been teasing her pet Fortune since they'd left London four hours ago. Yvette had seen the grey cat eyeing the thing from time to time on her perch on the bench beside her mistress. She'd only batted at it three times. Such restraint!

"London was unsuitable," Meredith said, wiggling her gloved fingers against her purple poplin skirt as if to direct Fortune's copper-colored eyes away from the tantalizing feather. "Too many people. We were lucky to spirit you into the War Office for your meeting and out again with no one being the wiser. Your enemies will not think to look for you at Carrolton Park."

"Because no one can find it," Yvette said, but she smiled as Fortune pounced toward her mistress' fingers, missing them by moments as Meredith pulled away.

Yvette scratched the plush seat, and Fortune's ears pricked, gaze narrowing in on the movement. Ah, to have such a life, with no more worries than where to play next. Her life had once been as pleasant, though it had changed forever the day the mob had come for her family.

Now the long hair her maid had faithfully brushed each night was cut short in curls about her head like a strawberry blond cap. It had been easier to care for when her cousin had insisted she serve as the lowliest chore girl in his home. In defiance, she had not changed it when Napoleon had demanded that she be brought to his court instead to serve his wife. How her cousin had preened that one of his family had been close to the Empress. As if she would ever have claimed her cousin Claude as family.

The coachman turned off the main road onto a graveled track that plunged deeper into the wood. The shadows lengthened this late in the day, multiplied until she felt them reaching into the coach with greedy fingers. She shivered and touched her wrist, where her dagger and sheath were strapped inside her sleeve.

What, was this fear? She had played the game of espionage, discovering secrets and sending them to Harry in England. She had matched wits with men on both sides of the Channel. She had been willing to risk her life to see the Corsican Monster brought down, her hated cousin humbled. The last time she'd known fear was when she'd been forced to live with him after Empress Josephine had left the court. Claude could not touch her here. If she did not fear him, she should not fear this earl she was about to meet or his dismal little park. But she wasn't about to trust him either. Time had taught her she had only herself to rely on.

The forest parted then to reveal a wide plain. Sunlight sparkled on a winding stream. Roan deer bowed low, as if offering homage to the emerald lawn. They glanced up complacently at the passing carriage, as if knowing themselves secure in this place. She could scarcely look away.

The lane led through iron gates fashioned to resemble ivy entwining around the letter C up over the stream and onto an area of golden gravel. A regal multistoried home with turrets at each corner sat serenely among the simplicity, like a castle in a child's storybook.

She blinked and turned to Meredith. "This is Carrolton Park?"

Meredith smiled, gathering Fortune in her arms as the carriage slowed. "It is indeed. I understand the current earl helped redesign it when he ascended to the title five years ago. I always thought he had good taste."

"I concur." The house was shaped like a U, with the open end facing the drive and spanned by a white marble colonnade. The warm stone of the rest of the building made the entrance look like a pearl in a gold setting.

Two footmen in blue livery hastened down the steps to help with the coach. Following them with a statelier tread was a tall, wide-shouldered butler. Black hair slicked back, he looked down his hawk-like nose at the coach, inclining his head as the footman handed down first Meredith and Fortune, then Yvette.

"Miss Thorn," he said, correctly divining that she was the leader. "Welcome to Carrolton Park. His lordship asked that you be brought to him at your earliest convenience. Would you care to refresh yourself first?"

He spared Yvette a glance, but his gaze was more kind than condemning. After all, he thought he was looking at Lady Carrolton's new companion, not the celebrated beauty who had once been the daughter of a *comte* herself.

She had tried to look the part of a poor relation. So much of playing a role depended on attitude and clothing. She had borrowed a plain navy gown from her friend Patience Ramsey, who was engaged to dear Harry. Miss Lydia Villers, whom she had recently met at Harry's Easter house party, had been persuaded to offer a straw bonnet, though, like Patience, she did not know exactly where Yvette would be hiding.

How Patience would laugh when she learned Yvette was to take up her previous position in this very house. Yvette hid her smile and kept her gaze respectfully down as she and Meredith followed the butler toward the house.

"I think it would be best if we speak to the earl first," Meredith was saying as they crossed the flagstone-floored courtyard behind the columns. Windows on all three sides regarded them with curious eyes.

"Very good, madam," the butler said, holding the double doors open for them.

They passed into a wide entry hall, and Yvette's smile broadened. Meredith had said the earl had good taste. She was wrong. If he had had any hand in the interior design, he had exceptional taste and an eye for beauty. The walls were the color of the mist over the Channel, the floor like the waves, patterned in white marble and a stone through which blue and purple swirled, much like Meredith's eyes.

Alcoves along the walls held Grecian statues, and fluted columns held up the entry to the stairway at the back, where the banisters and balustrades were made from silver-veined marble, the walls covered in carved reliefs of forests, bringing the setting inside.

The butler crossed to the door leading to what must be the north wing of the house and held it open for them. With a pang of regret, she turned away from the beauty. But the corridor proved equally wondrous. Light from the tall windows on one side made the tapestries on the other side glow like rubies, emeralds, and sapphires. Polished tables held Chinese vases and bronze sculptures. She recognized the prized Sevres porcelain in a bowl holding crimson roses. Napoleon would not be pleased to know his private pattern had been smuggled to England.

And who exactly had done the smuggling? Perhaps Harry, but surely not the earl!

Even more curious to meet the fellow, she followed the butler through the closest darkly paneled door into a withdrawing room. Everything glittered, for the bronze-on-gold pattern of the wallcoverings to the tall multi-armed standing candelabra to the gold filigree around the door and the fanciful gilt edging and button tufting on the armchairs and settee.

The man moving toward them in his simple coat and trousers did not seem to belong.

A man? No, surely a giant, one of the legends of this land. Had she stepped close enough, her nose would have bumped his breastbone. Instead, she could only gaze in surprise. The tweed coat stretched across powerful shoulders, and the tan chamois trousers encased legs worthy of the statues she'd just passed. Top it all off with a square jaw, warm brown eyes, and raven hair, and he was as impressive a specimen of a male as his house was a home.

He offered them both a bow. "Ladies. Welcome to Carrolton Park. I am Lord Carrolton, and I am delighted to be of service." He nodded to his butler. "Marbury, will you let my mother know that we will be up shortly?"

"Of course." With a dip of his head, the butler turned and saw himself out.

"Please, sit down," the earl said, striding back to the sofa near the fire. The deep voice made the request sound more like a command. "You must be tired from your travels, but I thought we should be clear on our course of action first."

What, did he think they were planning a campaign?

After so many years of working alone, daring to trust no one with her secrets, she found his assumption of collusion amusing. Yvette took a seat beside Meredith on the sofa, and the earl sat opposite on a dainty chair she could not credit would hold him.

"Excellent," Meredith said, settling back with Fortune cuddled close. "You received word from London, then?"

He nodded, leaning forward until his elbows rested on his thighs, black boots pressed deep in the ruby- and gold-patterned carpet. "I was informed that Miss de Maupassant has provided critical information to support England in its efforts against the French tyrant. Her efforts have put her life in danger. My task is to hide her until someone from the War Office comes for her." His lips turned up in obvious distaste. "Is it necessary that she pretends to be no more than a servant?"

Yvette spread her hands. "I am a servant, my lord. My family was guillotined, our lands and titles stripped. I now serve a noble cause, to stop this war and restore sanity to France."

He had paled at the mention of the guillotine. Most men did. Yet he could not possibly understand the reality of it, the horror, the shouts, the dull thunk as the blade came down. Here he sat, in his beautiful home, with nothing and no one to trouble him. She envied him that.

"It is best that no one knows her true identity," Meredith told him. "As I'm sure Lord Hastings told you, we've had some trouble already."

He nodded. "The spy Sir Harry caught. Hastings seems to think more are coming."

One more, if the boasts of the spy could be believed. His superior would be coming to finish the job. This new threat would meet the same fate as his predecessor: capture and imprisonment. There were too many in England waiting for him, her included.

"We cannot be certain," Meredith said to the earl. "But

make no mistake. Yvette de Maupassant is guilty of treason to the Emperor. The penalty is death. Therefore, she must disappear. I give you Miss French, your mother's new companion."

Yvette pasted on a happy smile, sat up tall, and fluttered her lashes for good measure.

The earl frowned, dark brows lowering until he looked rather formidable. Was subterfuge below him? Would he refuse her refuge after all? Had she come all this way for nothing?

Gregory, Earl of Carrolton, didn't like dissembling. It seemed cowardly, disrespectful. And he'd never been terribly good at it. His square-jawed face was too open, betraying his least emotions. The few times he'd shaded the truth as a child, usually to soften the blow of bad news, his tutors or his father had caught him immediately. Now the War Office wanted him to lie to his mother, his sister, and his staff. He couldn't help his qualms.

"I cannot stress the importance of keeping Mademoiselle de Maupassant safe," Lord Hastings had written. The wily marquis led an elite band of aristocratic intelligence agents, each hand-picked, their identities only hinted at on the *ton*. Together, they had uncovered secrets, brought down spies, and saved England from disaster time and again. That Hastings was asking Gregory to undertake even a tangential role in this work was a great honor. Gregory had been chafing at his inability to help with the war. Here was his chance to be of worth.

"Miss French," he acknowledged now, trying not to sound as doubtful as he felt about the new name. "And are you content in playing the role of companion?"

Once more she fluttered her golden lashes, blue eyes sparkling. That smile was all charm. "*Mais oui*. I assure you, it will be far easier than some roles I have undertaken."

Her lilting voice was confident, but she could not know his mother. The countess had run off three companions before Patience Ramsey had consented to stay for three years. Gregory suspected the good-natured blonde had remained because she had nowhere else to go. She had been a treasure, forever tending to his mother's many ills. But when she'd announced she'd found another position, he'd gladly let her leave. She deserved better than what they could give.

"If you have any trouble," he told Miss de Maupassant, "you must come to me."

Her smile tilted up, inviting him closer. "But of course, my dear earl."

He sat back in the chair, feeling his cheeks warm. He was never sure how to act around the fairer sex. Most of the ladies of his acquaintance acted as if they were fragile creatures. An ill-considered word, a firm glance, and they dissolved. The mincing manners employed by so many gentlemen on the *ton* seemed to please them, but the movements looked ridiculous on his larger frame. And the one time he had emboldened himself to propose, the lady had kindly let him know that he could never be more than a friend. No doubt he would have to marry one day to secure the line, but he was not looking forward to adding another lady to his already tempestuous household.

"You must treat her as you would any other staff member," Miss Thorn cautioned him, gaze pinning him in place. She had the purple-blue eyes of *Lavendula*, or at least that was how it seemed to his befuddled brain.

"Ah, but I am to be a companion," Miss de Maupassant said. "That is a special sort of staff, *non?*"

Gregory shook himself. "Yes. You'll keep my mother company from the time she wakes until the time she retires. I believe Miss Ramsey read to her, sang songs to brighten her day."

"How sweet," the Frenchwoman said.

That face was equally sweet, her bonnet and gown more practical than pretty, yet he struggled to see her being servile.

"Miss Ramsey took dinner with the family and attended church services and social gatherings with my mother as well," he continued.

"We may want to forego social engagements for the time being," Miss Thorn said, hand stroking the cat in her lap. The creature regarded Gregory with copper-colored eyes, tail twitching, and he sat straighter.

What was wrong with him? Was he seeking the cat's approval now? He could fell an opponent in the boxing square with one blow of his fist, slice a sapling in half with one swing of his cutlass, urge his horse over gate and gulley. He had spoken before Parliament, addressed His Highness, the Prince Regent. Why did one glance from a lady, even a feline one, make him want to run back to his greenhouse and hide among the plants?

"I'll do whatever is needed to keep Miss...French safe," he assured them, palms starting to sweat.

"Excellent," Miss Thorn pronounced. She stopped her hand as she gazed down at her pet.

The cat rose and stretched high on its paws, setting the lamplight to flashing on the white blaze that ran down her chest like a stream. She stepped off her mistress' lap onto the damask of sofa's upholstery.

"This is Fortune," Miss Thorn informed him. "Fortune, meet Lord Carrolton."

She was introducing him to her cat? How was he to react to that?

As if she'd spotted a plump mouse, Fortune leaped across the space between them and landed on his thigh. He held himself still.

Fortune eyed him a moment, then rubbed her head against the tweed of his coat.

Miss de Maupassant beamed. "She likes you."

"I suspect she likes everyone," he demurred, afraid to touch the lovely creature lest he inadvertently harm her.

"No, indeed," Miss Thorn assured him. "Fortune is quite refined in her opinions. You may pet her."

It seemed this was an honor too. Gingerly, Gregory stroked his hand down the silky fur. Fortune turned her head from side to side, and he obligingly rubbed behind each ear. Well, who would have thought?

Miss Thorn's smile spread. "It appears my work here is done."

Miss de Maupassant leaned forward, cocking her head to gaze at him out of the corners of her eyes. "But you will allow Meredith and Fortune to spend the night, *oui*? They have traveled far the last few days with me."

"Of course," he said. "And I hope you'll join us for dinner as well, Miss Thorn. I can have someone watch Fortune."

The cat glanced up at him as if she recognized her name, but her gaze seemed to chide him.

"My mother has been unwell," he said. Was he telling the cat or Miss Thorn? "The doctor advises us to keep her away from any sort of animal."

Fortune pulled back from him, hopped from his lap, and stalked off across the carpet, tail in the air. Had he offended her?

Miss Thorn inclined her head. "I understand."

That made one of them. "We keep country hours," he explained. "No need to dress. Say six?"

"Perfect." She raised her head to keep an eye on her pet, who seemed to be inspecting the standing candelabra.

Miss de Maupassant rose, forcing Gregory to his feet. "Thank you for your explanations and your hospitality, my lord. And now, you must introduce me to your mother. It has been a long day, and I have only so much charm to spare."

He nodded, but he was certain the nearly christened

Miss French was wrong. She had entirely too much charm. He felt it tugging at him even now. Would his mother take to it, or was this ruse doomed from the start?

CHAPTER TWO

In the end, Marbury the butler saw Yvette upstairs to meet the earl's mother. She understood the need. It furthered the fiction that she was a paid companion and not someone approaching the lady's equal. She just wasn't sure why she was disappointed the earl did not escort her himself.

He had walked her to the door of the golden sitting room. "If you need anything," he'd repeated, "you must let me know."

She'd offered him a smile. "I can take care of myself, my lord. You need have no concerns."

Miss Thorn had nodded agreement, while Fortune hurried to the door as if determined to leave with Yvette.

She could almost wish for the cat's company as she joined the butler now. That Mr. Marbury also had concerns was evident by the way his brows came down over his sharp nose.

"Did his lordship explain your duties?" he asked as they climbed the stairs past the sculpted stone forests.

"I am to attend to her ladyship from breakfast to bedtime," Yvette replied, lifting her skirts as they came out onto the navy carpet that ran down the upper corridor of the north wing.

"More than that," he assured her. "Lady Carrolton relies on her companion for advice on dressing, care for minor medical issues, and entertainment."

"*Bon*," Yvette said, gaze on the serene landscapes they were passing on the blue-silk-hung corridor. "I will make her happy."

Marbury stopped before a paneled door. "I am sure you will do your best, but I think you should know, Miss French, that the countess is rarely happy. I would not want you to set your expectations too high." His kind smile softened the words. "Yours is the most difficult position in the household. I will help you any way I can. I will introduce you to her ladyship now and return later to see how you're getting on. Good luck." Squaring his shoulders, he knocked on the door.

A frail voice, barely audible through the wood, said, "Come in."

Mr. Marbury gave Yvette an encouraging smile before making his face impassive and opening the door.

This room was as beautiful as the others, but darker, in part because the gold velvet drapes along one wall were drawn. A tall dresser, lacquered in the black and gold of the Chinese style, stood opposite a mirrored dressing table to match, with a handsome walnut secretary on the left. Bright marigolds clustered in a gold and blue Chinese vase on the mantle. Directly ahead was a great bed, the half canopy and hangings patterned with white lilies on a black background, gold thread picking out the center of each flower.

Pressed up against the headboard, fluffy pillows behind and around her, sat a woman as narrow as her son was broad. Even though it was still day, she wore a nightcap tied with ribbon and edged with lace and a cream-colored jacket embroidered all over with daisies, the dainty design at odds with her tight lips and stern expression.

"Your ladyship," Marbury intoned, "may I present your new companion, Miss French."

Yvette dipped a curtsey, rising in time to see the countess

wrinkle her long nose.

"French?" she complained in a nasal voice. "What sort of name is that? I warn you, girl, I won't stand for you putting on airs."

Well! Yvette glanced at Marbury for any sense as to how she was expected to respond. He tilted his head toward the bed. Yvette moved closer.

The lady had a certain elegance to her, features finely drawn, silver hair tightly curled around her pale face under the cap. She held herself so high she appeared to be supporting the pillows and not the other way around.

"I cannot help what I am called," Yvette said. "No more than you can help being a countess. But if my last name displeases you, you may call me by my first, Yvette."

The countess didn't respond to that offer, turning instead to eye the butler. "Why haven't you taken her bonnet, Marbury? Do you expect she won't last long enough to make it worth your time?"

"Certainly not, your ladyship." Marbury moved closer, holding out his hand, and Yvette untied the bonnet and offered it to him.

"Short hair!" The countess glared at her. "That won't do at all."

"I shall do my best to grow it longer by morning," Yvette said.

The countess blinked, but Marbury turned away before anyone but Yvette saw his smile. He bowed himself out.

"Well, don't just stand there," Lady Carrolton said. "Come sit beside me so I don't have to raise my voice to speak to you. I have a delicate constitution."

Perhaps, but she certainly had more spirit than most. Yvette moved to where a finely molded black-lacquered harp-backed chair stood waiting beside the bed and sat. Hard and uncomfortable, but what else would it be for a companion?

"I have high expectations," Lady Carrolton informed

her as if she wouldn't have realized as much. "As my companion, you must be available whenever I need you."

"From breakfast to bed," Yvette agreed.

She frowned. "Who told you that nonsense? I have a number of conditions that must be tended morning and night." As if to prove it, she began coughing. Not genteel little puffs but great racking whoops that bent her at the waist. One clawed hand waved toward the dressing table.

Yvette rose and slapped her on the back.

She jerked upright, eyes wide. "You struck me!"

"A practical technique to remove obstructions from the throat and lungs," Yvette explained. "You have stopped coughing, I see, so it must have worked. Should you start coughing again, I will administer it anew."

Lady Carrolton wiggled her shoulders as if trying to determine the extent of her injuries. "There's no need for you to administer it ever again. I am under the care of a number of very fine physicians. You'll find all I need in that case on the dressing table."

Interesting. Yvette went to fetch the thing. Bound in crimson leather with a brass lock and handles, it weighed heavily in her arms as she carried it back to her chair and set it on her lap.

"Open it, open it," the countess said, as eagerly as a child expecting a present.

Yvette snapped it open. Inside in a neat arrangement were vials and jars and contraptions. She picked up one that resembled long tweezers. A hand-written label on the side proclaimed its purpose.

"Finger stretcher?" she asked.

Lady Carrolton wiggled her fingers. "For cramps."

Did she play the piano that she overworked her hands? Yvette could think of no other reason for a lady of the aristocracy to tax her fingers.

Yvette returned the device to the box and picked up a vial instead. "Eye drops," she read.

Lady Carrolton nodded, edging forward on the bed. "I have rheumy vision. And there are nose drops for congestion, pills to block a bilious liver, medication for stomach complaints and to hurry or slow the bowel, plaster for bunions, and cream for warts." She sighed wistfully. "I don't get warts very often."

"For which we should be thankful." Yvette closed the case and set it aside. "So, you wish me to dose you whenever needed."

"Day or night," Lady Carrolton insisted.

Yvette glanced around. "Night is difficult. Where would I sleep?"

She waved toward a door beside the wardrobe. "In my dressing room."

Frowning, Yvette rose once more and went to look.

The countess' dressing room was nearly the size of her spacious bedchamber, with pale blue walls and a polished wood floor. Another dressing table and a Pier glass mirror sat along one wall, with wardrobes and trunks lining the others. Shoved between two was a low cot, perhaps four feet long.

All at once she was back in France, a child still shaking from watching her family guillotined. Claude, hand on her shoulder, pushed her up the stairs, past the floor where he and his wife slept, past even the servants' quarters, to the attic of the house. In the light from the door loomed old furniture and discarded paintings, all of them unwanted, just like her.

"This is where you will sleep," he had informed her. "If you work hard, you may earn yourself a blanket, but I wouldn't expect it soon."

She shuddered at the memory, then turned and marched back to the bedchamber. "*Non.*"

Lady Carrolton stared at her. "No? What do you mean, no?"

"No, I will not sleep on the floor like your dog."

The countess raised her head. "It's a perfectly fine cot. My previous companion slept on it."

"And left you," Yvette reminded her. She started for the door, her thoughts chasing her.

"Where are you going?" Lady Carrolton demanded. "You can't leave!"

She couldn't, but the despot on the bed must never know that. "I merely wish to look," Yvette told her, peering out the door. There were entrances to any number of rooms along the corridor, but most were too far away for her to hear the countess' call. But what about that door directly opposite?

"What is that?" she asked, pointing.

Lady Carrolton tilted her head to see around her. "A guest bedchamber, rarely used. Marbury generally puts our guests in the south wing."

"*Bon.* I will take it."

"But you'll never hear me from there," Lady Carrolton protested.

"*Certainement,*" Yvette told her, turning. "We will find you a bell."

For the first time since Yvette had entered the room, the lady smiled. "A bell?"

"*Oui.* A hand bell. When you need me at night, you must ring it, and I will come."

"Do you promise?"

Once more the woman sounded wistful, almost fearful, like a child begging for comfort after a bad dream. She knew the feeling, the need to know someone who cared was close, would be there no matter what happened. Thanks to the Revolution, she had lost anyone who might have filled that need. What had brought this daughter of the English aristocracy to such a state? Yvette might never know, but she could not ignore the need now.

She returned to her new employer's side and lay her hand on the countess'. "I promise. So long as I am your companion, you need not worry. Now, where is your maid? We must get you dressed. We have much to do."

He ought to stay out of it. Yvette de Maupassant—better get used to calling her Miss French—had lived through the Terror. Surely she could handle his mother. Yet as Gregory attempted to review the reports his steward had provided about their various holdings, his thoughts kept going to what must be happening upstairs. Had Miss French agreed to all his mother's demands? He knew they were many. Miss Ramsey had intimated as much before she'd summarily quit to take a position helping Augusta Orwell, aunt of his friend Harry. His sister Lilith was nearly as demanding as his mother. Of course, his father had had high expectations as well, but Gregory had always been able to satisfy them.

Perhaps he should just check.

He left his study to climb to the upstairs corridor of the north wing, where he, his mother, and his sister had apartments. Hands in his coat pockets, he strode down the thick carpet, quiet all around him. Lilith had gone riding that afternoon, one of her few pleasures, but surely his mother had not decided to nap with a new companion starting work. Yet as he approached his mother's rooms, he detected a surprising amount of activity. Maids darted from the servants' stair carrying linens. Footmen balanced furniture. Marbury stood along one wall, arms crossed over his chest, supervising.

"Is there a problem?" Gregory asked as he approached the man.

The butler drew himself up, missing Gregory's height by a scant two inches. "No, my lord. Just preparing a room for Miss French."

Gregory frowned. "Is there a reason she cannot use Miss Ramsey's room?"

Marbury's face remained impassive, but he thought he heard remonstrance under the tone. "Miss Ramsey had no room, my lord. She slept on a cot in the countess' dressing room."

She had? Small wonder the woman had left.

"That narrow thing we installed for the maid when my mother had influenza four years ago?" Gregory asked. "It was meant as a temporary arrangement and only for naps."

"I remember," Marbury informed him. "The countess had other ideas."

And still had, apparently.

"No, no!" His mother's voice was particularly strident as it echoed out of the unused room across from hers. "I said yellow. That is nearly mustard. Must I do everything myself?"

Gregory ventured into the room. He'd worked with his interior designer to make each of the one hundred rooms in Carrolton Park unique. This one had been inspired by spring, with sunny yellow walls, bed hangings patterned in jonquils and tulips, with matching fabric on the curved back chairs. The cornice of the bed and above each doorway was crowned with a gilded sun, its rays beaming out.

Against all that cheer, his mother, dressed in one of the black, lace-encrusted gowns she favored, looked a bit like a raven. Beside her tall, elegant frame, Yvette de Maupassant resembled a china doll.

And that hair! Cut as short as that of the infamous Caro Lamb, it curled about her piquant face in wild abandon. He could imagine running his fingers through the locks, silk springing beneath his touch.

He shook away the thought. Harry's note, which had accompanied Lord Hastings', indicated Gregory's friend had rescued her from a prison house after her espionage had been discovered. For all Gregory knew, her captors had cut her hair to shame her. He should not find the look so appealing.

"Gregory!" His mother smiled at him, wrinkles crinkling around her pale eyes as she raised her ebony-headed cane. "You came to see me!"

She made it sound a rarity for all he tried to check on her at least once a day besides dinner when he was in residence.

"Mother," he said, going to kiss her cheek. "You look busy."

"Very," she assured him, waving away the cream-colored linens a maid offered. "The blue, I said. I was very specific. Why do you all fail to listen?"

"They are doing splendidly," Yvette corrected her. "See how nicely the blue complements the gold? And cream lace on the pillow cases—so inspired!"

The maid bobbed a curtsey, blushing at the praise.

He left his mother directing another servant in the making of the bed and drew Yvette aside.

"I must apologize," he murmured, feeling like a hulking brute beside her. "I didn't know Mother had subjected her previous companion to sleeping on a cot."

She waved her hand. "It was easily remedied."

The bustling about him did not look easy. And he could not like the way the room's layout was being changed before his eyes. That black walnut trunk with the battered sides threw off the entire scheme. He looked to Marbury, who immediately came to him.

"My lord?" he asked.

"There's a maple wardrobe in the north wing," Gregory told him. "Have two of the footmen bring it here and remove that walnut monstrosity."

He inclined his head. "At once, my lord."

Yvette chuckled, the sound tickling him. "Monstrosity, he says. I am fortunate to even possess that."

Gregory kept his chin up. "And while you are here I am determined that you will be surrounded by beauty, Miss...

French."

She laughed again. "You must practice, my lord. I am a poor companion, the lowly Miss French." She fluttered her lashes in his direction.

"Perhaps you should practice," he said with a smile. "You look and act nothing like a lowly companion."

She made a moue. "But I am doing my best."

"French!"

At his mother's demand, Yvette hurried away from him. The sunny room seemed to dim. Once more he shook himself. What, had he been flirting? He was surprised he even knew how. She made every thought, every act, seem natural.

His mother may have taken the lead in redecorating, but he was fairly sure there was only one leader in the room, and that was clearly Yvette. Somehow, he thought Carrolton Park would never be the same.

CHAPTER THREE

M eredith Thorn exited her room, Fortune in her arms. She would have been willing to leave her pet with a kind maid rather than to carry her down to dinner, but no maid, kind or otherwise, had appeared. Indeed, the south wing, in which she was housed, seemed to be empty of human habitation as she headed for the stairs. She had just reached the landing when a voice stopped her.

"You there. You must be the new companion."

Meredith turned to the woman approaching from the north wing. Her hair, pulled back from her sculpted face, was dark brown, sleek as hot chocolate, but her eyes were so pale a blue as to resemble glass. She was tall for a woman, certainly taller than Meredith, and her physique in the austere, brown matte satin dress could only be called Amazonian.

"Lady Lilith, I presume," Meredith said, inclining her head.

"You presume a great deal," the earl's sister said. "You will address me as *my lady* or *your ladyship*. And I don't know who allowed that creature in the house, but I will not have my mother exposed to it. If you have not found another home for it by dinner tomorrow, I will have Marbury dispose of it."

Fortune leaned so far back from the woman that the cat pressed herself into Meredith's chest. Meredith refused to lower her gaze, much less grovel, as the earl's sister no doubt intended.

"You are mistaken, Lady Lilith," she informed her. "I am not your mother's companion. I am an acquaintance of the Duke of Wey and Sir Harold Orwell, who requested that your brother provide hospitality as I traveled through the area. I escorted Miss French, your mother's new companion here. If my dear Fortune is unwelcome, I will report to your brother's friends that I had to find accommodation elsewhere."

The most Lady Lilith would offer by way of apology was a slight shifting of her feet, setting her skirts to swaying. "No need to concern His Grace or Sir Harold. If Gregory agreed to let you stay, who am I to question him?"

There was no *if*. Did she think Meredith was lying? Did strange women appear on the stairs on a regular basis claiming invitation?

"The cat," Lady Lilith continued as she started down the stairs, "must stay in the stables."

"So long as you have a guest room in the stables," Meredith said, following her.

Lady Lilith didn't answer, but Fortune hissed at her back.

She thought they might all meet in the golden withdrawing room where she'd first encountered the earl, but Lady Lilith moved unerringly to another room along that corridor. They certainly didn't stand on ceremony at Carrolton Park.

The dining room was as lavishly appointed—pale green walls setting off rosewood furnishings—as the rest of the house. The earl, his mother, and Yvette were already sitting at the long table as Lady Lilith and Meredith entered the room. The earl hastily rose, nearly knocking over the heavy high-backed chair.

"Miss Thorn, so glad you could join us," he said, indicating the chair on his left.

His sister glowered at Meredith as she passed to sit below

her.

Across from Meredith, Lady Carrolton perked up. "Ah, a guest! Why didn't you tell me, Gregory?"

"You were busy with Miss French," he said, returning to his seat as Meredith took hers. "Mother, this is Miss Thorn, a friend of Wey's and Sir Harry's. Miss French, this is my sister, Lilith."

His sister turned her glare his way. Meredith had wondered why the powerfully built Lord Carrolton wasn't more involved in the war effort like his friend Sir Harry. Very likely that open face, that guileless smile betrayed every emotion. He had no idea he'd just insulted his sister by introducing Yvette to her as if she were her equal. If they weren't careful, he'd give away the game. A companion must always be less.

Before she could steer the conversation into safer waters, Lady Carrolton glanced at Fortune and began sniffing. A moment later and she sneezed with such force that the candles flickered in their silver settings. Lady Lilith looked pointedly at Meredith, then at Yvette, who smiled politely.

Marbury, who had been standing along the wall, stepped forward. "If I may, Miss Thorn, we have a saucer of cream and some tidbits for our other guest in the kitchen. If I may?"

Meredith glanced down at Fortune, who raised her head to regard the butler, then stretched up her paws as if begging him to carry her. Marbury picked her up and took her off.

The countess, however, continued to sniff.

"The case," Lady Lilith snapped to Yvette. "Where have you put it?"

"*Mille excuses*, my lady," Yvette said. "I did not realize it must be carried everywhere. Do you wish me to fetch it from the room?"

Lord Carrolton straightened as if he'd go for it himself.

His mother saved him the trouble. "Handkerchief!" she

demanded between sneezes.

"Ah." Yvette produced a silken square and offered it to the lady, who seized it and pressed it to her nose.

Meredith was simply glad that the footmen began bringing in the meal then.

Yet as food and wine flowed, the only sounds were the chime of fine crystal and the scrape of silver on china. Yvette ate daintily, smile vague. She seemed to have entered into the role of companion, saying nothing until spoken to. In fact, no one said a great deal. Were they so comfortable in each other's company?

Or so uncomfortable?

As the group dug into the final course of strawberries and cream, Lady Carrolton raised her head to appeal to her son. "French says I must have a bell."

The earl frowned. "A bell?"

"A hand bell," Yvette qualified. "So she can summon me when needed."

He nodded, but his sister set down her silver fork.

"And why would my mother need to summon you?" she demanded. "You should be on duty at her side, not gallivanting about the house."

Yvette's smile remained in place. "Me, I do not gallivant, your ladyship. But I will have to sleep on occasion, and I would like the countess to be able to summon me without having to climb from her bed."

Lady Lilith didn't respond, but she picked up her fork and stabbed a plump strawberry.

Oh, but it was good this situation with Yvette was only temporary. Meredith's new vocation was to find suitable positions for gentlewomen fallen on hard times. She would never have placed a client in such a house. Lady Lilith's cruel comments and sour disposition reminded her too much of her former mistress, Lady Winhaven.

Meredith had never planned to go into service, much less as a companion to an angry old lady whose domineering ways had frightened off most of her family. Meredith had been betrothed to be married, her love Julian Mayes off in London seeking his fortune. But Julian hadn't answered her pleas for help when her mother had died and she'd lost her home to a scheming relative. He had recently returned to her life after ten years' absence, and she was trying to accustom herself to the idea of being courted again.

Unfortunately, if she thought too hard she could still hear Lady Winhaven's sharp voice berating her for some imagined slight. The fire was too hot, even though it was the footman's job to stoke it, the water in her washstand too cold, even though that was the maid's purview. Meredith must be always on duty, ensuring that every little thing was perfect. Anything less resulted in a tongue lashing.

At least the woman had left Meredith a sizable inheritance that had allowed her to open her business. She had sworn that no gentlewoman in her care would ever suffer the indignities she'd endured in ten years of service. She only wished she knew a way to change Lady Lilith's outlook permanently. A shame she couldn't open a business for the reformation of the snippy!

"I think it should be silver," the countess said to no one in particular, and it took a moment for Meredith to realize she was still talking about her bell. "And big enough to really chime."

"You will wake half the household," her daughter complained.

Her mother drew herself up. "And why shouldn't I? This is my home. With your father gone, I may do as I please."

Lady Lilith cringed. "There are others in the household. I wish you would remember that."

"It is difficult to remember there are others when no one comes to see me," the countess said with a sigh. "I didn't even know we had company."

"Neither did I," her daughter said with a look to the earl. "I manage this household. I should have been told so

I could make the proper arrangements."

Like forcing Fortune to sleep in the stables. Good thing the earl and Marbury had made the arrangements instead.

"My apologies," her brother said, inclining his head in his sister's direction. "I should have thought to tell you and Mother. Now, perhaps we can turn to other subjects that might interest our guest."

His tone was mild, but his family's reactions were marked. Lady Lilith dropped her gaze to her food, but Meredith could almost hear her fuming.

Lady Carrolton went farther. Her eyes widened, and she clutched her chest. "Oh! Dear! Salts!"

Yvette offered her the salt cellar.

She struck it away. "No, you stupid girl. Salts! Smelling salts. In the case." She swooned against the back of the chair.

The earl rose, majestic even in his tweed coat. "Forgive us, Miss Thorn, Miss French. I'll see to her. Finish your dinners. Lilith, perhaps you can entertain our guest." As his sister sat taller, he went around the table to his mother's side and scooped her up in his arms.

"What are you doing?" she shrieked. "Put me down at once!"

In answer, he carried her out the door.

Lady Lilith turned to Meredith. "So, you are traveling, Miss Thorn. How soon will you need to continue on?"

Not soon enough, as far as she could tell. But could she leave Yvette in such bedlam?

Patience Ramsey was a saint. Yvette could think of no other explanation for the former companion's ability to survive three years of this. Yvette hadn't even made it through one day, and already she was willing to take her chances in London.

Well, nearly willing. There was much to be said for a home where no one tried to poison or shoot her. Both attempts had been made on her life since Harry had brought her from France. His superiors in the War Office were certain a French agent was stalking her, hence the need to hide until the villain was captured.

And what better place to hide? Besides being at the back of beyond, she was surrounded. If the French agent found his way to Carrolton Park, she might not even need to face him. He might succumb to one of Lady Carrolton's illnesses or drown in the acid of Lady Lilith's bile. Just the thought made her smile inch higher.

"Something you care to share, Miss French?" Lady Lilith asked as if she were a school mistress ready to scold a noisy child.

Yvette finished her dessert and rose. "Excuse me, if you please. I must see to the countess."

She could only hope Meredith could put Lady Lilith in her place as soon as Yvette was out of the room.

Lady Carrolton was back in bed when Yvette entered the suite. Her employer was tucked under the covers of the great bed, ribboned cap covering her tightly curled hair. Her son sat on the chair beside the bed, book open in his lap.

"'I never wish to offend,'" the earl read, head bowed over the page, "'but I am so foolishly shy, that I often seem negligent, when I am only kept back by my natural awkwardness. I have frequently thought that I must have been intended by nature to be fond of low company, I am so little at my ease among strangers of gentility.'"

He paused, frowning down at the book as if something had caught his attention.

His mother sniffed. "Idiot. He'll come to a bad end, you mark my words."

Yvette moved closer. "I can continue, my lordship. You will wish to see to your guest."

He rose, offering her the book, and his mother collapsed against the pillows, hand to her forehead. "Oh, my head! French, find the tisane."

It seemed she should find a way to wear the wretched case instead. She knelt and fished it out from under the chair. Immediately, the earl was beside her.

"Allow me."

He lifted it easily, set it on the bed, popped it open, and glanced through the bottles and devices, brow furrowed.

The countess lowered her hand, watching him.

"Perhaps," Yvette said, gathering her skirts to rise, "I should prepare a cool compress instead. Would you continue reading, my lord?"

"Of course." He sat, making the delicate little chair shudder, and found his spot in the novel. His mother's sigh sounded suspiciously pleased as she relaxed against the pillows once more.

Yvette took her time going to the washstand and wetting a cloth. He had a nice voice, warm, rich. It rolled through the room like the sound of the organ at Notre Dame. Small wonder his mother relaxed at the words. If Yvette closed her eyes, she could imagine herself at peace, safe.

No. Not safe. Not yet. Not until her enemy was captured.

She returned to the bedside, cloth in hand, and stopped. The countess' head lolled to one side, eyes closed and slim chest rising slowly and evenly. Yvette put her free hand on the earl's shoulder, feeling the strength beneath her fingers. "She sleeps."

He glanced at his mother, then eased the book closed. "A shame I'm not better at declaiming."

"*Non*," Yvette murmured. "You did not lull her to sleep. She just needed to know you were nearby to feel comfortable relaxing. *Vien*." She drew back from the bed, tossing the compress into the wash basin, and he followed her out into the corridor. Shutting the door, she faced him.

"Thank you, my lord. She is better when you are near."

He shook his head. "Only sometimes. At others, she shrinks away as if I am something to fear."

Was that the issue? Were the countess and her daughter afraid of the earl? He was certainly powerful enough to overcome any other person she had met in this house, with the possible exception of Marbury. Those hands could snap a neck.

"Some men like women to fear them," she acknowledged.

He stepped back, paling, mouth open and eyes wide. There was no dissembling with this one. He was horrified. "I assure you, I do not. I have never raised my hand to a woman in my life!"

But he knew how to raise his voice. It echoed down the corridor. Another moment, and he'd wake his mother.

She caught his hand, held it tight. "Peace. I do not doubt you. But something brought your mother to this point. All those pills and liquids, those devices. I cannot believe she is so ill. Did the physician truly prescribe them?"

"She has several physicians," he said, the tone of disgust approaching his sister's. "A fellow in Chessington, one near Hampton Court, and another in London. They all assure me they can make her well."

"And take your money," Yvette guessed. "Has she always been like this?"

He nodded. "Since I was a boy, but her symptoms have worsened over time, if tonight was any indication."

"I will see what can be done," Yvette promised.

His look softened. "Thank you, but that should not be your concern. You are not really her companion."

"Shh," Yvette cautioned, but a movement caught her eye.

Lady Lilith had entered the corridor from the stairs, leaving Meredith to her own devices far too early in the evening for hospitality. Yvette knew the moment the earl's sister spotted them, because she jerked to a stop and stared.

Yvette removed her hand from the earl's. "*Merci beaucoups*, my lord," she said, lowering her gaze and dipping a curtsey.

"I could not have lulled your *chère mere* to sleep without your help. I will attend to my duties now. *Bonne nuit.*"

"Good night, Miss French," he said. "Enjoy your rest. All will be well. I promise."

Enjoy her rest? She couldn't remember the last time she had even slept through the night. Sometimes rest was a long time coming as melancholy and loneliness crowded close. When she did sleep, her dreams held dangers: past, present, and future.

Tonight, she thought they would hold something else—a warm voice, a kind smile, and a promise that all would be well.

If only she could believe.

CHAPTER FOUR

Gregory watched as Yvette slipped back into his mother's room, then turned to meet his sister's glare.

"How dare you," she breathed. "Bringing your lover into this house. You're worse than Father."

He frowned at her. "What are you talking about? I met Miss French today, just as you did. And Father never kept a mistress."

"What do you know?" she retorted. "You were away at school and then off on your Grand Tour. The only reason you returned home was because Father died."

"Lilith." He kept his voice as kind as possible. "Father expected me to go to school and then tour the Continent. That's what most young men do to learn how to get on as a gentleman. Some days I think I'm still learning."

"Obviously," she snapped. "Or you would have let me know we had a guest."

How many times must he apologize? Lilith was right— if there were questions about staffing or food, Marbury would go to her first. But the staff were highly competent and generally agreeable. His sister had little to do when it came to resolving difficulties.

"At least Miss Thorn is only staying the night," Gregory pointed out. "She'll be no burden."

Lilith bared her teeth. "But Mother and I remain burdens, don't we? Poor Gregory, saddled with a sick mother and a spinster sister." She turned and stalked back down the corridor, hands fisted at her sides.

Gregory shook his head. He never considered his mother or sister a burden. As head of the family, it was his duty and honor to give them whatever support they required. They wanted for nothing.

So why was his sister so bitter? As a child, she'd been his mother's darling, quiet, but with flashes of brilliance. True, their interactions had been limited. His father had felt boys and girls should be reared differently, so Gregory had had a tutor until he went off to Eton and Lilith had had a governess until she came out. With her dark good looks and impeccable connections, she'd been expected to make an excellent match. But, after several years of making the social rounds, she'd declared herself on the shelf. Now it was all he could do to pry her out of the house to attend church services.

A shame his sister didn't have Yvette's spirit.

He started for his rooms at the end of the corridor. His mother and sister had been gently reared, their sorrows and trials seemingly minor, yet they both struggled to be pleasant. Yvette de Maupassant had lived through far worse, yet she could still smile. Just thinking about her coy looks made him smile as well.

But waking up to a brass clang wiped away any pleasant memories.

The noise echoed down the corridor, and he thought he heard the ravens in the woods around the house leap into the sky, protesting. He shoved back the covers and raced for the door, nightshirt flapping about his ankles.

His sister was in the corridor ahead of him, wrapper snug about her nightgown. "What is that din?"

The sound came again, from his mother's room. Before he could respond, the door to the room opposite opened. Smothering a yawn, Yvette stumbled across the corridor, creamy white nightgown hinting of her curves and bare feet sticking out below.

"I should never have suggested a bell," she muttered to herself. Nearly bumping into Gregory, she stopped, blinked, and focused on him. Pink sprang to her cheeks, and she looked away, only to meet Lilith's shocked stare.

She raised her chin and waved a hand. "Return to your rooms. I will see to the countess." She plunged into his mother's room, shutting the door and slightly muting the cacophony.

"You have to do something," Lilith said, voice desperate. "We cannot listen to that day and night."

"Agreed," Gregory said, hiding his smile. "I'll speak to Mother, right after I dress."

But when he ventured into his mother's room a while later, clothed in his usual tweed jacket and chamois trousers, he couldn't bring himself to remonstrate. His mother just looked so happy.

"See what Marbury found for me?" Sitting up in her bed, she clanged the massive brass bell that had probably once graced a cow's neck. She shook it so hard, in fact, that her whole body shook with it. So did the bed. Gregory tried not to wince at the sound.

"Excellent, Countess," Yvette said, seizing the bell with both hands. She must have taken time to change, for she was once more gowned in a plain, spruce-colored dress that seemed too large for her. "But I am here now, so perhaps we could avoid waking the dead."

His mother clung to the bell, but she must have decided not to fight against the determination on Yvette's face, for she released it with a sigh.

"Very well but set it where I can reach it if I need it."

"But of course." Yvette winked at Gregory as she passed. "I will put it on your dressing table. You may ring for me when your maid is finished preparing you for the day."

He thought his mother might protest, but she fluttered her fingers at them. "Go, go. I'll ring for you shortly."

Gregory followed Yvette out.

"Forgive me," she said, pausing in the corridor. "When I suggested she have a bell, I had no idea she would ring it so often or so loudly."

"Or take such joy from it," Gregory allowed. "I'll ask the silversmith in Chessington to make her something smaller."

"You can try," she said with a smile, "but I think she will want to keep the big one." She yawned. "*Excusez-moi.*"

He glanced closer. Darkness shadowed her blue eyes, and her curls seemed more tousled than the day before. "You need no pardon. Did she keep you up all night?"

"*Non.*" Her smile faded. "I have enough noises in my head to do that all by myself."

He sighed. "We are imposing. I was afraid this might happen. We'll reveal your true nature, find someone else to care for Mother."

Again she waved her hand. "You worry about nothing. I have faced far worse. Try pacifying the Emperor through one of his tantrums."

He could not imagine. "You were that close to Napoleon?"

She shrugged. "More so to his wife, but yes, I had the privilege of watching him take out his disappointments on her and anyone else within shouting distance. Your mother pales in comparison."

He chuckled. "I'm not sure if that is a compliment or an insult."

She laughed, deep and throaty, and something inside him rose to meet the sound. "If I compare you favorably to any Frenchman save my father, you should be very afraid."

Though he was certain his mother could not have finished dressing so quickly, from inside her room can the sound of a clang. Yvette made a face.

"I must go."

He caught her arm. "Are you certain? It would be easier

to confess our deception to Mother and Lilith sooner rather than later."

"And risk that others might learn I am here," she reminded him.

She could not know how infrequently his mother and sister left the house. But she was right. Once they knew, the servants would know as well, and word would get out.

She patted his hand. "Never fear. I can play my part. Remember to play yours."

That, he felt sure, would prove difficult. Whatever he did, his thoughts would likely drift to what must be happening overhead. Had his mother given Yvette some distasteful task? Had Lilith complained about some imagined slight? Had Yvette decided to wash her hands of the lot of them? How was he to focus?

On any given day, he had meetings with his steward or his agent from London, who saw to his holdings on the Exchange. He might hear a petition from the vicar or the leader of a charity requesting his support in some endeavor. He had bills to review from Parliament, the annuals of the Royal Society to peruse for ideas on improvements he might want to enact.

And his greenhouse was calling.

He wasn't sure when he'd first discovered his love of gardening. He could remember slipping from the house even as a lad to run down to the great glass buildings at the rear of the garden, where their head gardener raised the more exotic blooms as well as vegetables and fruits they would have been hard-pressed to grow otherwise during the colder months. There was something about plunging his hands into the rich earth, snipping off dead blossoms, and pruning branches for greater productivity that calmed his spirit, focused his mind.

His father had never understood.

"A gentleman has no need to dirty his hands, boy," he'd insisted. "He hires lesser men to do it for him. I will not allow you to debase yourself this way."

And so Gregory had stayed away. It hadn't been all that difficult while he was at school and on tour. And then he'd returned to a house empty of his father's edicts. He'd made it plain to the head gardener that one of the greenhouses was his, to do with as he pleased. No one else was to even enter without his prior approval.

He was planning his next steps—replanting the *Liliaceae* into deeper pots, coaxing the *Prosthechea cochleate* to keep blooming—as he ate breakfast when Miss Thorn appeared in the doorway. She must have left her pet with Marbury, for her hands were free. She waved Gregory back into his seat as he started to rise. Unlike Yvette, she looked rested and in complete control as she settled on the chair Perkins, their head footman, held out for her.

"Forgive me for intruding, my lord," she said, arranging her hyacinth-colored skirts. "But I was hoping to catch you this morning."

He straightened from his coddled eggs. "Something amiss?"

She nodded to Perkins as he offered her the gilt-edged porcelain bowl, and the footman spooned some eggs onto her china plate. "Merely protocol. I have placed a staff member in this house, and I'd like to ensure the situation suits all involved before moving on. Would you be amenable to me staying longer? It shouldn't take more than a day or two."

It seemed she was as concerned about Yvette and his mother as he was. He could not share his feelings in front of the watchful Perkins, so he nodded. "Of course. Stay as long as you like. We are indebted to you for finding us so able a companion."

Even if he could not think of Yvette as a servant.

Being a servant was more difficult than she remembered. At Claude's house, of course, she had been no more than a drudge, assigned to the lowliest chores like scrubbing the floors on her knees or emptying the chamber pots. Even after Napoleon happened to inquire about her, then command her presence at court, she'd had to bow and serve the ladies higher in position. Here she was almost one of the family, expected to dine with the earl and his sister and to entertain any guests the countess might have. But she was forever at the lady's beck and call. She didn't even have time to feel melancholy.

The countess began clanging her bell without fail by eight each morning, so Yvette took pains to be awake, dressed, and ready by that time. When she had first come to England, she hadn't been willing to allow a stranger like a maid to help her with her corset. It wasn't just baring the bruises from her prison ordeal that made her hesitate. Those were fading from what she could see over her shoulder in the pier glass mirror her new bedchamber boasted. No, after all the years of secrecy, the need to hide her inmost thoughts, she found it hard to allow anyone so close.

But Lady Carrolton's maid, Ada, was a dear girl, frightened of her mistress and not a little awed at her elevation to the role of ladies' maid. As she helped Yvette change, she confided that the previous maid had been discharged for poor service. Discharged in a fit of pique, more likely. Good thing the earl would not allow that to happen to Yvette.

He was consideration itself, stopping by to visit his mother mid-morning and again to take tea in the afternoon. He always included Yvette in the conversation, asked after her with such sincerity she knew he was still concerned about their ruse. At Yvette's urging, the lady consented to go down to dinner each evening as well, and the earl always walked her back to her suite and stayed to chat or read. He usually managed to lull his mother to sleep, so Yvette was able to slip out into the corridor with him afterward.

"You do not have to take such care of me," she'd said the second night. "Your mother is difficult, but I can manage." "And if I want to take such care?" he'd asked.

Something about the way he had gazed down at her had made her heart stutter in her chest. *Non, non!* This was not a grand ball, and she was not flirting. He was not offering more than a place of protection. She had a death sentence hanging over her head. Now was not the time to dream of taking a husband. After what she'd been through, she wasn't sure she'd ever feel safe enough to marry.

"You are too kind," she'd said, dropping her gaze. "Thank you. Until tomorrow."

He had bowed over her hand as if she were the lady her parents had wished for her to become, and she could not help her sigh as he'd walked away.

Miss Thorn also visited the countess twice a day and dined with the family in the evening. Yvette had slipped away once for a private conversation and knew her friend's concerns.

"So, you and Miss French are getting on well?" Miss Thorn asked the countess the third day.

"Quite well," Lady Carrolton pronounced. "She takes excellent care of me. I haven't had to resort to smelling salts in days."

Because she was enjoying all this attention. Yvette had a feeling that the countess' maladies sprang from boredom and a fear of neglect. Of course, she hadn't discussed the matter with any of the lady's physicians, so she made sure to keep the little red case handy.

Lilith always looked for it when she came to visit her mother, turning her haughty profile this way and that until she spied it, then glanced at Yvette as if she suspected her of hiding it. She was forever trying to direct Yvette, as if controlling the situation was all important. She alone watched Yvette as if trying to discover some dire secret that would allow her to discharge Yvette too. Why did she think Yvette was here? If she had been interested in stealing one of the priceless vases that lined the corridors, she would have done so and escaped by now.

Still, seeing Lilith alone with her mother gave her reason to wonder. She would take Yvette's seat beside the bed, forcing Yvette to find some corner to stand in. She wasn't sure whether Lilith took delight in inconveniencing her or was simply oblivious to the plight of servants. She and her mother would talk, and the conversation always started the same way.

"How are you today, Mother?"

Lady Carrolton would list a number of ills and then inquire, "And you?"

"Well, thank you," Lilith would say. "I believe the weather is improving."

"We'll have rain yet. You'll see."

How unlike the conversations at the Emperor's court. There everything had been veiled in innuendo, every look and word holding deeper meanings, and woe betide the person who could not navigate those waters. She had longed for a time when she could simply talk, without worrying whether someone might overhear or assume the worst. Her conversations with Lord Carrolton were like that—open, honest, much like the man himself.

Still, had the countess and her daughter nothing more to say to each other than comments about their health and the weather? What of shared memories? Plans for the future? What of hopes, dreams? She could not imagine anyone so narrow.

"Did Ada tell Lilith to wear the blue tonight?" the countess asked as Yvette was walking her down to the dining room the third night.

She'd been glad the lady had sent her maid and not Yvette. Telling Lady Lilith anything would never be easy.

"I believe she passed on your message, your ladyship," Yvette said as they took the first turn. "But I cannot say whether your daughter will heed your advice."

The countess pouted. "No one ever heeds my advice."

She doubted that. The woman would not offer it so freely if no one ever responded. "I would like to see your daughter happy for once."

The countess sighed. "So would I. She was a bright child, like a little bird hopping about, always cheerful. I blame that villain for the change in her."

What was this? "A villain?" Yvette encouraged her as they reached the bottom of the stairs.

Lady Carrolton paused in the entry hall, glancing about as if wondering whether the Grecian statues were listening, then leaned closer to Yvette. "A villain I will not name. However, a man paid her court the last year she went up for the Season. She never introduced me to him, which told me she knew he was beneath her. Her father refused to speak his name. He insisted the fellow was a fortune hunter and demanded that she cease receiving him. You mustn't mention the matter to my son. If he could discover the fellow's identity, he might call him out."

She struggled to see Lord Carrolton as the vengeful brother. And even if he was more of a bully than he appeared, would he go so far as to challenge this man to a duel? Had the fellow done worse than attempt to court Lady Lilith? Was that why she was so bitter?

Or did her anger stem at being denied the right to marry the man she loved?

CHAPTER FIVE

Yvette de Maupassant was a wonder. Only Miss Ramsey at her finest was as devoted. When Gregory woke, Yvette was already up and in his mother's room. She accompanied his mother to breakfast, served her tea, and sat beside her at dinner. She entertained her by reading, hosted visits from Miss Thorn and Fortune twice a day, and suffered through Lilith's presence. Each day it seemed his mother grew stronger and happier. She even agreed to venture outdoors the fourth day.

Marbury had set up a chair on the back lawn, and Gregory escorted his mother down the stone steps to it, so she need not use her cane. Yvette followed, arms laden with lap robes, which she tucked around his mother even though the day was warm. Both hands latched on the handle of the bell she had refused to allow out of her sight, his mother sat like a queen surveying her domain.

And it was a satisfying sight. His grandfather had built the house, a solid block at odds with the rolling vistas around it. Gregory had had it remodeled, inside and out, to take advantage of the natural beauty. Now, most rooms looked out on the fertile plain and woods. He'd removed the old formal gardens with their regimented paths and replaced them with lawn that swept down to the stream. In the woods beyond, bluebells (*Hyacinthoides*, he reminded himself) made a carpet of purple under the green canopy, and songbirds flitted among the branches, their cheerful sound ringing.

Fortune was particularly intrigued by the birds. Miss Thorn had brought her pet down to join them, jeweled collar fastened around the cat's neck with a leash attached. Fortune sat still, watching the woods with copper-colored eyes, whiskers twitching, and Gregory thought it was only a matter of time before she darted in pursuit.

Then his mother sneezed, and Fortune ducked behind her mistress' skirts, which were once again the color of *Lavandula*, like her eyes.

Yvette offered his mother a lace-edged handkerchief.

She eyed the silken square. "Aren't you going to help me blow?"

"*Non,*" Yvette said, turning her gaze to the view. "If you release the bell, you can do it for yourself."

His mother lifted the bell and gave it a good shake. Fortune dived under Miss Thorn's skirts.

Yvette tsked. "You have frightened *le chat.*"

His mother peered around Miss Thorn as if to be sure. Fortune poked her head out from under the skirts and eyed her back.

"Perhaps we can forego the bell," Yvette suggested. "The noise is making me deaf. I cannot hear it as well as I did. If you keep ringing it, I may not be so quick to respond."

Face turning mulish, his mother rang it long and hard. Fortune must have tried to climb up inside her skirts, for poor Miss Thorn swept to one side, picked up her pet, and marched off to a safe distance where she stood petting and crooning to the creature. Gregory felt for her.

"You are being unreasonable, Mother," he said. "Everyone who can see to your needs is present. There's no need to ring for them."

"Easy for you to say," she grumbled. "You're the earl. Everyone must do as you say. Wait until you're old and feeble, like me."

His mother had birthed children late. He'd overheard Society leader Lady Jersey telling another woman that some had expected she wouldn't be able to bear an heir at all. Still, she was approaching her sixty-first year. He didn't see that as so very old.

Neither did Yvette, it seemed.

"You are not feeble," she informed his mother. "You ring that bell like the strongest farmer."

As if encouraged, his mother grinned and swung the bell again.

"Oh, for pity's sake," Lilith said, descending the stairs behind them, dun-colored skirts trailing. "Will someone please take that away from her?"

His mother clutched the bell tight, but she didn't ring it again. As if determined to align herself against him, Lilith went to stand with Miss Thorn. Gregory could see Fortune peering up from her owner's arms as if unsure of his sister. He knew the feeling.

"Tell me about your estate," Yvette said, and he wasn't sure if she was addressing his mother or him.

His mother was certain. "Well, Gregory? Answer French. You've done a great deal to improve the place. I would think you'd want to crow."

He had never been the type to praise his own accomplishments. God had given him strength, vitality, and intelligence. He simply used them.

"Carrolton Park encompasses roughly ten thousand acres," he explained. "The house and gardens take up a small portion, the woods another portion, and the farm over that hill the rest."

She glanced up at him. "And what do you grow on your farm?"

Why was he feeling self-conscious? He could have told her the exact variety, the yield in bushels per year, but a gentleman wasn't supposed to be that invested in the things that brought him income. "Grain, vegetables, that sort of thing."

Her mouth quirked, as if his answer did not satisfy her.

"And what of you, my lady?" she asked his mother. "What do you love about it?"

His mother shifted under the lap robes even as Lilith and Miss Thorn ventured closer, as if drawn by the quiet conversation.

"I didn't like it when I first came here," his mother confided. "Too distant from anything I'd ever known. But you must admit it has a certain beauty. See the bluebells under the trees? When I was young, I'd walk through them and listen to the sounds of the wood, then gather armloads and bring them back to the house."

He didn't remember that, but the image of his mother as a young woman loving plants as much as he did was appealing. "We could gather some now, if you like."

Lilith snorted. "Oh, Gregory, really. What nonsense."

His mother nodded. "It was only a girlish fancy. Your father never liked the things and had the staff throw them out."

He didn't remember that either, but he felt as if he should apologize. "I'm sorry, Mother."

Her gaze was on the distance, though he thought he saw a sorrow equal to his own in Yvette's eyes.

"It matters not," his mother insisted. "Now Marbury brings me fresh flowers every day."

For once, something close to a smile hovered on his sister's lips. "Me too. Lilies, my favorite."

"I must thank him for the flowers in my room as well," Miss Thorn said with a smile to the butler.

"Actually, madam," Marbury started. Gregory shook his head.

"It was no trouble," the butler finished smoothly.

"And you, my lord?" Yvette murmured. "Do you love your estate?"

He smiled, gaze going out over the lush green. "I will

admit to admiring it greatly, Miss French. Others find it distant, but I like that it's set off by itself, with nothing crowding in. You can walk, you can ride, you can even dive into the stream if it suits you. There's no one and nothing to get in your way. And I like the bluebells. Your eyes are very similar in color."

He wasn't sure why he added the last part. She blushed, smile deepening, until he wanted to lean closer, perhaps press his lips to hers, see if they tasted as sweet as they looked.

He stood taller, made himself look away. She was a lady under his protection. He had no business thinking about what it would be like to kiss her!

He was relieved when their head footman strode out of the house to fetch him, announcing that they had visitors.

"The Duchess?" his mother asked, perking up.

"No, your ladyship," Perkins said, inclining his tawny head. "Two gentlemen to see the earl, a Mr. Mayes and a Mr. Villers."

Every lady reacted. Yvette stiffened from where she'd been attending his mother, Miss Thorn clutched Fortune close as if for protection, and the cat issued a hiss of challenge, to her owner or the visitors, Gregory wasn't sure. His mother beamed, and Lilith picked up her skirts and climbed back up the stairs at a pace he would not have credited to her. Even Marbury frowned in her wake.

"If you'll excuse me," Gregory said, more mystified than usual by the ladies of his household. He started after his sister, but his mother caught his arm.

"Ask them to stay for dinner," she ordered. "I want to meet them."

"I'll do what I can, Mother," he promised. He caught Yvette's eye, and she nodded as if in understanding. He hurried into the house.

He wasn't entirely surprised when their guests explained their purpose for visiting. He'd gone to school with Julian

NEVER ENVY AN EARL   53

Mayes, who had later distinguished himself as a cunning solicitor. His red-gold hair always looked as if he'd forgotten to comb it, but that didn't seem to make him any less popular with the ladies. Gregory had only heard of Julian's companion, a tall, sallow-complexioned fellow with pomaded black hair and a long nose.

"Carrolton," Julian greeted him as they met in the north withdrawing room. "May I present Beauford Villers. He's an acquaintance of our mutual friend, Lord Hastings."

An intelligence agent, then. Villers bowed, and Gregory nodded. He could see the potential for subterfuge in those grasping hands, the thin lips, the slim physique. Here was surely a fellow who would sneer at danger.

"Welcome to Carrolton Park, gentlemen," Gregory said. "Would you care to refresh yourselves?"

They declined, and Gregory used the excuse to dismiss Marbury and the junior footman, who had been hovering behind them. His butler was too well practiced in the role to show his surprise as he bowed himself out. Gregory motioned his guests into the gilded chairs.

Julian reclined with his usual grace, but Villers sat upright, gaze darting here and there as if expecting a French agent to pop out from under the settee.

"I'm sure you can guess why we're here," Julian said.

"The man after Miss de Maupassant," Gregory said. "Have you caught him?"

"No," Villers said with dark look.

Relief shot through him. Why? He should be as disappointed as the intelligence agent that the villain still moved through England, endangering Yvette. But a few moments' reflection revealed the reason for his relief. If the fellow was caught, Yvette would have no further need to stay.

Julian leaned forward. "We may not have caught him, but we think we have identified him. We have reason to believe Yvette de Maupassant's cousin Claude is in England and eager to take her back to France to stand trial for treason."

His hands gripped the arms of the chair. "Her family wants her dead? I was told they were gone."

"Her parents and brothers were guillotined," Julian said, voice as hard as the image it evoked. "This fellow assumed responsibility for her and took advantage of her introduction to Napoleon's court. It seems he was incensed that she'd defected. We have no reason to believe he's discovered her location, but you had to be warned."

Gregory nodded. "I'll protect her."

"Good man." Julian glanced at his colleague with less warmth. "Have you anything to add, Villers?"

The fellow shook himself and managed a brief smile. "How is your sister, my lord?"

Gregory blinked at the *non sequitur*. "My sister? Fine. Do you believe her to be in danger?"

"No, no," Julian hurried to assure him. "There should be no danger so long as no one discovers Yvette de Maupassant's true nature."

The doors to the withdrawing room popped open, and Yvette scurried into the room.

"Forgive the delay, *mon amis*. I had to hide the countess' cowbell and tell Lady Lilith to mind her own affairs. Now, what must I know?"

Men. They must have been discussing what to do about her situation, yet they all stared at her as if she'd floated down from the ceiling dressed in chicken feathers. Mr. Villers's mouth even hung open.

"*Vite, vite,*" she said, coming to join them. "You must be quick. Meredith is with her ladyship, but I will be wanted shortly."

Mr. Mayes brightened. She'd met the solicitor last month at Foulness Manor, the home of her friend Harry. Of course he would want news of Meredith—unless Yvette missed her guess, he intended to court the lady.

"Miss Thorn is still here?" he asked.

"For the time being," the earl told him. Then he stepped forward to take Yvette's hand in his. Such a large hand. Hers disappeared inside it, yet she felt perfectly comfortable.

"Miss de Maupassant," he said, "Mr. Mayes and Mr. Villers came to let us know they have identified the man pursuing you. You must be brave. It is your cousin."

The room dimmed. She must have swayed on her feet, for his hand slipped around her waist as if to hold her upright. She clung to his hand, to his warmth. She could not let her fear rule her.

"I should have known Claude would be involved," she made herself say. "I am only surprised he crossed the Channel himself. Where is he now?"

"We're not sure," Mr. Mayes admitted. "One of our best men, Lord Trevithan, nearly caught him in London, but he managed to escape."

He would, even from the dashing Lord Trevithan, who'd recruited her for a spy. Her cousin was a survivor. So many wrongs could be laid at his door, yet he always escaped capture, like a cockroach scuttling away from the light.

"You're safe here," the earl said in his deep voice, hand still holding hers. "He has no idea where you are."

Yvette shook her head. "He *had* no idea where I was. Why do you think he allowed you to see him in London? He wanted you to know he was in England. You hurried to tell me, and he will hurry to follow you."

Mr. Villers straightened, and Mr. Mayes' handsome face tightened.

"You're right," the solicitor said. "We were fools. Carrolton, there's nothing for it now. We'll have to find another place for Miss de Maupassant."

The earl stiffened, but once more the room seemed to darken. Leave Carrolton Park? She had only been here a few days, but she felt as if ribbons bound her to the place. Why? She owed them only her thanks.

But who would answer Lady Carrolton's bell?

Who would depress Lady Lilith's notions?

Who would smile encouragement to a beleaguered earl over dinner, share secrets and plans in the corridors?

He still had not released her hand, was gazing down at her, face troubled. Did he fear the danger she had brought to his beautiful home?

Or was he also troubled that she might leave?

"*Non*," she said, and his breath rushed past her as if he had been holding it in that magnificent chest. "My cousin is somewhere between here and London. If you take me away, he will only find us sooner. I will stay here, so long as the earl agrees."

He squeezed her hand, the merest of pressures, yet it seemed to echo inside her. "I am at your disposal, my lady."

Relief pulsed through her. She could not remember wanting more to stay.

"Very well," Mr. Mayes said. "Then let me beg a favor, Carrolton. Allow Villers and me to remain with you a day or two. If we make it appear our visit is merely social, the villain may return to London and try another approach to locate Miss de Maupassant."

The earl nodded. "You are both welcome."

Mr. Villers cleared his throat. "Perhaps I should stay at the local inn. I wouldn't want to put you out."

The earl chuckled. "In this house? We have more than a dozen bedchambers, only five of which are occupied. You will be no trouble."

His answering smile was sickly.

How odd. Mr. Villers and his sister Lydia had also been at Harry's disastrous house party at Easter. The dark-haired fellow had not endeared himself to Yvette, threatening to reveal her secret if she did not pay him well. But after an attempt on her life, he had become an ally of sorts. It seemed he was still working with Mr. Mayes or he would not be here now.

So why refuse the invitation? Was he so afraid of her cousin? From what she had heard, he had spent the last few years posturing to impress those with a title. Of course, that had been when he was trying to find a husband for his sister, who had recently declared herself more interested in pursuing science than a match. Still, to forego such an invitation was unlike the Beau Villers she knew.

What was the fellow up to?

CHAPTER SIX

He was holding Yvette close. Her hand was small and dainty, like the rest of her, yet he felt the strength in it. His mother and sister would have swooned to hear an enemy could be closing in. He'd moved to support her, yet she seemed composed, cool even.

"It is decided, then," she said with a look to Julian and Villers. "You two, the earl, Lady Lilith, and Meredith will make up a house party. Devoted companion that I am, I will encourage the countess to join you."

His mother was in for it now. Still, it would do her good to get out of her room more often.

"Excellent," Julian agreed. "I'm sure Marbury can arrange the details."

"I will be no trouble," Villers assured everyone. "A book in my room will suffice."

And here Gregory had thought him a redoubtable intelligence agent. Was the fellow so retiring, or so secretive? Yvette was frowning at him, and even Julian looked at him askance before turning to Gregory.

"It shouldn't take much to make this look like a house party," his friend said, rubbing his chin. "Tomorrow, you can take me on a tour of the estate, and we'll see if we can spot anything amiss."

Gregory nodded, but he felt a tightening inside. A foreign agent crept closer to his home, breathing danger.

He had never thought to find himself in such a position. Small wonder it remained on his mind as he saw his new guests settled and went to inform his sister and mother of the plans. Yvette had gone up ahead of him to alert Miss Thorn so she knew to play along. All the ladies were taking tea with his mother in her sitting room when he arrived.

This room had been decorated to his mother's specifications, with fanciful swirls marking the pink and blue panels of the ceilings and walls, a thick flowered carpet underfoot. The delicate gilt furnishings always made him feel like a lumbering bear. He declined to take the seat his mother offered and stood instead, but he only ended up looming over them all.

"I've invited friends to stay," he announced. "We'll be riding and playing billiards and that sort of thing, probably of little interest to you, but you're welcome to join us for meals and conversation in the evenings."

"Friends?" his sister asked, tremor in her voice. "Including this Mr. Villers?"

Gregory cocked his head. "You sound concerned. Has Mr. Villers offended you in some way, Lilith?"

She paled. "Certainly not. I hardly know the man."

Miss Thorn eyed her a moment before turning to Gregory. "I'd be delighted to join you, my lord."

"We will all join you," Yvette said with a look to his mother and Lilith. His mother nodded, but his sister said nothing.

"Perhaps we should start with a tour of the house," Miss Thorn suggested. "I'm sure your guests would appreciate seeing it in all its glory."

"*Mais oui,*" Yvette put in with a twinkle in her eyes.

Lilith rose. "I have no need. Excuse me." She hurried out.

"Meet me in the entry hall in a quarter hour," Gregory told the others, then strode after his sister.

He stopped her just as she put her hand on the latch to open the door to her suite. "Lilith, wait. Forgive me if I overstepped by not consulting you about the other guests. There's nothing to concern you. Marbury is making the arrangements."

She avoided her gaze. "It's your home. You can invite who you like. I'll do what I must to make you proud. Marbury may not have had time to inform Cook. I'll speak to her about the meals."

He nodded. "Thank you. I wish you'd join us. You must remember Julian Mayes. And I can introduce you to Mr. Villers."

"No need for an introduction," she said. Then she whipped open the door and disappeared into her room.

Gregory didn't follow. She deserved the privacy she was so set on maintaining. He only wondered why she felt the need to hide just as Beau Villers arrived at Carrolton Park.

Gregory found Julian, Miss Thorn, his mother, and Yvette waiting for him in the entry hall at a quarter past. Julian seemed more interested in eyeing Miss Thorn than his surroundings, and Gregory's mother appeared to be happy watching them both. As if she noticed as well, Yvette moved closer to him.

"And what is that lovely stone in the floor, my lord?" she asked. "I noticed it when I came in. It is unusual, *non*?"

Focused in such a way, he found it easy to explain his choices. His architect and interior designer had been surprised by his suggestions, but pleased to implement them, and Gregory had largely been satisfied with the results.

"It's Blue John," he explained. "A Devonshire stone. I saw it at Chatsworth, the home of the Duke of Devonshire, and thought it would look good here. You see, Carrolton Park is surrounded by green. Even in winter, our evergreens keep the land verdant. I wanted the entry hall calming, serene, different from the outdoors. Grey, white, and blue seemed appropriate."

His mother was staring at him. "Why, Gregory, I had no

idea you had such thoughts."

His cheeks were heating. He turned away from their admiring glances to hide the fact and pointed instead into the stairwell. "The Grecian motive continues here, but with brighter tones of silver and white, welcoming guests and family further into the house. The carvings depicting the forest remind us of the wonders to be viewed outside."

"So that's why the stones show trees," his mother mused. "I just thought it was pretty."

And it was pretty. A nice arrangement if he said so himself. Not out loud, of course.

As he continued leading them through the house, from the scarlet withdrawing room with its medieval tapestries in the south wing to the saffron silk walls of the long gallery, he couldn't help noticing the changes in his guests. Julian walked ever closer to Miss Thorn, until the lady's arm was tucked through his. His mother seemed utterly entranced by her own home, a fond smile playing about her mouth and eyes warm. Only Yvette seemed to be attending to his explanations.

"Your home is all the lovelier to me now that I know why you designed it this way," she murmured when the others stopped before a portrait of his father in the long gallery. "You have an eye for beauty, my lord."

"Yes," he murmured, gazing down at the red of her curls. "I do."

A blush stole over her cheeks, but she turned her gaze to his mother.

A good thing, too. Yvette was moving a moment before his mother gasped and clutched her chest.

Julian and Miss Thorn stepped away, looking troubled, as Yvette patted his mother's back. "Easy. Breathe."

"Salts," she rasped out.

Gregory was ready to run for the red case, but Yvette slipped her hand into a pocket and drew out a vinaigrette box. She held the screened brass under his mother's nose.

His mother took a deeper breath and started to slump.

Gregory moved to catch her. "I have you, Mother." As he had the other night, he lifted her in his arms. He could almost believe her claims about being feeble, for she felt so frail, as if he cradled a bird.

"I'll have Marbury send for the physician," Julian offered as Gregory started past.

He nodded his thanks and headed for the stairs.

Yvette trotted beside him.

"It was too much for her," Gregory felt compelled to explain. "The guests, the excitement."

"Perhaps," she said, but she frowned at his mother, whose eyes were tightly closed.

Yvette paced him to the room, skirts snapping as she tried to keep up. He laid his mother on the bed and stepped back. Julian must have alerted Marbury as promised, for the butler and Ada, his mother's maid, hurried in. The maid went straight to her mistress and smoothed his mother's skirts, face sad. His mother lay on the bed, face up, eyes closed, so still she might have passed on already. A chill went through him.

Marbury drew Gregory aside. "I've sent for Dr. Chase, my lord, and alerted Lady Lilith. Miss Thorn and Mr. Mayes would like to be of assistance."

"Thank them but assure them there's nothing to be done at the moment," Gregory told him.

Just then Lilith appeared in the doorway. She flung herself across the room and went down on her knees beside the bed.

"Mother, dear Mother. Can you hear me?"

Their mother cracked open an eye. "Lilith? Dear girl, how sweet of you to attend me in my hour of need."

Lilith's look was indeed sweet, as if she wanted only to see their mother well. Yvette's look was far less forgiving.

"You are awake," she said. "*Bon*. We will try sitting up now."

His sister rose in all her majesty. Ada cringed away from her.

"Sit up?" Lilith demanded. "Are you mad? She is ill, dying for all you know."

Yvette cocked her head, sunlight from the window shining on her curls. "Is she?"

His mother's hand fluttered to her forehead. "Oh, I don't know."

Color flamed in his sister's cheeks, and she pointed an imperious finger at Yvette. "You are what brought her to this pass, insisting that she rise and cavort about the house." She turned to him. "Gregory! I want this woman gone. Immediately!"

Lady Carrolton blinked as if surprised by her daughter's demands. Ada issued a moan. Marbury's face sagged. Yvette was more interested in what the earl would do. He had been having a private conversation with Marbury before his sister had stormed in. Now he looked to Yvette, anguish written on his readable face. She glanced to his sister, whose eyes gleamed with triumph. Lady Lilith knew he would deny her nothing, even if it inconvenienced him. How dare she put her brother in such a position!

Yvette could flatter and cajole. She had survived ten years among the new ruling class of France that way. But Lady Lilith wasn't a French aristocrat who could have her beheaded. She had no secrets Yvette could provide to the English to end the war. Neither her mother nor the earl would be served by her behavior.

"*Non,*" Yvette said, stepping closer to Lady Lilith and looking up to meet her gaze. "It is not for you to say where I go and when. I am your mother's companion, hired by the earl. They decide my fate."

Before the spiteful woman could speak, Yvette turned

to her mother, who was watching the whole scene avidly. "*Chère comtesse*, surely you do not wish me gone."

"Not in the slightest," the countess said, voice now strong and sure for one who was supposedly at death's door. "Though I do wish you wouldn't boss me around so."

As if anyone could. "I only suggest what is in your best interest," Yvette assured her.

"Really, Mother," Lady Lilith started, but Yvette crossed behind her to move up to the earl.

"And you, my lord? Do you wish me gone?"

"Never," he said, and the look in his eyes threatened to put her to the blush again.

Yvette spread her hands, turning to the countess. "*Bon.* I shall stay."

Lady Lilith turned on her heels and left the room. Ada bowed her head, but not before Yvette saw her smile. Marbury excused himself to wait for the doctor, but he nodded to Yvette as if proud of her.

The earl advanced to her side. "Will you be all right?"

"Why is no one asking me that question?" his mother complained.

"Fine," Yvette assured him. "And *merci beaucoups* for the encouragement."

He nodded, then raised his voice. "Mother? Dr. Chase is on his way. What can I do in the meantime?"

His mother patted the covers beside her. "Come. Talk to me. Take my mind off my troubles."

Though he had guests to entertain, a sister to placate, and doubtless a number of duties incumbent on an earl, he went.

Yvette moved around the room, repositioning the vaulted red case closer to the bed should the physician need it, lighting a lamp, drawing the velvet drapes. Lord Carrolton spoke little, mostly because his mother kept talking. But he listened, nodding and offering comment, gaze on her face.

She had never known a man to be so accommodating. The ladies she had served, all wives or mothers of men Napoleon had promoted to leadership, were used to their own company. Their husbands and sons might offer courtly attention in public, but in private each was consumed with their own interests. Gregory, Earl of Carrolton, gave all his attention to his mother, as if nothing could be more important in this moment.

What would it be like to be so valued? To have someone who put her interests ahead of his own, someone who thought only of what was best for her? To be truly loved?

Her heart rose inside her until she thought it would burst from her chest. Ah, but what a dangerous yearning. Since her family had been killed, she had kept her thoughts, her hopes hidden. If her cousin or men like him knew what mattered to her, they would take it away or use it against her. Until she was free of them, she had dared love no one. Did she dare now?

At length, the doctor came. The earl promised to wait outside the room for his verdict, offering Yvette a smile as he left. A narrow fellow, with thinning hair and a reedy voice, Dr. Chase bent over the countess and studied her warily as if she were a new species of thorn bush discovered growing in his garden. The countess stared back.

Finally, he straightened and turned to Yvette. "You are the new companion."

"*Oui.*"

He made a face. "French. I have no patience with this fad of hiring refugees from a country far inferior to ours."

Yvette bit the inside of her lip to keep from responding. "Have you been giving her the pills I prescribed?"

Yvette motioned to the red case, which was placed on the chair. "There are any number of pills, *monsieur*. Perhaps you would be so good as to tell me which ones."

With a frown, he opened the case and examined the interior, then drew out an amber-colored bottle. "These," he said, shaking the bottle at Yvette. "Twice a day, when she wakes and at bed. Should I write that down, or can't you read?"

"I read quite well," Yvette informed him. "English, French, and Italian. Why does the countess need such pills?"

"She has a delicate condition and a nervous complaint," he said with a nod to the lady, who nodded back.

"And with what am I dosing her?" Yvette asked.

He turned away. "A formula of my own devising. Nothing that need concern you."

Oh, the arrogance! She knew how to deal with such men.

"*Aiy!*" She dropped the bottle on the counterpane and brought both hands to her cheeks. "Oh, *non, non.* You must not ask me to do this. I will not poison the countess!" She dropped down beside the bed and clutched Lady Carrolton's boney fingers.

"Poison?" the countess asked, glancing from her to the doctor with a frown.

"Certainly not," Dr. Chase said, backing away from the bed. "Who said anything about poison?"

"That," said the earl from the doorway, "is what I would like to know."

Yvette peered around the countess' hand. Oh, but he was *magnifique!* His dark head was high, his eyes narrowed, shoulders back, and she couldn't have been surprised to see the host of heaven riding behind him.

The physician took a step away from him. "It's nothing, my lord. This girl is clearly overwrought. Perhaps I should prescribe something for her."

The earl stalked into the room, and the doctor scuttled back before him until he bumped against the wall.

"Miss French is in fine health," Lord Carrolton informed the quivering fellow. "What have you to say about my mother?"

"I have a delicate condition and a nervous complaint," the countess offered.

Yvette stood. "He wants her to take these pills but refuses to say what is in them."

"They must be good," the countess said. "They taste vile."

The earl raised a dark brow. "So, Chase? What are you giving my mother?"

The physician spread his hands, which were shaking. "Nothing, truly! I have found the complaints of older women rarely have to do with their health. A few sugar pills, coated with crushed bitter almond to discourage overuse, often satisfies."

The villain! Though Yvette had suspected most of the countess' maladies stemmed from the need for attention, a physician should have more courage to either treat her or let her know that she was well.

The earl, however, had stilled. "Bitter almond," he said in a low growl of a voice. "*Prunus amygdalus?*"

"Exactly. Harmless."

"How many years did you study to be a physician?" the earl demanded.

He blinked. "Number of years?"

"How many!"

He jumped. "I was tutored by Dr. Finch in London for three years before opening my own practice in Chessington. As you know, I have been attending Lady Carrolton for the last five years."

The earl's eyes were slits of fire. "And in all that time, you never encountered prussic acid?"

"I've heard the term, certainly," he sputtered.

"And prescribed it to the women under your care. I should have you up on charges."

"No, my lord, please!" He held up his hands, eyes goggling. "I beg you."

The fire in the earl did not die. It blazed from him, so hot she wondered the bed hangings did not ignite. "As magistrate, I hereby relieve you of duty to this parish pending further review of your practices. In the meantime, you will go to every patient to whom you prescribed those pills and confiscate the things. If any of your patients are feeling ill, refer them to another physician, one who actually cares about their wellbeing."

"Yes, my lord. At once, my lord." He gathered his things, bowed in the general direction of the bed, and fled.

"Am I going to die?" the countess asked in a shaky voice.

"No, Mother," the earl promised. "But we will examine every item in that case of yours to make sure nothing can harm you."

"Very well."

Yvette didn't like the docile way she spoke or how her hands plucked at the covers. She climbed to her feet. "I have not given you any of those pills. Did Lilith or Ada? Or did you take them on your own?"

"No." She transferred her gaze to her son and shrank deeper into the bed. "But I have never heard you talk that way before, Gregory. Perhaps you should compose yourself."

Yvette expected him to argue. Such fire did not leave a man so soon in her experience. But he paled, turned, and hurried from the room as if his mother had risen to chase him.

CHAPTER SEVEN

G regory strode down the corridor, but it didn't matter how fast he walked. He couldn't outrun the fear on his mother's face, the tremor in her voice when she requested that he compose himself. Ever since he had reached his full height at the tender age of fourteen, people had shied away from him. His father had made a joke of it.

"You have the physical prowess behind the political privilege, my boy. Use it to make them all quiver."

He didn't want to make anyone, least of all his mother, quiver. He had strived to be a gentleman—calm, composed, thoughtful. But how was he to remain pleasant and polite when the fellow chosen to care for his mother gave her nothing but sugar pills dipped in poison?

His hands fisted even now. He had a temper, seldom roused, but once heated it was difficult to cool. He wanted to hit something, rip something apart. That wasn't the gentleman he had tried so hard to be.

"My lord?"

Yvette's voice pulled him up, and he whirled to face her, dread settling on his shoulders like a cape. "What's happened? Is she sicker than we feared?"

She had every right to retreat from the demanding tone, but she put out a hand instead, as if trying to quiet an unruly horse. "She is fine. Set your mind at rest."

If only he could. He snapped a nod. "Then I will leave

you to it."

"Wait." She darted forward, head tilted to gaze up at him. "You are concerned, and not just about your mother, I think. It is understandable that you would be angry with the physician. He should not have treated her so poorly."

He nodded, drawing a breath. "But I could have made my point without resorting to ungentlemanly behavior."

Her smile threatened even as her lashes fluttered. "Ungentlemanly behavior? What is the English code of conduct when a gentleman discovers his mother is being poisoned?"

His smile broke free. "Why, we reach for a cup of tea and discuss the relative merits of syrup of ipecac and bleeding."

She shuddered theatrically. "Oh, too cold for me. I prefer a fellow who lets his passions out."

His smile left him with his comfort. "Alas, I haven't that luxury. Thank you for your concern, Miss de Maupassant, but I will be fine."

She put her hand on his arm. "Shh! I must be Miss French, particularly now. We do not know who to trust."

"I would trust my staff with my life," he assured her.

She pulled back. "I cannot say the same. You do not know my cousin. He worms his way into the lives of his victims, makes himself indispensable to them through flattery and favors, and then slips the blade between their ribs, smiling all the while."

The image sickened him. "You are safe here. Staff are on duty. No one can join us unnoticed."

"As you say," she replied, but her tone held a world of doubt.

"Go back to my mother," he said. "I'll return shortly."

With a nod, she went. And he went to consult Marbury. Perhaps if he made himself useful, he could shake off these feelings of anger and frustration.

Marbury had replaced the elderly man who had served as the butler when Gregory was a boy. Then the head footman, the imposing fellow had seemed the perfect choice for promotion. He was dignified, he was stately, and he was nearly as tall as Gregory. He also took a deliberative approach to running the household, thinking matters through before acting, a trait Gregory admired.

"How is the countess, my lord?" he asked when Gregory found him in the corridor near the kitchen.

"Well for now," Gregory said, "but I'd advise soup for dinner, something clear, easy to digest."

Marbury inclined his head. "I will inform Mrs. Clarke."

Their cook was generally flexible about such things. "The countess will also require a new physician," Gregory continued. "But we can determine who to approach another time. For now, you must know that I have been informed there is a criminal in the area."

Marbury raised his chin as if eager to take on the miscreant himself. "Indeed. Is there reason to believe the house is at risk?"

"He's not a thief," Gregory said. "I'm more concerned with the safety of the ladies under my roof. I want the doors locked each night, with a footman patrolling the corridors. Keep up our habit of having each door watched during the day. Hire extra staff if needed, but Miss French and I must meet any man before he starts his duties."

"Miss French?" Marbury asked with a frown.

"I have found her to be an excellent judge of character," Gregory temporized, feeling his cheeks growing hot at the half-truth. "Not that you aren't, Marbury, but two heads are better than one."

"As you say, my lord."

Why did he get the impression his butler doubted him as much as Yvette did? At least Gregory had every expectation that Marbury would obey his orders. Having done what he could for the moment, he returned upstairs to check on his mother, and Yvette.

The room seemed quiet as he approached, so he eased

open the door without knocking. Yvette was seated in the chair beside the bed, head bowed and lamplight reflecting in her curls. She was continuing to read the book he had found on his mother's dressing table, *Sense and Sensibility* by an anonymous lady. His mother lay on the bed, eyes open and smile pleased. Even Ada had paused in her work, standing in the doorway to the dressing room, to listen to Yvette's soft, lilting voice. It was the very picture of family domesticity. He wanted to join them, but he hated to interrupt. In the end, he closed the door and went to his room to refresh himself before dinner.

His family often said little during meals, but tonight the quiet weighed on him. Yvette remained with his mother, while Lilith and Villers had requested a tray instead of coming down to dinner. Gregory ate with Miss Thorn and Julian, but he might as well have been alone the way the two of them had eyes only for each other. As if loath to part from them, Miss Thorn remained after his staff had cleared away the food and left.

"Given the news that came from London, how long do you intend for Yvette to continue at Carrolton Park?" she asked, gaze moving from Julian to Gregory.

"For a while," Julian said. "Though if her enemy followed us here, as she suspects, it would be best to keep her out of sight."

She nodded, then returned her gaze to Gregory. "And you have taken steps to protect her, my lord?"

Gregory sat taller under her regard. "I have. Rest assured that she will be safe."

"And will you stay for the duration?" she asked Julian.

"Alas, no," he answered. "I'll stay for a few days to make good the fiction of a house party, but I must let Lord Hastings know the latest development. I could escort you back to London, if you'd like."

She raised her chin. "I cannot leave while my client is in danger."

NEVER ENVY AN EARL   73

Gregory could have told Julian that patronizing smile would have ill effect. His words weren't much better. "Now, dearest, she really isn't your client. You were kind to escort her here to further the ruse of her being a paid companion, but you bear no responsibility for her."

Her jaw hardened. "Only the responsibility of a friend. Or do you still not understand the distinction?"

Julian leaned back in his chair. "I thought we'd settled that."

Gregory glanced between them. The lady's eyes flashed a warning. Julian's look was implacable. Interesting. He'd always admired his friend's carefree attitude. Little ruffled him, which was one of the traits that made him a good solicitor. It seemed Miss Thorn was the exception.

She rose now, tall and imposing, and he and Julian stood as propriety demanded.

"I should check on Fortune," she said, voice decidedly chilly. "She, at least, has always supported my best interests. Good night, gentlemen." She was out the door before either could respond.

Julian fell back into his chair. "Well, that's a leveler."

Gregory sat more slowly. He'd never considered himself good at these sorts of personal discussions, but he wanted to help his friend.

"Is there a problem?" he asked.

Julian studied his hands on the white tablecloth. "Apparently so. Miss Thorn and I once had an understanding. I went to London to set myself up, so we could marry. She disappeared without a trace. She apparently wrote asking for my help after her mother died. The letters never reached me. She doesn't think I tried hard enough to find her. She may be right."

He glanced up. "But how many times must I apologize? Can't she see the man I have become?"

"Apparently she expects more," Gregory said. "You'd stay if you thought me in danger, yet you ask her to leave her friend behind."

"Because staying puts *her* in danger," Julian protested. "Am I not allowed to put her needs first?"

"Perhaps," Gregory suggested, "you should ask her what she wants before telling her."

Julian blinked. "When did you grow so wise about women?"

Gregory laughed. "I'm surrounded, old boy. I ought to have learned something."

Even if most days he wasn't so sure of it.

The countess had just finished her broth and bread, complaining between every bite, when Meredith arrived with Fortune. Yvette had never been so glad for the company. Though the earl had promised to return, the only other person she'd seen was Ada. The little maid took the tray to return it to the kitchen now.

"I wanted to see how our patient is getting on," Meredith said, approaching the bed. Fortune regarded the countess as if she were a particularly ripe piece of cheese.

Lady Carrolton sneezed, a delicate squeak compared to her usual loud blows. It still made Fortune start.

"You should have left the cat behind," the countess said. "It cannot be sanitary in a sick room."

Meredith held Fortune closer as if concerned she might be taken from her. "I daresay she bathes more often than most people."

The countess drew herself up.

Yvette spoke first. "As you can see, Miss Thorn, her ladyship has recovered her usual spirit. Now we just need to strengthen her enough to rise again."

Lady Carrolton made a face. "I won't improve eating that slop Cook sent up tonight. Where's my mutton? A nice filet of salmon?"

"Tomorrow," Yvette promised. "We must make sure the poison is out of your system first."

"Poison?" Meredith asked with a frown.

The countess brightened. "Yes! You'll never credit it. My physician tried to kill me."

Meredith's brows shot up, and Lady Carrolton went into excruciating detail about the plot against her. At some point, Meredith released Fortune, who set about navigating the room, starting with the underskirts of the bed. Yvette let the countess talk. For once, she had a justifiable reason for being the center of attention.

"I'm glad the earl turned him out," Meredith said when the lady paused for breath.

"Yes, but what am I to do about a physician now?" Lady Carrolton demanded.

"Perhaps you have less need for one," Yvette suggested. "You are strong of spirit, your ladyship. I suspect your body is not far behind."

Lady Carrolton sank lower in the bed, tugging up the covers. "Nonsense. I'm a frail old lady. Who knows how many days I have left?"

"Who knows how many days any of us has left?" Yvette countered.

Something thumped beside the bed. The countess clutched the covers. "What is that?"

Meredith bent and retrieved Fortune. "Merely a curious kitty. She admires your red case, Lady Carrolton."

The lady began blinking her eyes. It was only a moment before she called for eye drops or a handkerchief. Yvette nudged the case under the bed.

The door opened just then to admit Ada. Yvette rose from her chair and motioned the girl closer.

"Here is Ada," she told the countess. "She will comb your hair for bed. I'll just step out with Miss Thorn. Ring if you need me."

By the light in the lady's eyes, she couldn't wait to take

up her bell again.

"You are handling her marvelously," Meredith said when Yvette had closed the door behind them. She stroked Fortune, who wiggled as if determined to get down and explore the long corridor as she had the bedchamber. With a smile, Meredith bent and let her pet go free. The cat scampered down the carpet.

"Lady Carrolton is a termagant,"Yvette agreed, watching the cat pounce on a bit of fluff drifting along the floor. "I have seen worse."

"I'd like to prevent you from seeing worse again," Meredith said. "Julian wants me to return to London with him, but I cannot like leaving you alone when danger could be approaching."

Yvette shrugged. "I have lived with danger most of my life. I treasure your company, Meredith, but if you have business elsewhere, go."

She sighed. "I should look for my next client. Viscount Worthington has a sister unhappy in her role as chatelaine, I hear."

"You hear a great deal for having been gone from London for days."

She smiled. "I learned of the lady some time ago, but Patience Ramsey had greater need." Her smile faded. "As do you."

Behind her, Yvette heard a door open. Fortune raised her head, fluff sticking out of one side of her mouth, then scampered back to Meredith's side as Lady Lilith swept toward them. Her head was high, her gaze on the distance, as if unaware of their presence, or at least unwilling to acknowledge it.

"Your mother is well, your ladyship,"Yvette called to her. "She is preparing to sleep just now."

That drew her up short. She eyed Meredith. "I hope you didn't bring that cat into the room."

Meredith bent and picked up her pet. "I bring Fortune

everywhere with me. But I didn't stay long. I didn't want to tire your mother. And I wanted to explain that I will be returning to London with Mr. Mayes and Mr. Villers."

Meredith had explained that to Yvette, not the countess, but then, Lady Lilith was not aware of the relationship between Meredith and her mother's new companion.

At the mention of their other guests, something sparked in Lady Lilith's pale eyes. "Mr. Villers is leaving?"

"In a day or so," Meredith said. She turned to Yvette. "But I will stay if I am needed."

"We will be fine," Yvette assured her.

With a nod, Meredith excused herself and took Fortune off.

"It seems you made a friend," Lady Lilith commented. The tone lacked its usual bite.

"*Mais oui,*" Yvette agreed. "Friends are far better than enemies. I am not your enemy, you know."

Lady Lilith kept her gaze on her mother's door. "I know."

"But perhaps Mr. Villers is?"

It was a calculated shot. Lady Lilith had been so vague about the matter when she'd spoken with her brother and the countess. Yvette fully expected fire and brimstone to rain down on her now for being so impertinent as to ask.

Instead, Lady Lilith washed white. "You've heard the rumors, then?" she asked, hands worrying before her dark gown.

So, there was some scandal involved. Did the earl know? Doubtful, or he would never have allowed the fellow in the house. Still, it explained Beau Villers's reticence in accepting the invitation.

Yvette made herself shrug, hoping to encourage a confidence.

"They aren't true," Lady Lilith hurried to assure her. "He didn't take advantage of me."

Quelle! What had she stumbled into? "And he should not," Yvette scolded.

She dropped her gaze. "No, of course not. He merely showed interest that some remarked on as unseemly—singling me out to walk alone in the park, meeting me to ride three days in a row. He raised expectations. But he wasn't the fellow for me. In truth, I think he wanted me to introduce Gregory to his sister."

Mr. Villers had apparently tried to interest her friend Harry in his sister Lydia as well. He had been shocked last month to discover she preferred the appellation of bluestocking to wife. Lydia Villers was happily engaged as an assistant to the amateur apothecary Augusta Orwell, Harry's aunt, who was trying to develop the perfect healing balm for skin conditions.

"Mr. Villers has that reputation," Yvette commiserated. "I am glad he did not ruin yours."

Her mouth tightened. "A kiss on the hand on a moonlit balcony should not count as compromise."

"No indeed," Yvette agreed, watching her. "Yet you are hiding from him as if you had cause for shame."

She raised her head at last. "My shame is that I did not manage to attract his interest. Father forbid me to encourage him. But Mr. Villers was easily the most presentable, the most stimulating man ever to show his appreciation of me. I would do anything to capture him as my own."

Yvette stared at her. So much passion, for Beau Villers? Yet how could she doubt the lady? Eyes flashing, color high, she was every bit the winged fury, the avenging angel. Mr. Villers would have to have been a fool not to see the lady's attributes. A shame he actually was a bit of an idiot.

Yet if he could make Lady Lilith happy, why not encourage the match? Surely the earl would not oppose it as his father had.

"You could still have him," Yvette informed her. "He failed to marry off his sister, but he still craves entrance to the aristocracy, I think. Show him you can give him that. Show him the vibrant woman that you are."

She blinked. "Me? Vibrant?"

Yvette put her hands on her hips. "Hair like night, eyes like lightning, figure better than that of a Greek statue. What man would refuse?"

She touched her hair as if she had never considered herself in such a light.

"All you need do is encourage him," Yvette insisted. "Be bright, be delightful. Flirt, flatter his consequence. The usual things ladies do to attract the male."

Her hand and face fell. "Oh, French, I have no experience in such things."

Yvette lowered her hands. "And I have enough experience for us both. I will show you. Together, we will be invincible."

CHAPTER EIGHT

All his guests and family presented themselves for breakfast the next morning. Gregory wasn't sure what to make of it. Novt knowing their preferences, he instructed Marbury to keep the sideboard loaded—ham, kippered salmon, and bacon; poached eggs in cream sauce; pickled asparagus; and various pastries. Julian and Villers loaded their plates, and Perkins assisted Meredith, Yvette, and the countess, who looked far better than she had yesterday.

Lilith was the last to enter, head high and steps graceful. The men popped to their feet, and Villers nearly spit out his tea.

"Please, don't trouble yourselves on my account," she insisted with a regal wave before going to select her breakfast.

Gregory and the others sat, but not before he caught Yvette smiling as if she knew something he didn't.

Conversation remained congenial, with enough people asking after his mother's health that she glowed with pleasure. Villers showed Lilith similar attention, insisting on filling her plate the second time himself. His sister gazed after the fellow wistfully. Perhaps he should ask Julian a few more questions about the intelligence agent while they were riding around the estate this morning.

His mother had other ideas.

"I shall go outside," she announced as breakfast was ending.

Julian met Gregory's gaze and shook his head ever so slightly. Right. While fresh air would do his mother good, she would no doubt expect Yvette to accompany her and they didn't want to advertise her presence.

"You are still recovering, Mother," Gregory tried.

Her face tightened. "I feel much better. French says I must get out more."

Yvette smiled. "Indeed you should. What about the courtyard in front of the house? We should be sheltered there from any cool breeze."

And any prying eyes. Gregory nodded. "Excellent idea."

"*Bon.* I'm sure you wish to join us, Lady Lilith."

Lilith, who had been smiling across the table at Villers, started. "Yes, yes of course." She turned to Gregory. "That is, if you and your friends will join us as well."

Julian's smile was polite. "Certainly."

And so a short time later they all regrouped in the flagstone-tiled courtyard between the north and south wings. The construction had been designed to allow the sun-heated stone to help warm the house in winter, while breezes during the summer cooled the stone and house. Marbury brought out a chair for the countess, who sat with her usual queenly air, surveying the rest of them. But instead of sitting in one of the other chairs that had been set up near her, with a view out the portico to the lawn and woods beyond, his sister brought out battledore rackets.

Miss Thorn declined, but Yvette seized one, and she and Lilith were soon batting the feathered cork back and forth, their skirts fluttering. His mother and Miss Thorn watched, calling encouragement and applauding. Villers hung behind them, looking a bit like a moon-struck calf.

"What do you know of Mr. Villers?" Gregory asked Julian as they strolled along the portico.

Julian shook his head. "He's a decided nuisance, if you ask

me. For years he shoved his poor sister into the arms of any titled gentleman who made the mistake of looking twice, hoping to worm his way further into Society through her marriage. Now he seems to have decided his fortunes will be made in espionage. I suspect he's just gathering intelligence he can use for blackmail."

Gregory stared at him. "As bad as that?"

Julian smiled consolingly. "At least he'll be leaving shortly."

Gregory glanced to where Villers was enthusiastically applauding his sister, whose color was high as she curtsied in his direction. "Could he have feelings for Lilith?"

"Doubtful," Julian said, deflating the last of his hopes. "Your sister has a way of scaring off suitors."

Marbury approached just then, and Gregory nodded for his man to speak.

"I have been informed," he said, falling into step beside Gregory and Julian, "that the gamekeeper encountered a stranger in the woods last evening. He believed the fellow to be a poacher, but I thought you would want to know, my lord."

Julian jerked to a stop, and Gregory and the butler paused as well.

"Do you have a description?" Julian demanded. "A location?"

"I regret that it was dark," Marbury said. "The most we know is that the fellow appeared to be dressed in rough clothing. And as to location, I believe it was in the woods overlooking the back of the house."

Julian met Gregory's gaze. "It could be our man."

"Or a poacher, as my gamekeeper noted," Gregory replied. "We don't get many, but it is early in the season with not much available to harvest. Someone might be hungry enough to risk it."

Julian glanced at the players. While he and Gregory had spoken, Villers had traded places with Yvette and was lobbing the shuttlecock to Lilith. She returned it with far more force, making Villers dive for it.

"There's one way to know for sure," Julian murmured, fingers stroking his chin. "Allow him to view his prize and see if he takes the bait."

Heat flushed up Gregory, and it was all he could do to keep his voice civil. "That will be all, Marbury. Thank you."

With a bow, his butler moved to the side of the courtyard.

"You asked me to keep Miss de Maupassant safe," Gregory told Julian. "Do not ask me to risk her life."

Julian reddened. "Lord Hastings asked you to assist in a matter that concerns the security of our nation. We cannot allow a French agent to escape."

"Then catch the agent," Gregory said, turning away. "My duty is to my household."

"Your duty is to England," Julian argued, following him. "Or do you forget the oath of loyalty you swore to the King when you ascended to the title?"

Gregory pulled up to face him. "Of course not. But there must be another way."

"I could request the local militia to surround your estate," Julian offered, "but one man could easily slip through. Making Miss de Maupassant more visible would be more effective."

"For you," Gregory said.

Julian nodded to where Yvette was bending closer to Gregory's mother, cheeks pink from her exertions. "She's tougher than you know. She watched her family die. She served as a drudge to her cousin, surviving his taunts and blows. She sat beside Empress Josephine at one point, always capturing information she could send to England. She wouldn't balk if I asked this of her."

Very likely not. Already he'd seen the strength in her in the way she dealt with his mother and sister. "Then let it be her decision," Gregory said. "I will abide by her wishes."

Meredith stood by the countess, arms feeling empty without Fortune in them. Lady Carrolton's maid, Ada, had promised to look after her pet so Meredith could join more fully in the activities of the house party. She should be watching the game or conversing with the countess, but her gaze kept going to Julian.

He had always been handsome and engaging. She'd been enamored of him for years before he noticed she wasn't a child anymore. A decade had tempered the boyish grin into something stronger, a smile that turned her insides to jelly when he looked her way. Now his face was stern as he argued some point with the earl. By all accounts, he was an excellent solicitor, well gifted in persuasion. Look how easily he had persuaded her that he still cared.

How would he react if he knew the truth?

She refused to shudder and alert those around her to the turmoil that thought engendered. Lady Winhaven's fortune had come at a price. If Julian knew about the scandal, would he still feel inclined to court her?

She made herself smile as he and the earl strode up to them. But he did not address her, turning instead to Yvette.

"Miss French," he said, as if she were no more than the companion she played, "I am helping the earl consider whether to press charges against this charlatan who endangered Lady Carrolton's health. I'd like to ask you a few questions." He bowed to the countess. "With your kind permission, of course, your ladyship."

The countess hitched her lap robes closer. "You should be asking me the questions, sir. I was the one poisoned." She coughed for good measure.

"Ah, but your description this morning at breakfast was so thorough," Julian said smoothly, "that I find I only have questions of a nature that you might find personal."

Her eyes lit. "Personal?"

Yvette patted her shoulder. "It is nothing, your ladyship. I will only be a moment."

The countess muttered, but Julian and Gregory led Yvette a little ways away.

"Well?" the countess demanded of Meredith. "Don't just stand there. I'm stuck in this chair, but you can move. Draw closer so you can hear what they're saying, then report all to me."

She ought to refuse, but, truth be told, she was curious as well. With a nod to the countess, she edged nearer.

"So, he is here, my cousin," Yvette was saying. "How can you chase him into the light?"

Cousin? He must be the French agent Harry had feared would come after Yvette. That he had been confirmed in the area sent a chill through her.

"That's just it," Julian said. "The only way to capture him is to draw him out of hiding. I know I cautioned you to stay in the background, but now may be the time to show your hand. He'll try to attack, and we'll catch him."

Meredith gasped. Julian glanced her way, brows up in surprise. Which shocked him more, that she would eavesdrop or that she would disapprove of his monstrous plan? She stalked up to them.

"Refuse," she told Yvette. "You do not owe them your life."

"But I do," Yvette said with a sad smile. "I would not be free if Harry and Mr. Mayes had not come for me."

"Nevertheless," the earl said, gaze on Yvette, "I cannot like this. What sort of gentleman puts a woman in danger?"

"What sort indeed?" Meredith said with a look to Julian.

His face didn't soften. "The sort who understands that sacrifices must be made for the greater good."

"Easy to say," Meredith retorted. "You're never the one to sacrifice."

"Peace," Yvette said, reaching out one hand to Julian and the other to Meredith. "It is my decision, and I agree

with Mr. Mayes. It is more important that we capture my
cousin before he endangers others. Besides, it will not be
so terrible. I will have the earl to protect me."

Lord Carrolton did not look comforted by this statement.

"And Villers," Julian said. "I can escort Meredith back to
London and alert Lord Hastings. Villers can stay here and
lend a hand."

"*C'est parfait,*" Yvette declared.

But Meredith could not agree to the perfection of
the plan. She'd go with Julian if that was the best for all
concerned, but she could not like how this plan endangered
Yvette and could endanger the earl and his family. It made
her realize how little she knew Julian Mayes.

"Well?" the countess demanded when Yvette led
Meredith back to the lady's side. Lilith and Mr. Villers had
ceased playing and now promenaded along the portico
in conversation. Their heads were not as close together as
Yvette would have liked, and they did not hold hands, but
at least they were being friendly.

She could not say the same of Meredith and Mr. Mayes.
The lady had refused to take his arm as they returned to
the countess, and he stood stiffly beside the earl where
Yvette and Meredith had left them.

"What did they say?" the countess asked, glancing from
Meredith to Yvette and back.

"Mr. Mayes believes you will do better without that
physician," Yvette told her. "I agree. You should get out
more—driving, to church, to visit friends."

"Tea," she proclaimed. "I go every week to visit the
Duchess."

"The Dowager Duchess of Wey," Meredith explained to
Yvette. "Though she may be too busy for a visit at the
moment. Her son, His Grace, is marrying a week from

today."

Lady Carrolton reared back. "What? Why haven't I received an invitation? Lilith! Lilith!" She fumbled with the blankets. "Where is that bell?"

"Safely inside,"Yvette informed her. She was just glad to see Lady Lilith hurrying toward them.

"What is it, Mother? Are you unwell?"

"I am much put out," her mother declared. "Miss Thorn says Wey is marrying next week."

Lady Lilith glanced around by way of apology as Mr. Villers joined them, and the earl and Mr. Mayes ventured closer as well.

"Yes," the earl's sister said. "We received an invitation. I didn't think you would want to attend given who he is marrying." She lowered her voice as if even saying the words was shameful. "His daughters' governess."

Meredith's eyes flashed. "An intelligent, caring, lovely woman. His Grace is quite fortunate."

"I'd say the fortune will fall on the governess," Mr.Villers drawled with a chuckle at his own wit. "You are wise to stay away, Lady Lilith."

The countess pouted. "I want to go. There's sure to be a fine wedding breakfast."

Mr. Mayes stepped forward. "And I'm certain His Grace would be distressed if his mother's dearest friend did not attend. If you doubt you will be strong enough, take Miss French with you."

What was he doing? It was one thing to try to force her cousin's hand here in the quiet of Surrey, where the villain could be contained. But at a wedding? Too many people could be hurt if something went wrong.

The countess raised her chin. "We'll go. All of us. Gregory can escort us. Wey will expect you at his side. I'm surprised he didn't ask you to stand up with him."

"That honor was given to me," Julian said, inclining his head as if humbled by the request. "And Sir Harold Orwell and his family will be in attendance as well, including your sister, Mr. Villers."

Villers started.

Lady Lilith turned his way. "Then will you attend, Mr. Villers?"

Yvette could see the struggle in him. He truly disdained this governess who was marrying above her station, yet how could he forego the opportunity to mix with a duke and his friends? She still could not like the idea of attending herself and possibly bringing danger to the wedding party, but she could help Lady Lilith achieve her dream.

"But of course a gentleman of Monsieur Villers's standing must attend," Yvette said. "His absence would be remarked upon. And weddings are such pleasurable affairs—the ladies look so lovely; the gentlemen begin to dream of their own brides."

Lady Lilith cast Mr. Villers a quick glance. "Well, perhaps we should go, for Mother's sake. The Duchess *is* a particular friend."

"*Bon.* Then you will have no need for my services."

"Or mine," the earl put in. "Villers can escort you and Mother."

His mother frowned. "But Wey will expect you."

She knew what he was doing. Every thought glowed from that open face. Much as he wanted to wish his friend happy, he would never leave Yvette alone while danger threatened.

Mr. Mayes shook his head. "I know you're not a social gadfly, old man, but you really must do your duty this time."

Lord Carrolton shifted on his feet. Just as Mr. Villers was torn between two social strictures, he had been torn between two duties. Mr. Mayes was reminding him of what he considered most important.

"We'll all go, then," he said, jaw hardening. "Villers, may I have a word with you?"

Paling, the intelligence agent followed him and Mr.

Mayes back to the portico. Lady Lilith gazed after them, sigh so deep it ruffled Yvette's curls.

"Vibrant," Yvette whispered, and she straightened and pasted on a smile.

"Now what are they talking about?" the countess demanded.

"Really, Mother," Lady Lilith remonstrated. "Gentlemen must have a moment to themselves, just as we do."

"*Certainement*," Yvette said, watching them. But she would have given a great deal to know why Mr. Villers looked so uncomfortable with the conversation.

She did not have an opportunity to ask until after dinner. The countess seemed to have recovered her spirits and kept her hopping. Meredith helped, bringing in Fortune. While the cat still made the countess sneeze, Lady Carrolton was amused by her antics and was even persuaded to dangle a bit of lace for the cat to pounce on. Lady Lilith was conspicuous by her absence. Yvette could only hope she was spending time with Mr. Villers.

They all retired to the golden withdrawing room after dinner. The countess, Lady Lilith, and Meredith were conversing politely by the fire with Mr. Mayes. The earl motioned Yvette and Mr. Villers to one side.

"Mr. Villers has agreed to stay when Mr. Mayes escorts Miss Thorn to London tomorrow," the earl told her. "He is unconcerned about the stranger in the woods."

Mr. Villers' smile was overly confident. "I think you have the right of it, Carrolton; it's just a poacher."

"I hope so," the earl said, gaze on his family. "When it comes to the ones I love, I tend to be overprotective."

Villers paled and excused himself to go stand by Mr. Mayes.

"You are angry with him?" Yvette asked.

The earl raised his brows. "No. I'm more concerned about this situation. You should not be made into a worm on a hook."

"So long as you catch the fish with me still intact, I will not complain," Yvette assured him.

"You have every right to complain," he argued. "I've heard stories about how you were treated in France. Abominable."

It had been. She wasn't sure why it felt good to hear him acknowledge it. "That life has ended. I must choose a different way. Though I am sorry to tell you that, however this ends, you will still have to find another companion for the countess."

He closed his eyes with a groan. "Don't remind me."

"Ask Meredith. She is determined to find gentlewomen in distress new homes."

He opened his eyes. "She's the one who found another position for the last companion. I'm not sure she approves of my household."

"Your mother and sister are improving."

"Because of you. I see the difference you make, Yvette. Thank you. I've never met anyone like you."

Warmth danced through her. How pleasant to talk, with no deadly intent, no political positioning, no reason to posture. He made it feel easy, effortless. She could imagine resting her head on that broad chest, his arms wrapping around her, knowing herself safe, treasured, loved.

Her breath caught, and she stepped back. "I should see to the countess."

Disappointment flickered across his face, but he inclined his head, and she hurried away instead of doing as her heart demanded and throwing herself into his arms.

CHAPTER NINE

Mr. Mayes, Meredith, and Fortune left the next morning. Yvette went out with the earl, Lady Lilith, and Mr. Villers to see them off. The morning was cool, mist rising from the grass to shine like silver in the air. Fortune cuddled close to Meredith, tail twitching, as if she couldn't wait for their next adventure. Knowing her cousin could be watching from the woods, Yvette felt more like an archery target, set up in the meadow and expecting the arrow to find her.

The feeling wasn't unusual. She'd been living under the shadow of discovery for ten years, ever since a dark-haired stranger had spoken to her at a ball given by her cousin. She had been trotted out, all dressed up, to prove Claude was treating her well.

"My condolences on the loss of your family, Mademoiselle de Maupassant," the fellow had murmured in perfect French as he'd led her through a gavotte. "If you have ever wished for something beyond this narrow existence, I can help."

She hadn't been sure what he'd meant, but the scowl on her cousin's face had said that Claude disliked the fellow, and that had enough to encourage her to further the acquaintance.

At eighteen, she'd thought it highly romantic, meeting at first with the dashing stranger, who had turned out to be

Lord Trevithan, England's top intelligence agent, and later Harry or his men to pass on secrets. This was her way to avenge her parents, to strike back at the indignities heaped upon her. Her work might help topple the tyrant, restore her beloved country to some sense of peace.

But, as the years went by, her position had become ever more precarious. Once she had been presented at court, her cousin pushed her forward, knowing that where she was accepted, he would be also. Every time she sent word to Harry, she'd felt a dozen pairs of eyes watching. Each smile, each movement, was calculated. The stress had been her undoing. She still wasn't sure what had alerted her cousin, but he'd discovered her deception and imprisoned her in Calais. Now that she had escaped the punishment he intended for her, he would look for every opportunity to recapture her. She shivered just thinking about what would happen if he succeeded in dragging her back to France.

As Mr. Mayes's carriage took him and Meredith off, the earl reached out and settled Yvette's shawl higher on her shoulders, fingers brushing her neck. The second shiver had nothing to do with her cousin. She wanted to lean into the earl, feel that strength around her. A shame she could do no more than play the companion. But friends had proven fickle before, family fallible. She did not trust easily now.

"I think I'll avail myself of your excellent stable," Mr. Villers announced as they turned for the house. "Care to join me for a ride, Carrolton?"

Lady Lilith had brightened at his words, until he invited her brother instead of her. Face darkening, she turned and swept up the steps to the house. The earl frowned after her, but Mr. Villers seemed oblivious.

"I must return to my duties," Yvette told them. She bobbed a courtesy, as might be expected, and climbed the steps, fully aware that both men were watching her.

"How do you do that?" Lady Lilith demanded. She was waiting just inside the double doors, as if ready to pounce. "Mr. Villers couldn't take his eyes off you, and he didn't even think to invite me to ride."

Yvette suspected the ride had more to do with checking the area around the house than pleasure. All the more reason not to include Lady Lilith. But she could not tell her that.

Instead, she looked her up and down. "You are determined to capture his attention, then."

She nodded eagerly.

"Then I suggest some changes. We will collect your mother and see what can be done."

Ada had already dressed the countess for the day and brought her breakfast. Lady Carrolton looked up with equal eagerness from the chair near the hearth in the sitting room as Yvette and her daughter entered her suite.

"What's happened?" she demanded. "Why wasn't I told?"

"Nothing happened, Mother," Lady Lilith said with a sigh. "Miss Thorn and Mr. Mayes left for London. Mr. Villers is staying."

"And your daughter would like to make a good impression," Yvette added.

Lady Carrolton raised her feathery brows. "A good impression? Have you feelings for the fellow, Lilith?"

Lady Lilith looked down her nose. "Certainly not."

"Not yet," Yvette amended. "But he is handsome in his own way, *non*? And he has a certain presence."

Lady Lilith sighed again. "He does indeed."

Yvette advanced on them both. "Then today, we will work to emphasize the lady's attributes. Come, we will start with her toilette."

She must have been sufficiently commanding, for both women followed her from the room, Lady Carrolton leaning on her cane.

Yvette had seen Lady Lilith come out of her suite

often enough that she knew which door was hers on the long corridor. She was not prepared for what lay inside. Lady Lilith's rooms were done in shades of rose, from the flowered chintz on the upholstery to the blossoms woven into the carpet.

The sitting room boasted chairs and a chaise lounge framed in rosewood, the bedroom a box bed with roses carved into headboard, footboard, and cornice. Gilded vines tied back the chintz bed hangings and velvet drapes. Pink lilies, delicate and dewy, peered out of a silver vase on the mantel. With the sun coming through the window, it was as if Yvette had wandered into a garden.

She directed Lady Lilith to sit at the mirrored table in her dressing room while the countess sat on a harp-backed chair nearby.

"Your coloring is dark," Yvette explained, meeting the lady's gaze in the gilt-framed mirror. "You can emphasize the mystery."

Lady Lilith frowned. "How?"

"Smile, like so." Yvette gave her a knowing look, one corner of her mouth tilted up.

Lady Lilith mimicked her, then spoiled it with a grin. "Oh, my. I see what you mean."

"And your hair should not be so severe," Yvette continued. "Allow a few curls to come free." She tugged the sleek tresses out of the bun, where they fell to tease the lady's cheek. "*Bon*! You see how it hints of something more within?"

Lady Lilith turned her head from side to side. "Oh, yes."

Yvette straightened. "And then your dress. Crimson, I think."

She paled. "Oh, I couldn't wear something so bold."

"Why not?" Yvette strode to the closest trunk and shoved up the lid to lift the tissue paper that protected the dresses inside. Sorting through them, she frowned. Each layer held dark, drab gowns—grey and navy and brown and puce. The material might be rich—satin and velvet and lustring—but everything was understated.

As Yvette straightened, Lady Lilith shook her head. "Don't bother with the others. One is more of the same and the other holds nothing but black from when we were in mourning for Father."

Lady Carrolton coughed. For once, it sounded like more of an attempt to catch Yvette's attention than a demand for it herself.

"Lord Carrolton preferred that we did not dress in bright colors," she told her when Yvette met her gaze.

Yvette frowned. "But why would the earl protest such a thing?"

Lady Lilith rose. "My father felt women should not call attention to themselves. He preferred to think of us as frail creatures requiring his instruction and protection."

Was that why his son was so protective? Had he inherited such a restrictive view? She could not believe it.

"Then perhaps it is good he is not here to stop us," she said, turning for the trunk again. There had been a few dresses, one a blue several shades deeper than Lady Lilith's eyes, that might suffice.

Behind her, she heard someone sigh. The voice that spoke was the countess'.

"How odd. I hadn't realized I was still living by his edicts. My husband was quite forceful in his opinions. And he could not abide anyone disagreeing with him. I told myself it was wicked to feel glad he was gone, but a part of me was relieved not to have to face him again."

"I know, Mother," Lady Lilith murmured. "I felt the same way."

Another difference between them. Yvette had mourned her father for years. He had been a gentle soul, more interested in the paintings he collected than currying favor at court. He had always encouraged Yvette to dream. The former Lord Carrolton sounded just the opposite. Had he done nothing but berate his wife and daughter?

She glanced from Lady Carrolton's trembling mouth to Lady Lilith, who had hunched in on herself, and knew it was the truth. Small wonder Lady Carrolton felt the need for commiseration, if she had received none from her husband. And Lady Lilith clung to the control her father had taken from her. If he had had the prowess of his son, he would have been intimidating indeed. It seemed neither his wife nor his daughter had been successful in challenging him. Like Napoleon, he had ruled this household, and anyone who had disagreed had been made to feel his wrath.

The injustice of it burned through her.

"I will tell you a secret," Yvette said, lowering her voice. Both women looked up in surprise. "Before I became a companion, I worked for years for my cousin. The rest of my family was gone. He should have been my protector, seeing to a better future for me. Instead, he put me to work in the vilest of jobs. And if he should come upon me while I was scrubbing the floors, he would laugh at me before aiming a kick my way."

Lady Carrolton bared her teeth. "The swine."

"Oh, yes, he is the vilest pig, and I malign the pig by saying so. But I would not let him win. I would not forget who I am, the woman I wish to be." She turned to Lady Lilith. "Who do you wish to be, *mademoiselle*?"

Lady Lilith straightened to her full height, a valiant Amazon. "A woman of breeding and taste."

Yvette turned to the countess. "And you, your ladyship?"

The countess gazed at her daughter. "The mother of the most beautiful lady in England."

With a cry, Lady Lilith ran to throw her arms about her mother. Yvette turned away to give them a moment of privacy.

Yet their stories were not so easy to turn from. It seemed the former Lord Carrolton had been a despot. Had he taught his son to be the same? Was that why Lady Carrolton had become so still when her son raised his voice? Had she feared he would lash out at her in anger?

Yvette had come to expect such behavior from her cousin. If Gregory, Earl of Carrolton, ever treated her with such contempt, she knew it would hurt far more.

Gregory returned from his ride with Villers to find the house strangely quiet. It was generally that quiet, but he'd become accustomed to having his guests underfoot.

The woods had been just as quiet. The birds were silent, as if holding their breaths. Nothing moved among the bluebells. What had frightened the typical woodland creatures away?

"Look there," Villers had said, pointing to where a metal snare lay among the flowers at the side of the riding track. "You see? You do have a poacher."

Perhaps, but poachers generally hid their work so as not to get caught and to better lure in their prey. This snare was too obvious. Either Gregory had an inexperienced or stupid poacher on his land, or someone wanted him to think as much. He'd snapped the trap and returned home.

He could not help a feeling of foreboding as he climbed the stairs with Villers now. It was as if a thundercloud hung over the house, and he kept waiting for the lightning to strike.

As they reached the landing, Villers excused himself to change out of his riding clothes. Gregory nodded and went to do the same, heading down the north wing while Villers turned for the south. He had not traveled half the length when he heard voices from his sister's suite. The door was ajar, so he peered in.

"The eyes," Yvette was saying as she stood beside his mother near the hearth. "Do not forget the eyes."

Seated on one of the rosewood chairs that graced the suite, in a low-necked blue gown he had not known she possessed, Lilith fluttered her dark lashes. She'd done something with her hair. The curls on either side of her face softened the firm line of her jaw.

"Oh, Mr.Villers," she said in a sultry voice."How you do go on. I've never met a man so witty."

"What are you doing?" Gregory asked, pushing the door open wider.

His sister stiffened, and his mother curled in on herself.

Yvette turned to meet his gaze. Her look too had changed, but it had nothing to do with her hair or clothing. He had not realized how much he enjoyed her approval until he saw something less.

"Your sister is completing her toilette," she informed him."You embarrass her by your presence."

There he went blushing again. "Forgive me. When you have a moment, I'd like to discuss plans for the rest of the day."

Lilith rose, all grace. "It's all right, Gregory. You may enter."

Feeling a bit like a schoolboy brought before the dean, he moved into the suite. The lilies on the mantel were beginning to wilt. He frowned at them, frustration building.

His mother straightened. "It's time I retired to my room. I've been gallivanting about entirely too much. You can come read to me later, Gregory, if it isn't an inconvenience."

"I'd be delighted, Mother," he said."Would you like me to escort you now?"

"*Mais non,*"Yvette said. "You cannot retire, my lady. Did you forget we promised Lady Lilith we would go shopping for a new bonnet for the wedding?"

"Yes, Mother," Lilith said, moving to join her. "We want to look our best on such a festive occasion."

"Oh, all right," his mother grumbled. "Might as well show up the governess."

They wanted to leave the estate to shop? They were intent on cutting up his peace. Still, if Yvette's cousin came after them here, it would be far easier to deal with than at Wey's wedding.

"We'll go to Chessington, then," Gregory said. "I'll have the carriage brought around. Mr. Villers will no doubt want to accompany you."

"No!" his sister cried.

Even as Gregory frowned, Yvette moved to his sister's side. She murmured something that sounded like *breeding and taste*.

Lilith drew in a breath. "Forgive me, Gregory. Of course your friend may accompany us. I was merely concerned he might find the outing dull. He's no doubt visited far better shops in London."

It was her protection and not the shopping that required the fellow's company, but Gregory could not tell her that. "Chessington is likely livelier than Carrolton Park."

His sister blushed, and he realized belatedly she might take it that he found her company lacking.

"Will you be attending us as well, my lord?" Yvette asked.

He looked to her. Her face was bland, her look diffident. If he did not know better, he would have thought her no more than a servant. What had he done to make her retreat into this shell? Or was she merely better than usual about playing her part?

Well, if she could play servant, he could play earl.

"Certainly I'll accompany you, Miss French," he said. "Nothing could keep me from my mother and sister's sides."

Or hers.

CHAPTER TEN

He did not look like a villain. Yvette tried to reconcile the open face of the earl, seated across from her and the ladies in the carriage, with what she had learned about his father. Since finding them in his sister's room, he had worn a slight frown, as if he simply wasn't sure of any of them. She shared his concern.

She'd seen how easy it was for her cousin to pretend. In public, Claude was all charm, suave, sophisticated. Everyman's friend, Napoleon had once called him. The Emperor could not know how true the statement was. Claude was capable of being friendly to men. It was the women, even his own wife, he held in contempt.

She watched how the earl and the women in his life interacted as the driver let them off on the high street of Chessington. Lady Lilith was correct—the cozy hamlet was a far cry from London. A few red brick shops with glass fronts clustered around an inn, where some older men sat under a spreading oak, telling tall tales no doubt. More wagons than carriages trundled past. On a hill in the distance, the steeple of a church pointed heavenward.

Likely used to the quaint surroundings, Lord Carrolton offered his mother his arm and slowed his steps to match her pace as they moved away from the carriage. He bent his head to listen to her usual litany of complaints—the day was overcast; she hated the rain; the flowers in the box in front of the shops made her sneeze; the cobbled pavement hurt her feet. Never once did he betray frustration or chagrin.

Lady Lilith and her wished-for swain were a contrast. She walked beside Mr. Villers toward the shops, but he did not offer her his arm, and he did most of the talking, sneering at the plebian surroundings while extolling the virtues of London. Still, Lady Lilith did not seem unhappy.

She seized Yvette's arm the moment they entered the millinery shop. The two lady owners—sisters by the similar look of their round faces, neat brown hair, and wide blue eyes—were already curtseying and fussing over the countess.

"I have no idea what to buy," Lady Lilith whispered to Yvette, gaze darting from the white wicker cages that would become bonnets to the spools of bright ribbon that would decorate them.

"Allow me," Yvette said.

Disengaging, she joined the countess and the shopkeepers. "*Bonjour*, madams. I am Miss French, the countess' new companion. We are here for the finest of headdresses to wear to His Grace the Duke of Wey's wedding."

Out of the corners of her eyes, she saw Mr. Villers sidle up to Lord Carrolton for a word. The two men stepped outside.

The two sisters stepped forward. One brought over a somber black velvet bonnet with glass-eyed blackbirds on it. The countess reached to take it from them, but Yvette waved it away.

"*Non, non*! Lady Carrolton must have something regal, befitting her station. A satin turban, perhaps, trimmed with pearls."

The sisters exchanged glances, then looked to Lady Carrolton.

"Well, go on," she ordered them. "You heard what I want."

One sister curtsied again, then hurried to the back of the shop. The other glanced at Lady Lilith before addressing herself to Yvette. "And for her ladyship?"

"Blue velvet of a shade to compliment her eyes," Yvette said. "High crowned, with ostrich plumes."

"Oh, daring." With a smile, the woman headed toward the front window.

Lady Lilith took the shopkeeper's place beside Yvette. "High crowned? I already stand taller than half the men in the room."

"You are an Amazon," Yvette told her. "Be proud of it."

She was watching the countess and Lady Lilith try on more appropriate headdresses when the earl returned and touched her arm. She stiffened at his touch and made herself smile. "*Oui?*"

He tilted his head, and she joined him near the front window.

"Villers is strolling the area around the shop, to make sure you are safe," he murmured. "But I must ask: have I offended you in some way?"

He looked so concerned, brow furrowed and eyes tight. Was he only posturing?

"I do not know," she replied. "Perhaps we can find time to talk later."

He nodded and stepped back, and she went to advise on the headdresses.

In the end, they left with three pieces: a turban in royal purple, trimmed in pearls and white satin ribbon for the countess; a sky blue velvet shako with white ostrich plumes curling from the top and black satin braiding crisscrossing the front for Lady Lilith; and a close-fitting green velvet bonnet with a spray of pink silk roses along one side for Yvette.

The countess had insisted on the last. "I want you to look good, too," she said when Yvette protested. "Patience Ramsey will no doubt be attending. She must see that my new companion is far superior."

Yvette felt a pang. She had spent some time with Patience, who was to marry Harry, and knew the compassionate woman must have made a fine companion. Still, the countess had forced her to sleep on a cot. Lady Carrolton was being far more generous with Yvette. How would she feel when she learned of Yvette's deception? Always before those she had deceived had been complicit in the Emperor's crimes. They had, in a sense, deserved any disappointment in her. Lady Carrolton and her daughter were innocent.

And extremely eager to put her suggestions into practice.

They commandeered her for the rest of the day, begging her help to go over each item in their wardrobes, from ballgowns to gloves, pelisses to ear bobs. Yvette was able to locate several day dresses, an evening gown, and a ballgown suitable to Lady Lilith's dark coloring. Others could be made passable with the addition of a fichu or shawl draped to advantage. The rest Yvette suggested donating to the staff.

"Would they want such things?" Lady Lilith asked, making a face at the pile of silk and wool.

"If not, they will know where to sell them," Yvette assured her.

Lady Carrolton's wardrobe was more difficult. Most of her recent gowns were black; the older gowns were a bit behind the fashion. Yvette chose several that could be altered, including an amethyst-colored silk gown in matte satin that could be ready in time for the wedding.

"You take this one," the countess commanded, shoving an orchid-colored dress at Yvette. "Far too frivolous for me."

Yvette accepted the dress, fingering the gold lace overskirt. "Why did you buy it, then?"

"My husband insisted on it."

The lace felt hot in her hands. She fought off the feeling.

By wearing it, she was in no way condoning the actions of the former Lord Carrolton. And if the dress was seen at the wedding, perhaps it would become associated with happier memories.

Between the countess' usual needs and Lady Lilith's requests for advice, however, Yvette was prevented from having a private word with Lord Carrolton until the following day, after services.

She had forgotten it was Sunday until she answered the countess' ring and found her dressed to go out. Ada too wore her best dress, blue with a dainty white collar.

"I suppose you're a Papist," Lady Carrolton accused Yvette as she settled the lady's breakfast tray across her lap on the chair by the hearth.

"*Mais non,*"Yvette said, straightening. "The Emperor and the Pope are not on the best terms. But it has been a while since I attended services."

In truth, her first real church service in a decade had been two weeks ago—had it truly been so short a time?—when she'd attended Easter services with Harry and his bride-to-be. The simple chapel, the heartfelt prayers, had been so different from the pomp and circumstance that was every part of Napoleon's court. There people attended services to see and be seen, and she had always been aware that she was on display. Today she need not fear. Her cousin would not dare attack her in church—too many witnesses and too few means of escape. She could truly worship.

St. Mary the Virgin in Chessington proved to be the home of the steeple she had seen the previous day. The tiny church stood high on a hill overlooking the green fields. The warm rough stone of the exterior, the cool interior with its sharply arched windows and doors appealed to her immediately. The vicar was a middle-aged man, appropriately serious in his demeanor. Seated in the walnut box pew between Lady Carrolton and the earl, voices raised in prayer around her, she felt herself relaxing.

Thank You.

The prayer came easily, from the depths of her. She drew in a breath and smiled at the cross over the altar.

As the service progressed, however, she became more aware of the earl beside her, the way he shifted when the vicar called for reflection, the way his hands gripped the back of the pew when he rose or sat. His expression was as solemn as the vicar's, and when he bowed his head to pray, she could feel his devotion. He couldn't be a bully, could he?

A sandy-haired deacon came forward as the services ended.

"I have a duty to perform," he informed them all, adjusting the spectacles on his short nose. He lifted a piece of paper and read from it. "I publish the banns of marriage between Sir Harold Orwell of Foulness and Patience Ramsey most recently of Carrolton Park. This is the first time of asking. If any of you know cause or impediment why these two people should not be joined together in Holy Matrimony, ye are to declare it." He folded the paper and smiled hopefully at them all.

No one spoke.

Lady Lilith puffed out a sigh.

Lady Carrolton waited until they had exited the church before speaking her mind.

"Married!" she cried as they walked under the ivy-wrapped iron arch that held the lamp over the gate in the hedge. "You told me Patience Ramsey was too good to be my companion, Gregory, but I never believed it. I didn't believe that upstart Sir Harold when he claimed to be engaged to her. My Patience, married to a baronet." She frowned at her son, who was escorting her. "Why haven't you married? Must I die before seeing grandchildren?"

Lady Lilith stifled a sob and ran for the coach. To Yvette's surprise, Mr. Villers hurried after her.

The earl started forward, then must have realized he

could not drag his mother with him and pulled back.

"This is not the time or place to discuss this, Mother," he said, manly jaw tight.

She sniffed. "It never is. You should have pursued Charlotte Worthington. Her brother encouraged you."

Why did Yvette have a sudden urge to yank out Miss Worthington's no doubt shiny hair? She hadn't even met the woman!

"I did pursue her, Mother," the earl informed her as they approached the carriage. "She decided we would not suit." He turned to help his mother up into the coach as the coachman steadied the horses.

So, the lady he had pursued had turned him down. What did she know that Yvette had missed?

Yvette continued to watch him warily, as if she expected him to leap from the carriage and run alongside. Gregory had wracked his brain, but he could think of nothing he had done that might have caused her to take him in dislike. But then, the behavior of some women baffled him.

His mother would have to bring up Charlotte Worthington. The sister of a good friend, she was tall and graceful, with auburn hair and wise grey eyes. Wise enough to see through him.

"You don't love me, Gregory," she'd said, patting his hand after he'd had the courage to suggest their friendship might be something more. "And I cannot abide the idea of being one more pretty decoration in your home."

He certainly hadn't intended her to be a decoration, even if she was lovely to look upon. Then again, what did he know about the roles a wife could play? His mother had been a recluse since he could remember. Worth's mother was gone, as was Harry's, and there was no one quite like Harry's aunt Gussie, who had raised him. Of Gregory's close friends, only Wey had a mother highly involved in his life. The Dowager Duchess of Wey was still mourning the death of her husband, but she'd been known to take a hand in politics and advocate for the less fortunate. Did other wives do as much?

Not that he had much chance of finding out at the rate he was going.

He made sure his mother was settled in the carriage, then turned to hand in Yvette. As he did so, a movement caught his eye. A stranger was watching them from the corner of the hedge, where it turned around the churchyard. As he shifted, the sunlight gleamed on strawberry blond curls escaping his cap.

Gregory seized Yvette by the waist and bundled her into the coach.

"Gregory!" his mother scolded, while Yvette stared at him.

"Stay here," he ordered, "and keep away from the windows."

His mother's eyes widened, but Yvette nodded and pulled her back against the seat.

Of course, the fellow was gone by the time Gregory reached the spot. The grass appeared to have been trampled, but he could have said the same about much of the area around the church following services. Likewise, a fellow in a tweed cap fit in all too well with the people heading back into the village.

"Is this where you saw him, then?" Yvette asked.

He spun to find her just behind him. "What are you doing? I told you to wait in the coach."

"I am not good at obeying orders," she said, glancing around. "Besides, it is plain he has fled."

Gregory drew in a breath. "If it even was your cousin. I cannot know every man in the area, though I have met many. What color hair does he have?"

"Like mine," she said, fingering a curl escaping from the

bonnet his mother had purchased for her. "I do not think he realized how much I would resemble him when he insisted my head be shaved." She shrugged.

He could not be so cavalier. The fellow had been here, less than twenty feet away. He could have shot from cover, killed her before anyone would have been the wiser. And Villers, who was supposed to be helping Gregory guard Yvette, was…

Standing on the other side of the coach, bending his head toward Lilith!

Gregory grabbed Yvette's hand. "Back in the coach. Now."

She did not resist, but she didn't like it. Her hand was stiff in his. "I am not your prisoner, my lord."

"Until I know you are safe, you might as well be."

Now she dug in her heels on the soft ground. "I can help."

"Not now." He picked her up and deposited her in the coach once more. Turning, he found his coachman and the remaining parishioners staring at him.

"Servants," he said before moving around the coach.

Villers and Lilith seemed oblivious as he approached, her color high and his voice low. Had the miscreant gone so far as to kiss her? Gregory grabbed him by the collar.

"You are shirking your duty, Mr. Villers," he said, lifting the fellow to the toes of his shiny shoes. "I have half a mind to make you walk back to the house, but that would leave me short-handed."

"Gregory!" Lilith cried. "Release him!"

Villers was making unconvincing gagging noises. Gregory pushed him in the direction of the carriage door, opened it, and thrust him in.

"I don't need your assistance," Lilith informed him, lifting her skirts to clamber in after the fellow. Villers slumped onto the rear-facing seat and refused to meet Gregory's gaze.

By the time Gregory climbed in, his sister had taken his seat next to Villers and was apologizing. Gregory squeezed in next to his mother, whose gaze darted about the coach as if she wasn't sure which person was more interesting. Yvette was worse. She stared straight ahead, as if seeing nothing and no one.

"I assure you, I don't know what came over my brother," Lilith said to Villers as the coach started out.

Villers was attempting to salvage his cravat, which Gregory's grip appeared to have wrecked. "No reason to apologize, Lady Lilith. The earl is correct. A gentleman has a duty to all the ladies he is escorting. I will only say that my admiration of you made me oblivious to everything else."

She slid closer, lower lip trembling. "You are a true gentleman, Mr. Villers, unlike some." The look she cast Gregory was all venom.

"Alas," Yvette said into the silence, "it is easy for a bully to wear a pleasant face."

Sandwiched between his mother and the wall, he winced. Bully, braggart, bruiser—the names had been easily applied by those who saw only his size and not the man beneath it. Sometimes he felt like a lion in a cage—the very things that made him who he was were viewed as dangers to those around him.

Even, it seemed, by the woman he had vowed to protect.

CHAPTER ELEVEN

She had hoped he was different from so many of the men she'd known. Her father was the one good example she had. He had been devoted to his wife and children, his death a senseless act, as tragic as the burning of the paintings he loved. Lord Carrolton had seemed kind, yet what was she to make of his behavior at the church? Such brute force! Such command! The change in him was as great as if Fortune had turned into a mountain lion.

He said little on the drive back to the house, sitting with arms crossed over his chest and lips tight. Lady Lilith and Lady Carrolton kept their heads down and their thoughts private. Only Mr. Villers seemed confused by the tension, glancing from the earl's sister to him, opening his mouth and then shutting it again. He finally looked to Yvette in appeal. She could only shrug.

As soon as they entered the house and Marbury stepped forward to take the ladies' wraps, the earl turned to Yvette. "Miss French, a word if you please."

Lady Carrolton sighed and shambled over to Yvette's side as if assuming she would join them.

"Alone," he added.

The countess' lower lip trembled as she peered up at her son. "You aren't going to discharge her, are you?"

In the act of draping the countess' pelisse over his arm, Marbury froze.

Lady Lilith's reaction was far stronger. She gasped and rushed forward. "Gregory, no! Whatever she did, it wasn't her fault. It was mine."

Her mother drew herself up. "Nonsense. It was mine. If you must punish someone, let it be me."

Yvette stared at them. They feared what he might do, yet they were willing to take the blame onto themselves. No one had ever done as much for her since her family had been killed.

The earl was staring as well. "I don't intend to punish anyone. I simply wish to speak to Miss French about a matter that occurred at the church. I promise not to shackle her in chains or put her on bread and water."

Marbury relaxed.

Lady Lilith slumped, then raised her chin in her customary hauteur. "Well, if I learn otherwise, I shall be very put out with you, Gregory. Come, Mother. It seems we will have to fend for ourselves."

Lady Carrolton leaned closer to Yvette. "Tell me everything he says." Her whisper carried around the entry hall.

"Am I to be included in this conversation?" Mr. Villers asked as Lady Lilith and the countess climbed the stairs, Marbury right behind.

"No," the earl said. "I'll have words with you later."

He paled, but he inclined his head and excused himself.

The earl motioned Yvette into the corridor and walked with her to the golden withdrawing room, opening the door to let her in. For once, the gilded and bronzed decor did nothing to lift her spirits. He shut the door and turned to face her.

"I asked you to wait in the coach."

The words came out clipped. He was still in high dudgeon. She would not fight fire with fire. Yvette wandered to the marble hearth and ran her hand over the smooth surface. "You ordered me to hide. That was counter to the plan. If my cousin does not see me, we will not see him."

"He saw you all right." He strode to the window and snapped shut the drapes as if trying even now to shield her. "And I saw him."

"You might have caught him if you hadn't insisted on protecting me," Yvette informed him as the room darkened. "I know you British thrive on chivalry and romance, but in this game, *monsieur*, you must think with your head, not your heart."

"My heart is entirely the problem." He stalked back to her. My, but he was large. She had to tilt her head back to meet his gaze. Those brown eyes were sagging, his spirit as well, she thought.

"This isn't a game to me, Yvette," he murmured. "I cannot think like Julian Mayes. I realize the goal is to stop your cousin from harming others, but harming you is equally repugnant."

And that was the difference between Claude and the earl. Her cousin cared nothing for the carnage in his wake. Sometimes she thought he thrived on it. This man cared too much. Still, she could protect herself. Perhaps it was time he realized that.

She slid away from him along the hearth. "You are big and strong. Few can match you. You rely on this."

He shook his head. "I like to think I have more on my side than brute strength."

"*Oui*. Honor, valor. You look at me, and you see a frail creature in need of your protection, a seedling to your oak."

He did not refute her.

Yvette kept her voice sweet. "But I am not helpless, my dear earl. I survived the Terror, the treachery of Napoleon's court. I know when to fight and when to cry peace." She moved closer, rested her head against his chest. She thought he was more surprised than she was when his arms came around her.

In a flash, she had slipped away, blade springing easily to her hand from the sheath on her wrist. "You see? I am no one's fool. You do not have to treat me like a child."

He stared at the dagger, glittering as brightly as his withdrawing room. "Where did you…"

"I carry it, always. At night it is under my pillow. I am no novice to danger, my lord."

He shook his head again. "So you have no need of me. And here I thought the War Office was finally going to allow me to participate. I'm nothing but a backdrop in the play."

Yvette lowered the dagger with a frown. "You wish to be in danger?"

"No," he corrected her. "I wish to be of use. Our nation faces a threat that could well end us. What sort of man sits idly by? But I have a responsibility to this estate, the people who depend on it. I cannot simply ride off to war."

Very likely not, though he had the physique to do well as a warrior. Had the Carroltons descended from the northern hordes that had once conquered this land and even sacked Paris? She could imagine him standing at the prow of a ship, sword raised and teeth bared. But she had a feeling that while his comrades would rush to the fray, he would have stayed to protect the widow in the village.

She sheathed the dagger in the scabbard. "We are both of us misplaced. My parents intended me to marry a count and be a wife with nothing more to do than tend roses and plan banquets."

"Would you have been happy?" he asked.

"Perhaps. It was all any of us knew then. Now? I have seen too much, done too much, to return easily to that life."

"And I am constrained to the life I have." He sighed. "What would you have of me, Yvette? I cannot stand by and watch while you are in danger."

"I do not ask it of you. We must work together, you and

me. My cousin is now certain, if he was not before, that I am in your house. He may even have allowed you to see him, so you would know he was coming. He wishes to strike fear in us. Instead, we will be ready for him. Like the French royalty, we will eat, drink, and be merry as the mob approaches the Bastille."

He grimaced. "Not the best analogy. Louis and his queen were destroyed."

"We will not be," Yvette told him. "The king and queen could not understand the frustrations of the people. I know how Claude thinks." She paced away from the hearth and back again, chewing her lower lip. "The agent he sent to Harry's tried to kill me twice, once with a shot from cover and the other with poison."

He looked white against the gold of his wall coverings. "If we keep inside and hire no new staff, you should be safe here."

Yvette shook her head. "Still you think of protection. We must bring him closer if we wish to capture him. He must have an opportunity to strike in which he thinks he can escape." She eyed him. "You have men in the woods, *non*?"

"My gamekeeper," he allowed.

"And grooms to attend you."

He nodded.

"Then I must visit the forest. I will go tomorrow to gather bluebells for the countess. You will send men ahead to surround the area. When Claude shows his hand, we will capture him and end this madness once and for all."

She was so fervent. Her eyes flashed, her skin glowed. He could imagine men marching behind her all the way to the palace gates. He would have been one of them.

Still, he doubted it would be so easy to draw her cousin out of hiding. The man was adept at escape.

"And if that doesn't work?" he asked.

She wiggled her lips as if chewing on a thought. "If we cannot lure him out here, he may strike at this wedding. We could send your men ahead to watch the road and add one to the servants working at the celebration. My cousin must think me an easy target."

He still didn't like her being a target at all, but that dagger proved she was ready to take on anyone rash enough to accost her.

They plotted strategy for a while longer, then she raised and lowered her slender shoulders as if stretching them. "I should go. The countess and your sister will be worried."

He smiled. "I've been half expecting them to storm the doors."

She eyed the portal as if expecting the same. "They wished to protect me. I am amazed."

The words came out before he could stop them. "You inspire acts of valor."

She dimpled. "Why, my lord, you truly are a romantic."

If only his cheeks did not betray him. He could feel them heating. "Nonsense. If you see Marbury on your way, tell him I'm ready for Mr. Villers."

She started for the door, then looked back. "Will you tell him our plan?"

Gregory smiled. "*Certainement.*"

She answered his smile and left.

His smile faded. His mother and sister seemed certain he would beat or discharge Yvette over some infraction even though he tended to be the most lenient of employers. He still wasn't sure what Yvette thought of him.

And Villers thought him a fool who would allow the fellow to dally with his sister.

The intelligence agent came in a short while later, walking gingerly as if the gold and ruby carpet was as hot as coals.

"You wished to see me, my lord?"

Gregory motioned him into a chair. Villers perched on the edge as if ready for flight.

Gregory sighed. "Why are you in my house?"

Villers blinked. "Surely you know. I was sent to protect Yvette de Maupassant."

Gregory leaned forward. "Then why, when we were out in public, where anyone might approach her, did you leave her side?"

Villers threw up his hands. "We were on hallowed ground! No one would dare trouble her there."

"You give the villain more credit than I do." Gregory leaned back. "In fact, I'm fairly certain Claude de Maupassant was watching our every move."

Villers shook his head. "You must learn to be more trusting, my lord. We were perfectly safe, I assure you. I would have noticed anything untoward. I am trained for this sort of thing, you know."

"Indeed." Gregory crossed his arms over his chest. "And what sort of training does Lord Hastings provide his agents these days?"

Villers flicked a piece of lint off his trousers. "I'm afraid that is privileged information, my lord."

The popinjay! Given Julian's comments about his abilities, Gregory began to think the fellow had no experience whatsoever. "Then allow me to share with you some equally privileged information. Claude de Maupassant was at the church. I saw him."

"What!" Villers surged to his feet. "Where? Why didn't you capture him?"

"Because," Gregory gritted out, "I was too busy protecting Yvette. Alone."

Villers sank back onto the chair. "Oh. I see. So, he got away."

"For now. Yvette intends to make herself more visible the next few days to attempt to lure her cousin out of hiding."

His pallor said he liked the idea as little as Gregory did, but he nodded agreement. "I will do my duty, my lord."

"Good," Gregory said. "Now, care to explain why you were attending my sister after church instead of doing your duty then?"

Villers blew out a breath. "I never could ignore a lady's tears."

"Tears?" Gregory frowned. "Why was Lilith crying?"

"Those banns." He shook his head. "Can you imagine? A woman of delicate sensibilities like your sister, hearing that her mother's companion was to wed a baronet while she languishes on the shelf. It was not to be borne."

He hadn't realized Lilith regretted her single state. He had never seen her go out of her way to seek a husband, if that was her goal.

"I would hope my sister to be magnanimous enough to be happy for the woman," Gregory said. "This is an excellent opportunity for Patience Ramsey, and I gather Harry is over the moon."

"Utterly besotted," Villers said with a curl of his lip that told Gregory his feelings on the matter.

He thought he knew at least partly why Villers was as bitter as Lilith about Harry's upcoming marriage. Gregory clasped one knee with his hands. "My condolences, old fellow. I know you hoped Harry for your sister."

Villers shrugged. "Lydia has made her choice, for all I think it beneath her. Playing with chemicals in a laboratory." He shuddered. "Sisters."

Gregory felt for him. He too would have liked to see his sister well settled. Sometimes he thought Lilith's frustrations stemmed from having little on which to expend her skills. A house of her own, a challenging occupation, or a noble cause might help.

"I also wish the best for my sister," he said aloud. "Which is why I must ask your intentions."

Villers stiffened. "Intentions?"

"Come, now. Strolling alone together, standing heads bowed in the churchyard."

"I told you—I was comforting her," he protested. "As any gentleman would."

"Then you have no feelings for my sister."

He adjusted his cravat as if it were suddenly too tight. "I never said that."

"You don't seem to be saying anything at all," Gregory pointed out.

Villers shifted on the chair. "Lady Lilith is one of the most magnificent specimens of womanhood it has been my pleasure to meet. I treasure her friendship. But I was under the impression you would never countenance a match between us."

Interesting. Lilith had certainly shown her preferences for the fellow. If the feelings were mutual, a match might benefit all around.

Gregory studied his fingers. "That would depend. As her brother and head of the family, I must look to her best interests. What do you offer her?"

Villers sank lower. "What would you consider? I have no title, no estate, and my fortune is barely sufficient to meet my needs."

"Such honesty," Gregory said, looking up, "is a start."

Villers raised his head. "Truly?"

"Truly."

He straightened. "Excellent. Then let me confess that in my devotion I fought a duel last year in your sister's honor.'

Gregory started. "What?"

Villers froze. "Few knew of it. I wouldn't have mentioned it now, except you said honesty…"

"Yes, yes. But why did you need to defend my sister's honor?"

He raised his chin. "You'd have to speak to her about that. I will say no more on the matter. Word of a gentleman."

Gregory rose, and Villers put up his fists to shield his face.

NEVER ENVY AN EARL   119

"I'm not going to strike you!" Gregory thundered.

Villers peered over his fists. "You'll pardon me if I don't believe you."

Gregory stepped back. "Believe me or not. I have never raised my fists in anger."

"Well, I wouldn't admit that in public, old boy," Villers said, lowering his hands. "We are supposed to be protecting Miss de Maupassant. We wouldn't want the enemy to think you'd gone soft."

First he was a bully, and now he was a coward. He couldn't win. He nodded to Villers. "I will consider the matter between you and my sister, but I make no promises. A great deal will depend on how Lilith feels and whether you can support her."

Villers stood. "I understand. You will want a gentleman of sterling character, impeccable address, and high social standing for your sister. I'm certain my attributes speak for themselves."

Far more than he knew. Gregory could only hope his sister would see that as well.

CHAPTER TWELVE

Lady Carrolton and Lady Lilith were waiting for Yvette in the countess' sitting room.

"Did he berate you?" the countess demanded.

"Did he order you from the house?" Lady Lilith beseeched.

Yvette held up her hands. "Peace. All is well. He was only concerned that I was distracted today from attending to you."

"It's Beau," Lady Lilith said, worrying her hands. "Gregory doesn't approve."

"He said nothing of the sort," Yvette assured her. "Continue as you have, and see how Mr. Villers responds."

The earl's sister nodded slowly. Yvette did not doubt Lady Lilith had already succeeded in attracting the gentleman's attention. She did, however, wonder whether she'd succeeded in making her point with Lord Carrolton. The important thing was to capture Claude. He needed to remember that.

Accordingly, she made doubly sure her dagger was in place before leaving her room the next morning to the sound of the countess' bell. As if he had been waiting for her, the earl was standing in the corridor, clad in his usual tweed coat and chamois trousers, and wincing at each clang.

"Do not answer immediately," Yvette advised him. "She

likes the noise."

"She likes the power," he corrected her with a smile. It faded as quickly as it had come. "Send for me when you intend to go to the woods."

Yvette put her hands on her hips. "The earl would not accompany the companion."

"But the companion could come upon the earl out for a stroll," he countered.

Her hands fell as she laughed. "Very clever. You are learning."

Unfortunately, the countess was not. She fussed about every little thing that morning, until Yvette began to think she really was trapped in the role of companion. Only when Lady Lilith and Mr. Villers came to visit was Yvette able to excuse herself long enough to put the plan into action.

The day was overcast as she exited the house through the front door. Clouds hung heavy, bottoms scraping the treetops, and the breeze smelled moist with the promise of rain. Mr. Marbury had loaned her a wicker basket, which she looped over one arm as she lifted her navy skirts to start down the stone steps. She caught no sign of any other staff member as she crossed the wide swath of lawn, though a family of deer bounded away to the wood at the sight of her.

They saw the trees as shelter, but a chill went through her as she approached the shadows. She could only hope the earl's men were standing by, as she'd suggested.

Like a gentle tide, bluebells lapped at her hem as she moved deeper into the trees. Their rounded heads bobbed in the breeze while birds sang above. Small wonder the countess had come to gather the flowers when she was younger. Yvette bent and plucked an emerald stalk.

"Lovely day for a walk."

That familiar deep voice made the tension slide further from her shoulders. She straightened to smile at the earl.

What, had he been in hiding as well? She could not credit the trees were thick enough to obscure a man of his size. Yet his coat was rumpled, and a leaf lodged in the dark of his hair. Her hand was moving to take it out before she thought better of it, but she stopped herself from touching him.

She was a companion. She must seem like a companion.

"A lovely day indeed," she made herself say, dropping her gaze humbly to the purple carpet below. "The countess wished me to retrieve some flowers for her room."

"Allow me to be of assistance."

Those hands could have yanked up enough to fill her basket in one swipe, but he bent and carefully selected a flower before straightening and handing it to her.

"The gamekeeper and two grooms are watching," he murmured as she laid the flower with the other in the basket.

"Thank you, my lord," she said aloud. "I would not wish to detain you."

There was a decidedly determined light in his dark eyes. "It is no imposition. Anything for my mother." He selected another blossom and offered it to her. As she reached for it, his fingers brushed hers, and a tremor went through her.

"You will frighten him away," she whispered, carefully laying the flower in the basket.

He shook his head but raised his gaze to look deeper into the trees. "I believe there's a larger patch just there. Excuse me." He moved beyond her.

She drew in a breath and tried to focus on the flowers. With so many so close she could catch the cool, clean scent of them. A shame she could not simply stop and enjoy it. A part of her must remain alert for any strange sound from the trees, any movement in the shadows. She bent and picked several more of the blooms, depositing them in the basket.

The songbirds fell silent.

She should not show that she noticed. Claude must not know her fear. He must think her blithefully unaware. She gave the basket a little swing as if she hadn't a care in the world.

Something cracked in the forest behind her.

And everything exploded. A grey-haired man dove out of cover on the left and raced toward the sound, only to have a younger blonde crash into him from the right. They went down in a tangle of arms and legs, flattening the bluebells and sending birds into the sky. A third fellow appeared from in front of her and leaped his comrades to disappear into the forest again. And, like a minotaur surprised from his lair, the earl stalked out of the forest and thundered past her to follow his only man still standing.

Yvette shook her head, set down the basket, and attempted to help her would-be rescuers to rise. She was just reassuring the gamekeeper that she was fine when the earl returned.

"Potter is on the trail," he reported. "Thurston, James, circle around past the greenhouses just in case he doubles back."

With a nod of respect to the earl and her, his men headed off.

"They will capture your cousin," he promised.

Relief was stronger than the scent of the flowers. "You saw him, then?"

"No," he admitted. "But if he caused that noise, he won't get away." He bent and picked up the basket. "Allow me to escort you back to the house."

How could she argue? If his men were in pursuit of her cousin, Claude would be running for his life. If he had been watching from a distance, he would know he stood no chance of capturing her while the earl was so close. Either way, she might as well give up, for now.

Gregory escorted Yvette back to the house, careful to stay between her and the trees. His men were clever and loyal, if a bit too eager. He should have realized his gamekeeper Thurston and the younger groom James might leap to action prematurely. Still, no harm done. If Claude de Maupassant had ventured near, he would shortly be in custody. And Yvette would be free.

He glanced at her as they climbed the steps to the portico. She hadn't deigned to don a hat or bonnet, and her curls looked bright against the grey of the day. There was no tension in her slight shoulders, only confidence in her walk.

"How do you do it?" he asked.

She laughed as they came into the shelter of the flagstone courtyard. "Your sister asked me a similar question. Am I such a mystery to you?"

"At times," he admitted. "Your perseverance in adversity amazes me."

"And what choice do I have?" she asked. "Persevere or die. I am not ready to die yet."

"I'm glad." He stopped her close to the doors, loath to return inside where he ought to pay her no notice if he was to play his part. "When this is over, Yvette, you will need a place to stay. I want you to know that Carrolton Park will always be open to you."

Her smile tilted up with her eyes. "*Merci beaucoup*, my lord. But I think your mother and sister will not know how to deal with Miss de Maupassant the French lady any more than they know to deal with Miss French the companion."

"They already care about you," Gregory said. "I see it in how they relate to you."

She glanced up at him through her lashes. "And you, Gregory? Do you care?"

Far more than he should, if the use of his first name could make him feel this pleased. "Of course," he answered. "You are here under my protection."

"Oh, *oui*. For the good of the nation."

"Yes, exactly," he agreed. He only wondered why he felt as disappointed by the fact as she sounded.

The doors opened, and Marbury glanced out. "My lord? I believe the countess would like Miss French's attention."

The clang of the cowbell rang through the house.

"I will go," Yvette said to no one in particular and hurried past the butler into the house.

Marbury remained attentive. "Is there anything you need, my lord?"

Gregory sighed. "No. But I'm expecting a report from Thurston. Bring me word the moment he returns."

"Of course." Still Marbury waited, and Gregory belatedly realized he still held the basket of bluebells. He offered it to the butler with a sheepish grin.

As it was, he had to wait another long hour before Marbury came to the study to report. This room, of any of the others in the house, was his alone. The furnishings, from the walnut box desk to the white bookshelves with their classical pediments, were large and sturdy, everything well organized, simple and elegant. In this room, if only for a moment, he could convince himself he was the master of all he surveyed. He leaned back in the leather-bound wingback chair behind the desk as Marbury recounted the tale.

"They found no one in the wood, my lord. Mr. Thurston asks if you'd like to bring on other men to patrol."

With the size of the estate, even the entire population of Chessington couldn't cover every acre.

"No," Gregory said, "but tell him to remain vigilant."

Marbury saw himself out, and Gregory went to find Yvette.

She was with his mother, sister, and Villers in the music room, and he stood for a moment in the doorway to admire the tableau. Gowned in a navy gown of fine silk with a cream-colored ruff gathered at her neck, Lilith stood behind the gilded spinet, voice sweet as she sang a country ballad about a tragically lost love. Villers and Gregory's mother were seated in the little white spindle-backed chairs that graced the room, the intelligence agent looking particularly entranced.

Yvette sat on the spinet's bench, gaze focused on the sheet music before her and fingers moving unerringly as she accompanied his sister. Even with her plain gown and studious look, she outshone every lady in the room, the blazing sun to their mellow candles. He wanted to draw closer, bask in the warmth.

Lilith finished and curtseyed to Villers's enthusiastic applause. Gregory applauded as well as he moved into the room. Yvette looked up eagerly, and he shook his head just the slightest. She sagged on the bench, and he cursed himself for dimming her light.

"The voice of an angel never sounded sweeter," Villers was telling Lilith as Gregory approached.

"You are too kind, Mr. Villers," Lilith murmured, lashes fluttering. "I could be persuaded to sing another if you'd like."

"Ah, such a dilemma," Villers declared, tilting his head as if to see up under her lashes. "If you sing by the spinet, I will have the delight of listening, but if you stay to converse, I will have the joy of you at my side."

Is that drivel what women expected from the men courting them? Small wonder Charlotte had refused him. He must have looked as disgusted as he felt, for Yvette rose from the spinet and shook out her hands as if to draw attention to herself and away from him.

"*Fini*," she announced. "His lordship obviously came for other purposes."

Put on the spot, all gazes turning to his, Gregory managed a smile. "It was nothing of import. When you have a moment, Lilith, I'd like a word."

Villers stepped back from her. "I've monopolized the lady's time quite enough. Until this evening, my dear Lady Lilith." He took her hand and bowed over it. Lilith pressed her hand close as he left the room.

His mother levered herself to her feet with her cane. "What's Lilith done to displease you now, Gregory?"

Did they think he did nothing but scold? "Nothing to concern you, Mother," he assured her. "We'll only be a moment."

Lilith shrank as if expecting a lecture, but his mother made no move to leave the room.

Yvette stepped between him and his mother. "Come, *comtesse*. We must return to your room and change for dinner."

His mother drew herself up, no doubt to protest.

"We will, of course, have to ring for Ada to help us," Yvette added.

His mother grinned before she schooled her face. "Well, don't keep me waiting, French."

"Certainly not." Turning her face so neither his mother nor his sister could see, Yvette winked at him before accompanying his mother from the room. Gregory could only smile after her.

Lilith stood taller. "What did you need of me, Gregory?"

He turned and nodded her toward the nearest chair, then drew up the sturdier bench opposite her for his own seat. "I wish to speak to you about Mr. Villers."

Her nostrils flared as her breath came faster. "I won't give him up. Not again."

Gregory frowned. "Again? Has he courted you before?"

"As if you didn't know." Her face was unyielding, a mask of righteous indignation.

"I don't know," he informed her. "You haven't set foot in London since before Father died, as far as I recall, and I don't remember Mr. Villers visiting the area before."

Her eyes narrowed to slits of ice. "Father never said

anything to you?"

Foreboding crept up on him. "No. Should he have?"

She relaxed suddenly, and he heard her draw a breath. "No. There was no reason, I suppose. I met Mr. Villers in London. He showed some interest in me while you were gallivanting about the Continent. Nothing came of it. I am enjoying renewing our acquaintance now."

He wished he could believe that that was all to the matter, but he recognized the signs of evasion. Her gaze refused to meet his, and she was twisting her fingers together in her lap. He took a deep breath and launched into the worst of it.

"And what of this duel he fought in your honor last year?"

She gasped, hands clasping before her dark bodice as her gaze rose to meet his. "He fought a duel? How romantic!"

"Perhaps," Gregory allowed. "But he refused to say why such a duel was necessary, so I cannot say."

She dropped her hands. "Don't you dare browbeat him! He was defending my honor. You said so yourself."

Gregory leaned forward. "Why did your honor need defending?"

"Most likely gossip." She bit off the words as if she'd like to sink her teeth into the people who had spread the tale. "Why do you think I left Society? Mr. Villers showed me only the most courteous of attentions, but some people were so jealous they put about that he had ruined me. It was nonsense. The tale must be circulating even now. Hence the need for him to defend me." She sighed happily.

He could not be so delighted. "Who would say such things about you, must less be willing to duel over them?"

She sniffed. "We have many enemies."

"That," Gregory said, "I highly doubt. It sounds as if this whole mess is Villers's fault. He showed undue attention, he didn't honor you with a proposal of marriage, he put you in a position that encouraged gossip to start."

NEVER ENVY AN EARL   129

"No," Lilith said, rising. "You mistake him. He has ever only put my needs first."

When Gregory shook his head, she raised hers. "I knew it! You will never accept him. You're just like Father, standing over us, imprisoning us in this house." She turned and ran from the room, and Gregory could only stare after her.

Standing over them? That had never been his intent, even if he was the tallest. He had tried not to be the least overbearing. And imprisoning them? He was the one who encouraged them to get out! He felt as if the world was tipping, and he could not find his footing.

Still, one thing had not changed. He had work that must be done—protecting Yvette and his family. He would continue to do that to the best of his ability, no matter what his sister and Beau Villers thought.

CHAPTER THIRTEEN

Though Yvette ventured out again on Tuesday, no one attempted to accost her, and there were no more sightings of strangers in the woods. She spent the rest of the day Tuesday working with Ada to prepare Lady Carrolton and Lady Lilith for the trip to the Duke of Wey's estate for the wedding. While they would not be spending the night, each lady required her hair to be washed, trimmed, and styled. Lady Carrolton insisted on beauty treatments. Yvette made sure the earl looked over everything before allowing his mother to put it on herself or in herself. There must be no repetition of the prussic acid incident.

Lady Lilith seemed more agitated than Yvette had expected about the wedding. Mr. Villers had spent a great deal of time in her company—riding, taking tea, playing games on the lawn. Yet there was a certain defeat in her attitude, particularly when the earl was around.

"How have you earned your sister's wrath?" Yvette asked when they all took a turn about the rear lawn before dinner Tuesday. It had rained earlier, but the sun had since consented to shine. Golden light spilled across the green, setting the grass, the woods, and even the glasshouses at the back of the space to glittering.

The earl watched as Villers strolled along, Lady Lilith's arm tucked in his. "I'm not entirely sure."

And the fact saddened him. His eyes turned down at the

corners, until he reminded her of a chastised puppy. Best to change the subject. She turned to the view across from them. "And what do you grow in your glasshouses?"

He shifted, blocking her view of the buildings. "Vegetables, fruits, the usual things."

"So that is how you had strawberries before everyone else," she said with a smile. "Your gardener must be very talented."

He was blushing again, and this time she wasn't sure why. "He does what he can, given other priorities," he murmured. "Would you care to play battledore, Yvette?"

There was something sweet, something endearing about the way he used her first name. He had not protested when she'd called him Gregory recently. Perhaps he would allow the familiarity in private.

They left early in the morning on Wednesday for the wedding. Yvette felt that chill again as she headed for the stairs. Who knew what Claude might do and when? She could almost wish she wore something more practical than the orchid-colored dress Lady Carrolton had given her. The small bodice hugged her curves, and the graceful skirts overlain with lace would not make running easy. Still, the way Gregory stared as she came down the stairs made the dress feel perfect.

His mother and sister were in fine looks as well, though Lady Carrolton wore a black pelisse to protect her amethyst-colored gown from any travel dirt. She had been persuaded to leave her cane and bell at home. Lilith too wore a pelisse, but Yvette had had her drape a cream Paisley shawl patterned in red and blue about her shoulders. Mr. Villers's eyes lit in appreciation as she came down the stairs, new bonnet on her dark hair.

Gregory allowed the fellow to sit beside his mother and sister. That left Yvette to sit next to him on the drive. His sister smiled her thanks to him, but he didn't fool Yvette. He hadn't entirely arranged the seating out of generosity.

He was worried and still thought he could protect her better than she could.

Something zinged through her as the coach set out. Perhaps Claude was waiting along the way. Perhaps today would be the day they captured him and ended his tyranny over her. Perhaps she would finally be able to go on with her life.

And what would that life be?

She felt no need to enter Society, posture as Lady Lilith was to catch a man's attention, yet what else was there for her here in England if not marriage? She had no trade outside espionage. Despite her unexpected success with Lady Carrolton, she had no desire to continue in service. After what she had done for England, Lord Hastings would likely be glad to find her a house somewhere. She could reach out to the other émigrés, build the life of gentility her parents would have wished for her.

She just wasn't sure what she wished for herself.

She was disappointed that nothing happened on the hour drive through the countryside north to the Thames. The green fields, the dark woods, rolled past, until she could see the ribbon of grey in the distance, boats dotting the expanse. The Duke of Wey's home sat on a hill overlooking the island on which it was built. The stones glowed in the sunlight as if even the house was celebrating.

"Terribly plebian," Lady Lilith murmured to Mr. Villers as the coach rolled through the crowded streets of the village below the house, on the way to the church. "Look at these people. Shouldn't they be working?"

"I understand Wey gave everyone in the area the day off," Gregory said. "He told the businesses he would make up any lost income."

"Frivolous extravagance," Lady Lilith said, tossing her head so that the ostrich plumes bobbed on her bonnet.

"A wise use of his wealth," Yvette countered. "She was the governess, his bride. Considered beneath him. If they marry quietly, some will say he is ashamed of her. What better way to say he believes her his equal than to marry her in front of everyone?"

The earl nodded thoughtfully.

And everyone it was. The little stone church was so crowded some of the locals were relegated to the yard beyond. Yvette glanced around as Gregory led them up the pebbled path, keeping her close to his side, but she did not spot Claude among the dozens of eager strangers. Neither did she see him in the chapel with its delicate arches overhead, though Lady Lilith and Mr. Villers nodded to a number of people. Several gentlemen raised their quizzing glasses to study the earl's sister as she passed. Yvette smiled.

As a particular friend of the family, Gregory had been saved seats near the front. Lady Carrolton sat upright in the dark boxed pew, head high, face regal. Yvette sat between her and Gregory, then rose as the groom and his attendants came in. The duke was tall, with dark hair and a heart-shaped face. He looked resplendent in a suit of grey superfine, waistcoat shot with silver. Julian Mayes stood beside him, also in a grey suit, though his waistcoat was blue satin striped. His gaze roamed over the attendees, then rested as his mouth turned up. Yvette did not need to turn to know he had likely spotted Meredith. She would have to look for her friend when services ended.

The church quieted, and everyone turned to watch the bride walk down the aisle. Dressed in a grey gown that turned to silver as she moved, the duke's beloved was a sturdy-looking woman with dark hair and an easy smile. Her attendants consisted of three girls, one young enough to have just barely entered the schoolroom. They wore rose-colored satin dresses and carried sprays of roses bound with white satin ribbons that matched the ribbons in their hair. Several of the guests smiled fondly as they passed. His Grace looked utterly besotted as he took his bride's hand and pledged his love.

"I, Alaric, Duke of Wey, do take thee, Jane Kimball, as my lawfully wedded wife."

For some reason, Yvette glanced at Gregory. Was that longing on his face? Did he wish for an adoring wife to manage his home, fawn on his friends? Gaze at him so trustingly? Could she play that role? Did she want to?

A cheer went up as the vicar pronounced the duke and his bride husband and wife. Some of the aristocracy looked shocked by the display, but Yvette could only smile. It seemed the duke and his duchess were much loved by their staff and tenants.

"But will anyone receive them?" Lady Lilith was murmuring to Mr. Villers as they started out of the church. A select group—Gregory and his family among them— had been invited to attend the wedding breakfast at the duke's home afterward.

"We will," Gregory said, and no one gainsaid him.

Yvette stayed behind Lady Carrolton and Lady Lilith as they navigated the receiving line inside the vast entry hall of the house. Floored with flagstone, the space soared three stories to a painted ceiling. Gregory looked right at home with the hosts of heaven riding into battle above him.

Though many of the guests were ogling the new duchess as if she were a rare bird, she smiled as they were introduced to her. Several frowned or blinked after she spoke to them, and, as Yvette and Gregory neared the couple, Yvette began to see why.

"I won't remember your names," the new duchess was telling a viscount and his wife. "But I'm glad you could join us."

The little girl beside her, curls golden and eyes bright, tugged on her skirt and pointed. "Look, Mrs. Kimball, it's Lady Quarrelsome."

Lady Carrolton drew herself up, and Lady Lilith took equal affront, while Yvette hid a smile at the accurate appellation.

"Remember to say *Mother* now, Belle," His Grace murmured to the daughter from his first marriage before turning to the countess. "Lady Carrolton, Lady Lilith, Mr. Villers, thank you for joining us."

"Yes, well, quality will out," Mr. Villers said with a look to Lady Lilith.

The duke smiled at his bride. "It will indeed."

She blushed under his regard, then turned to Yvette as Gregory began speaking quietly with her husband. "You must be the lady who took Patience Ramsey's place as companion. Any thoughts of hemlock yet?"

Lady Carrolton sniffed. "It wasn't hemlock. It was prussic acid."

"Inventive," the new duchess said.

Yvette laughed. Seeing Lady Carrolton's scowl, she adopted a more servile look. "I am honored to serve two such fine ladies."

"Indeed," Lady Carrolton said. "Let us make room for others. Everyone wants to look at a seven-day wonder." Mr. Villers took her arm and offered his other to Lady Lilith, and they sailed past.

"I look forward to seeing you at weekly tea," the bride said to Yvette with a wink as she followed. "And I won't make you sit along the wall."

"The impertinence," Lady Carrolton fumed as they moved up the stairs and into a long gallery with the other guests.

"The cheek," Mr. Villers agreed.

"The disgrace," Lady Lilith lamented.

"I like her," Yvette said.

They found a spot to wait for the newlyweds to lead them into the dining room. While Lady Carrolton, her daughter, and Mr. Villers spoke with friends, Meredith materialized out of the crowd and moved in next to Yvette.

"You look well," she said.

"You do not," Yvette replied, noting the darkness under

her eyes. "What's happened?"

Meredith brushed down her lavender skirts. "Nothing. Can you say the same?"

So, she was worried too. "*Mais oui.* I understand my cousin has been seen, but he has not approached me."

Meredith seized her arm and drew her closer. "Then they insist on that ridiculous scheme to parade you to all and sundry."

"I agreed to it," Yvette reminded her. "It is for the best."

A head taller than anyone else in the room, Gregory was moving toward them. He nodded in greeting to Meredith, then lowered his head and his voice to take them both into his confidence.

"I spoke with Wey," he murmured. "He has heard of no strangers in the area recently."

Yvette glanced around. She could not see over the people crowding close, but there were dozens in attendance, silks and satins bright against the darker wool coats of the gentleman. "How would anyone know? His tenants and staff would not recognize all the lords and ladies who have come for the wedding, much less their servants."

"True," he allowed, "but I feel better with Wey being aware of the situation."

Meredith did not look comforted. The poor duke—to have his wedding interrupted for intrigue! Yvette had been hoping to put an end to her cousin's villainy, but perhaps it would be better if he did not attempt to reach her today.

Gregory glanced around the gallery, the joyful faces of most of the attendees at odds with the more solemn faces looking out of the paintings on the wall. Even though far fewer had been invited to the wedding breakfast than the service itself, at least one hundred people gathered round, and that discounted the footmen wending their way among the guests with crystal goblets on trays. Most of those attending he knew. Worth and his sister Charlotte, the Duke of Emerson and his older daughter, lords and ladies from around the area.

He couldn't help his grin at the entourage quickly approaching.

"Harry!" He stuck out a hand, and the baronet shook it gladly. Sir Harold Orwell still looked like his pirate forebears—swarthy, confident, and nimble.

"And Miss Ramsey," Gregory added, bowing to the lady on his friend's arm.

His mother's former companion smiled sweetly. Gregory had always thought her aptly named—nothing seemed to ruffle the dark-eyed blonde. She had certainly blossomed since leaving Carrolton Park. He couldn't recall her wearing anything as pretty as the pink gown with roses embroidered at the neck and hem. Or had his mother been the one to decree she only wear navy and grey?

"Lord Carrolton," Patience said with a curtsey. Then her eyes brightened. "And Meredith and Yvette! It's so good to see you!"

Gregory's mother and sister turned at the sound of her exclamation.

"Ramsey!" his mother cried.

"Your ladyship," she acknowledged as they and Villers moved closer. "Lady Lilith, Mr. Villers."

Though Gregory sometimes missed the social nuances, there was no mistaking the chill in her tone.

"How do you know Miss French?" Lilith demanded.

"Well, I..." Patience turned to Harry in appeal.

Harry put his arm about her waist. "Carrolton asked Patience's advice as to whether Miss French would suit you. I can see she has done well in the position. You all look stunning."

Yvette and Meredith looked pleased by the compliment to her efforts. Villers nodded approvingly, Gregory's mother preened, and Lilith smiled complacently. Gregory could only marvel at how easily lies slipped from his friend's tongue. Patience had met Yvette when Harry and Julian had rescued the Frenchwoman from a prison house on the Continent. To keep others from questioning Harry's activities, Patience, who had joined the household to assist Harry's aunt in her apothecary studies, had pretended to be betrothed to the baronet so she could cover for his absences. Their false engagement had led to a true love.

"You remember my aunt," Harry continued, motioning to someone across the room. "Mr. Villers's sister has been staying with us as her apprentice."

Gregory bowed to the tall, spare woman in navy who strode up to them, a pale-haired blonde in a frilly white dress at her elbow. "Gussie. Miss Villers."

Augusta Orwell had never been one to stand on ceremony. She shook hands all around, causing Gregory's sister to raise her brows and their mother to lower hers. Villers's greeting to his sister was surprisingly cool as well, but Lydia Villers didn't seem to notice, for the sunny smile remained on her pretty face. Those big green eyes did not give credit to the intelligence inside.

"I must brag on Lydia," Gussie told them all now. "She recently made a discovery that is highly promising for my formulation. Cod liver oil."

Every woman but Miss Villers made a face. She giggled. "You wait. When you see what it does for your skin, you won't mind the smell."

Somewhere a bell rang with a silvery tinkle.

"Mine is far superior," Gregory's mother muttered.

"Ladies, gentlemen," Julian called. "We will be going in to dine shortly. I wanted to take this opportunity to toast the bride and groom."

Around them, the room fell silent, all eyes on the happy couple standing beside him at the head of the room, arm in arm.

"Wey," Julian said. "I've known you since we were lads. I've seen you grin as you took your horse over a jump, smile at the antics of your daughters. But I have never seen you as happy as when you married your beloved Jane."

The duke's gaze was all for his wife.

"Jane," Julian continued, "I can safely say I've never met a more forthright, caring woman, capable of stepping into the role of wife, mother, and duchess." As she blushed, he raised his goblet. "To the Duke and Duchess of Wey—long may they be as happy as they are today."

"To the Duke and Duchess of Wey," the guests echoed, glasses high.

Yvette caught Gregory's arm before he could take a sip. "There," she whispered. "Behind the duke."

He saw who she meant immediately. A footman stood slightly behind Julian and the bride and groom, as if ready to usher the guests in to dine. Her cousin must have dyed his hair, for the once-red curls were now a dirty brown. Still, Gregory was certain it was the same man he'd seen in the churchyard.

The guests began making their way toward the dining room. Gregory refused to wait.

"Watch the ladies," he advised Harry before starting forward himself. His size made it easy to shove his way through. A hand on his coat told him Yvette was following. He caught Julian's eye and jerked his head toward their quarry.

Julian was cooler than Gregory could have been. He struck out his goblet in the fellow's direction. "You there. Fill this and be quick about it."

Yvette's cousin hurried forward with his bottle. He had just finished pouring when Gregory reached their sides.

Julian's smile was triumphant. "You are mine."

What happened next was a blur. The Frenchman hit the stem of Julian's goblet, ramming the glass up and into his face. Dropping the bottle, he pivoted around Gregory and seized Yvette. Gregory whirled to block the exit as the other guests streamed past, unknowing.

The Frenchman's smile was ugly. "What will you do? I hold her life in my hands."

"*Non*," Yvette said, bringing her heel down on his instep. He reacted, and she broke free to fling herself at Gregory. Catching her close, he turned and sheltered her from whatever was coming, his body wrapped around hers.

"Stop him!" Julian's voice pierced all other conversation in the room. Suddenly aware of the danger, women cried out. Men exclaimed. Feet pounded against the carpet. Gregory refused to move, refused to think. All he knew was that he had to keep her safe.

"My lord," she murmured, curls tickling his chin. "Gregory. You can release me. He has fled."

He shook himself and uncurled from around her.

She offered him a tremulous smile. "You make a very fine shelter, *mon cher*. Now, let us see if Mr. Mayes makes an equally fine stallion."

CHAPTER FOURTEEN

They did not catch Claude. Somehow Yvette knew they wouldn't. Her cousin had escaped the house and disappeared among the revelers in the village, making him impossible to locate. Perhaps if she had been closer...

She might be dead. As it was, she hadn't even had time to slip out her dagger. And she could not forget how Gregory had wrapped himself about her, cocooning her in safety. He had been willing to take a bullet or a blade for her. What honor! What valor!

"We gave them something to talk about," Lady Carrolton crowed as they rode for Carrolton Park later that day.

"Apparently so," Lady Lilith replied, pulling her shawl higher. "Chasing a footman about because he attempted to pick Mr. Mayes's pocket. What sort of staff does His Grace hire?"

"The sort he marries," Mr. Villers quipped, and the ladies tittered.

What a relief that they believed the story Julian Mayes had put about as to why he, Mr. Villers, and several of the male guests had gone chasing after a footman right before the wedding breakfast was to be served. Most of the other guests appeared to believe the story as well, despite the bruises forming on Mr. Mayes's handsome face. She had felt as if she should apologize to the new Duchess of Wey, but the lady had been overheard to laugh at the matter.

"At least they stopped talking about me for a while," she'd said.

"Still, Gregory," Lady Lilith said now, gaze turning to her brother seated across the coach and next to Yvette, "I never understood why you felt you must gather French so close."

Gregory's cheeks turned red, and his mouth worked as if he were struggling to come up with an answer.

Yvette had pity on him. "I saw the act, your ladyship. It was my first thought to pursue the villain. The earl prevented me from being so foolish."

He cleared his throat. "Yes. Quite."

She was glad he didn't elaborate. The look on his face betrayed everything to anyone looking closely. He didn't like the fact they must lie to his family. He was chagrinned he couldn't think of a more convincing story. And he was still worried about her.

It would have helped if they could have had more than a short conversation with Mr. Mayes and Mr. Villers as they regrouped before going in to the wedding breakfast.

"Can we stop this nonsense and ensure Miss de Maupassant's safety?" Gregory had demanded.

"No," Mr. Mayes had said, jaw stubborn. "The plan's working. We nearly had him."

"Nearly being the operative word," Gregory pointed out.

"It would have helped if others had been as attendant," Mr. Mayes replied with a look to Mr. Villers.

He threw up his hands. "What do you expect? The fellow could strike anywhere, at any time. How am I to explain that I am stuck to the companion's side?"

Mr. Mayes frowned. "You have a point."

"You are courting Lady Lilith, *non?*" Yvette challenged.

He glanced at Gregory, who was scowling. "I was considering it."

"*Bon.* To her you are devoted. I am merely the chaperone."

Mr. Mayes nodded, brow clearing. "Excellent. Be on

guard, gentlemen. I'll report the incident to Lord Hastings and relay any instructions. Expect me at Carrolton Park in the next few days."

"And Meredith as well?"Yvette had asked.

He had glanced to where her friend was talking with the new duchess. "I'll see what I can do."

Oh, if only she'd felt comfortable bringing Fortune with her. Meredith forced her trembling hands to still.Yvette's cruel cousin had been in this very room, a threat to her friend. Still, Meredith's first thought had been to help Julian.

He made his way to her side, dark blotches on his handsome face. She wanted to touch him, hold him, but propriety demanded that she keep her distance.

"That was eventful," she made herself say.

His smile was tight. "Not eventful enough. He escaped." He glanced down. "And my cravat is ruined."

It was. Crumpled beyond repair and purple from the wine that had spilled. "Better that than your face. If the crystal had broken…" She couldn't finish.

He took her hand. "I'll be fine, Meredith. The greatest wound is to my pride.We were so close."

Far too close, but she decided not to belabor the issue. "And what now?"

"Carrolton is takingYvette back to the Park.Villers will remain on duty, for all that's worth. I'll speak to Hastings and report to them.Yvette wondered if you'd be willing to accompany me."

"Of course."

His smile deepened at her quick answer. "I need to clean up, but I can escort you in to breakfast if you'd like."

A few guests still loitered in the gallery instead of going in to the buffet. One, in fact, was heading in their direction, blue eyes bright and brown hair tightly curled around her narrow face. Panic poked at her. Meredith grasped Julian's arm and attempted to steer him toward the breakfast room.

The little woman, a few years her junior, detoured to meet them. "Pardon the intrusion," she said in a high sweet voice, "but I believe I know you. Aren't you Miss Rose, companion to Lady Winhaven?"

Worse and worse! Her stomach plummeted to the soles of her feet. Yet there was no use denying it. Julian knew her real name. He was frowning at her as if he had never seen her before.

"Once," Meredith allowed. "How good of you to remember. Miss Pankhurst, is it not?"

"Yes, indeed." Like startled birds, her fingers fluttered before her sky blue gown, but Meredith knew it was gossip rather than a perch she hoped to find. Distantly related to her former employer, Miss Pankhurst survived on being asked to dine to spill all she knew.

"How have you been?" Meredith asked, hoping to forestall the woman. "You were living with your brother when last we met."

Her lips turned down, making her crooked nose look longer. "Yes. Poor Georgie passed away, and I have been assisting Miss Worthington ever since. But what of you? What adventures you've had! I was astonished about the scandal."

She would not leave off. "Some are always keen to take advantage of misfortune," Meredith allowed. She turned to Julian, who was watching the exchange. She could not read the look in his eyes. "Mr. Mayes, do not allow us to detain you."

Miss Pankhurst tsked. "Certainly, sir. Your efforts were admirable, but your cravat was punished. You must see to it."

"Yet how could I use such a feeble and vain excuse to force me from such pleasant company?" Julian countered with a winning smile. "You were talking about a scandal, I believe."

"Surely not at a wedding," Meredith tried, but her nemesis brightened and stepped closer to Julian.

"You hadn't heard?" she asked, patting an errant curl back into place. "Oh, it was quite sensational. I am related to Lady Winhaven, you know. I'm related to half the finer families in England." She tittered, the sound like fingernails on a blackboard to Meredith's nerves.

"Lady Winhaven," Julian mused. "The elderly heiress who died last year?"

"The same. Miss Rose was her companion."

She could not breathe. "It's Miss Thorn now, and I really must insist we head in to breakfast. We wouldn't want to disappoint the bride."

Miss Pankhurst darted to block her way forward. "I merely wished to offer my condolences. How difficult it must have been for you." She looked to Julian instead. "Lady Winhaven allowed minor matters to overtax her, I fear. I understand she was attempting to persuade Miss Rose as to the proper way of behaving when she dropped dead of apoplexy."

The memory loomed up, halting all other thought more surely than Miss Pankhurst's titter. One moment her employer had been shouting at her, face its usual florid color, the next she'd choked and collapsed, eyes staring at the ceiling. And after the shock had faded, joy had surged up, because Meredith was finally free. And that feeling had only made guilt come crashing down.

"I prefer not to speak of it," Meredith informed her tormenter now. "If you'll excuse me, I should find a seat."

"Allow me," Julian said, taking her arm.

Miss Pankhurst tried one last time to detain them, but Julian sailed past as if her calls were no more than whispers in the wind.

He saw her to a seat not far from the head table, where

she knew a chair was waiting for him. Bending low, he murmured, "You cannot allow such drivel to disturb you. Will you be all right if I go clean up?"

She nodded. If he stayed, she'd only find herself answering the questions that must be crowding him. As it was, she sat and smiled and made conversation with those around her, but she didn't taste one bite of the wonderful wedding breakfast.

He would cut her off. Miss Pankhurst must not have put two and two together and realized that Meredith had received a bequest from her late employer, but Julian would remember the case now that the horrid woman had brought it to his attention. Meredith's lawyer had done all he could to keep her name out of it, and she had changed her name to prevent any connection. But there were some who still whispered that Mary Rose had killed her mistress and profited from her death.

Surely, he wouldn't abandon her immediately. He had escorted her to the wedding, so he must return her to London. When he rejoined her just as she was making her farewells to Jane, she was so tense she thought she might snap in two. She flinched as he handed her up into his curricle.

He didn't speak until he had directed the horses east.

"Why didn't you tell me?"

"Why didn't you ask?" Meredith countered, voice sharper than she'd intended. "You have been content to forget the gap in our relationship—that time between when you left to seek your fortune and when you discovered me again. I explained that I had been a companion."

"But not the circumstances," he protested. "I begin to see why. Alexander told me about the case."

Of course he would. Alexander Prentice had been Julian's mentor, the solicitor who had set him on the path to success. He had represented Lady Winhaven's heir, who had attempted to have the will dismissed, for it left Meredith

NEVER ENVY AN EARL 147

with a sizeable bequest he had believed she didn't deserve.

"The woman was demonstrably negligent," the older solicitor had argued before the magistrate. "Why, her incompetence may well have led to her mistress's demise. She should be tried for murder, not rewarded."

Meredith shuddered at the memory. "It was a very dark time, Julian. I don't like discussing it. It has no bearing on who I am today."

One hand on the reins, he reached out the other to cover hers on her lap. "But it does, Meredith. You survived an ordeal—the harsh treatment, the trial. That changes a person, makes one stronger."

It did indeed. No more was she willing to allow injustice to overpower her. "Your mentor thought otherwise."

"Alex was arguing a case," Julian said. "I don't have to agree with him on his approach or his opinion."

Meredith glanced his way. His smile gave her hope. "Then you won't disassociate yourself now that you know the truth?"

"Never," he vowed. "I don't berate you for what happened. I admire your courage. I only wish I had been there to help."

"So do I." The words came out far too quietly. As if he thought so too, Julian pulled the horses to the grass at the edge of the road, drew the vehicle to a stop, and turned to take her into his arms.

"Forgive me, my sweet Mary," he murmured. "I've missed so much, left you when you needed help. Alex never told me the name of Lady Winhaven's companion. If he had, I would have found you sooner."

She wanted to believe that. So much had conspired against them. Was it possible they might still have a future, together?

CHAPTER FIFTEEN

M r. Villers could not put the plan in place and request
Yvette as chaperone for him and Lady Lilith as soon
as they returned to Carrolton Park. Lady Lilith and her
mother repaired to the countess' dressing room, where
they proceeded to criticize everyone at the wedding as
they changed out of their finery. Yvette took a moment to
change as well and came back to find them still at it.

"And the Duke of Emerson," Lady Carrolton
complained as Ada helped her into her dinner dress. "The
older daughter was passable, but I understand the younger
daughter thinks she might be a painter. He needs to take
a stronger hand."

"That is nothing compared to Sir Trevor," Lady Lilith
argued, patting her hair into place after changing her
gown. "I heard he married the daughter of the fellow who
was caring for the estate he inherited."

"Is no man willing to marry within his own class?" her
mother lamented.

Lady Lilith put her nose in the air. "Apparently not. You
will recall the duke had his choice of three imminently
suitable ladies—"

"Including you," her mother agreed.

"—and still he wed his governess. I am disappointed
with Mr. Villers, as well. All this talk of marriage, and he
never so much as asked to hold my hand."

"But how could that be?" Yvette asked, all innocence. "The earl instructed me to act as chaperone while Monsieur Villers courts you."

Lady Lilith gasped. The cruel lines around her mouth disappeared, and light gleamed in her pale eyes. "Truly?"

"*Mais oui.* If you doubt me, ask your brother."

"I will." She hurried off.

Yvette didn't see her or Gregory again until they all gathered for dinner. As she entered, the countess leaning on her arm, Mr. Villers was making conversation with a blushing Lady Lilith. Gregory started toward them, and Mr. Villers glanced up, turned white, and dropped his gaze to the damask-draped table. He did his best to keep his distance from Lady Lilith for the remainder of the evening, excusing himself early. Gregory watched him go.

"Gregory hates him," Lady Lilith moaned as Yvette prepared to bid the countess good night. Her daughter paced the bedchamber, dark skirts swirling. "Beau will never declare himself with such animosity."

"Surely your brother wants what is best for you," Yvette told her.

Lady Lilith met her mother's gaze. "That's what Father used to say, and here I am alone."

The room felt colder, as if the specter of the dead earl had passed by. Yvette waved a hand to dispel the thought. "I will speak to the earl, tell him how you feel."

Lilith brightened. "Would you?"

Lady Carrolton held up one hand as if to bless her. "Excellent idea. He's less likely to take his wrath out on the staff. Be cautious, though, French."

Be cautious. As if she could be anything less. As it was, she half-expected to see her cousin leering at her from behind a statue in the elegant entry hall as she ventured downstairs, preparing to pounce from behind a tall Oriental vase in the corridor, or lurking in the corner of the beautiful withdrawing room. He was none of those places. And neither was Gregory.

She approached Mr. Marbury in the end. The butler was in the kitchen, discussing the next day's plans with the cook. Like every other room at Carrolton Park, this one bore the mark of its master. The walls were a warm cream, the cabinets a sunny yellow that was reflected by the polished copper pots and pans. Palm fronds and pineapples in greening copper topped the tall metal supports that braced the high ceiling. The solid work table in the center of the room boasted a marble top, and the brick hearth held a round black cast-iron door for a roaster. Napoleon would have been jealous.

"Pardon me, Monsieur Marbury," Yvette said with a curtsey. "I am to deliver a message from Lady Lilith to the earl. Can you tell me where he is?"

The butler held out his large hand with a sigh. "I shall deliver it."

Yvette grimaced. "I regret that it is not on paper. I have memorized it."

"Then report it to me."

She lowered her gaze. "It is of a personal nature. I promised to tell only the earl."

Marbury sighed again, lowering his hand. "Such doings, Mrs. Clarke."

"In my day servants knew their place," the older, heavy-set cook said, patting her silvery curls.

"Ah," Mr. Marbury said, "but you are not a servant, are you, Miss French?"

Yvette stilled. Had she given herself away? Did he know? She raised her head to scan his face. His smile was kind, his look fatherly. She drew in a breath.

"*Mais non*," she said with a smile. "I am the countess' companion."

He nodded. "Very well. His lordship is the greenhouse. He does not appreciate having his work interrupted. I will escort you and explain the matter to him."

Disappointment clung to her as they exited the kitchen
for the yard. It took little thought to realize why she
suddenly felt blue. She had been hoping for time alone
with Gregory. She didn't want to share him with anyone,
even Marbury.

Still, as they set off across the lawn, she was glad for the
butler's strength beside her. The greenhouses stood a little
ways from the house, very likely so as to keep out of the
building's shadow, and the only light came from inside and
the feeble moon tangled in the trees. In the darkness, she
would never have seen her cousin approach. Then again,
he would not easily see her if he was watching the house.

They reached the closest greenhouse, and the butler
opened the door. Warm, moist air rushed out, along with
the scents of earth and life. As she stepped inside, she gazed
about.

The greenhouse was a long, low structure with a peaked
roof, the metal scaffolding supporting the glass like a
skeleton of some gigantic creature. Pots along either side
held dark earth, silvery ash, rounded rock from a river
bed, and water that sparkled in the lamps hung by chains
from the roof. Here and there, larger pots supported broad,
vibrant green trees heavy with the round dimpled fruit of
oranges. Tables down the center groaned under the weight
of pink lilies, purple asters, and frilly marigolds, all under
the glittering black of the night sky.

It was still easy to spot the large man in the tweed coat.

He was standing at the closest table, sleeves rolled
back and gaze focused. His hands were black with soil;
perspiration beaded his brow, likely from the heat of the
room. In front of him lay dozens of smaller pots, fragrant
blossoms bobbing as he picked up a container. How gently
those big hands cradled the plant, how tenderly he moved
it into a larger pot.

Marbury waited until he had finished before clearing
his throat. Gregory looked up, eyes blinking as if recalling

himself from a long distance. "Marbury? Miss French?"

Yvette curtseyed.

"Miss French has a message from your sister," Marbury explained. "It is of a personal nature and rather urgent, from what I've gathered. May I leave her with you to explain?"

Gregory nodded, and Marbury withdrew.

The earl shook the dirt from his hands and strode forward. "What's happened? Has your cousin been sighted again?"

Yvette shook her head. "*Non, non.* It is truly about your sister I must speak. She is very concerned about Monsieur Villers. She believes he would propose if you would encourage him."

His face tightened. "I'm afraid I can't do that."

She frowned up at him. "But why? He is not the most admirable fellow, I agree, but your sister is fond of him."

"He's done nothing to prove himself worthy of her, and I will not countenance an alliance until he does."

Once more, he was all conviction, all command. Still, she could feel his concern, for his sister, for her. She wanted to ease the tension.

"So, tell me," she said with her best smile. "What do you do here in the night?"

"Nothing of import."

She didn't believe him, and she wasn't ready to leave his company so soon. She wandered to the table, then turned to gaze up at him. "I think it is of more importance than you claim. You have a secret passion. You must tell me."

A secret passion. With her looking up at him through lashes gilded by lamplight, he could easily confess he was coming to care about her. To think her cousin had approached her not once but twice chilled him. And he could not seem to get through to Julian or Villers that this approach of making her the bait was madness.

So, he'd taken refuge in the one place he knew, the one place where he could make a difference. The one place his size and strength were immaterial. Even his friends might laugh had they known. The powerful Carrolton, playing in the dirt.

"It's just a hobby," he insisted.

She touched the tip of her finger against a bloom, and he felt as if she'd caressed his cheek. "But you take such care. And you do not keep these wonders to yourself. I have seen such blossoms before—on your mother's dressing table."

He nodded. "They are her favorite."

Her smile was soft. "How kind. The countess said Marbury was filling her vase. But it was you."

"She wasn't getting out much, you see," he felt compelled to explain. "Or at least she didn't until you arrived. I thought it might cheer her to see them."

"And this?" she asked, moving on to the *Hemerocallis*.

He smiled at the bright, tri-petaled blossom. "Lilies. For Lilith."

"And you are starting something new, I see," she said, regarding the row of pots where bulbs were just sprouting.

His throat felt tight. "I planted them last fall, but I've been trying to force them to bloom early. *Iris xiphium*. Some call them *fleur-de-lis*."

She stilled. "The flower of France."

He couldn't answer.

She turned to face him, lips soft. "You want them to open, for me?"

Why did he feel like a child who'd been caught with his fingers in the sugar bowl? "I thought they would remind you of home."

She flung herself at him, wrapped her arms as far as they would go around him. "Oh, Gregory, how you honor me."

She trembled against him. He put his arms around her, bent his head until his chin brushed the curls of her crown.

Like silk. And she smelled of roses—*Rosa*. Even as he marveled, he heard a sound that ripped through him.

He thrust her back from him. "Are you crying? I never intended, that is I hoped..."

She laughed through the tears shining on her cheeks. "*Non, non, mon cher*, you mistake me. These are tears of joy. No one has ever been as thoughtful to me as you. *Merci beaucoups.*"

He drew in a sigh of relief. "Oh, good. Well, then, you are very welcome. Now, I should get you back to the house before Mother and Lilith wonder what's become of you."

She took the arm he offered her but held him in place. "First, *mon coeur*, you must tell me. Why are you so set against Monsieur Villers?"

He sagged. "Must I?"

"*Mais oui*, for I must have something to tell your sister. I have seen him at his worst at Harry's home, so I can understand your reluctance to accept him."

"He's useless," Gregory said. "He's supposed to be on guard, and he's done nothing but flirt with Lilith."

"True. He looks to his own interests first. When he threatened to blackmail Harry, I was equally angry with him."

He jerked back. "What! He threatened Harry?"

Yvette patted his arm. "Have no fear. Harry and I dissuaded him. I thought perhaps he had learned his lesson. He agreed to help Lord Hastings, after all."

"Very likely to avoid prosecution, if he's attempted to blackmail others," Gregory muttered.

"Perhaps. But he does seem to admire your sister. Could not love make him strong?"

He shook his head. "You have been through so much, yet you still believe in the power of love?"

Her smile was sad. "One needs to cling to something."

Cling to me. The words almost came out before he clenched his teeth against them. He had offered his heart

before—in the calm of an English withdrawing room—
and been dismissed. He had no right to offer it to her now,
not while she was so uncertain as to her future.

"Will you consider the matter?" she pressed. "Your sister
is actually happy with him. It is so good to see her smile."
She waved a hand toward the plants. "Is that not why
you work here? To create something that will bring your
mother and sister joy?"

It was. The simple acts brought him peace, reminded him
of the man he wished to be. A man who cared for his
family, who looked to the needs of others.

Though at the moment, his need to hold her was nearly
his undoing.

"Very well," he said. "I will attempt to tolerate Beau
Villers. But if he hurts Lilith in any way, I will not be
accountable for my actions."

All humor vanished from her face, and he almost called
the words back. The best he could do was offer her his arm
again and escort her out, leaving his peace behind in the
greenhouse.

CHAPTER SIXTEEN

W hat was she to make of him? Yvette watched Gregory over the next few days. He was as good as his word, treating Villers with cordiality even though at times his face showed his conflicting feelings. As if he hadn't noticed, the would-be intelligence agent lavished praise on Lady Lilith, seldom straying from her side from breakfast to dinner. Lilith bloomed under the attention, her laugh warm, her smile bright. And that only made her suitor more determined to please her.

There was no further sign of Claude. Yvette made a point of asking Gregory or Mr. Villers each day, when she could escape her duties.

"He won't dare show his face," Mr. Villers had bragged. "We scared him all the way back to France."

Yvette had smiled at him. "I doubt that. It will not be his face you see, *monsieur*. It will be the flash of the blade before it strikes."

That had wiped the sneer from his mouth.

But with Lady Lilith getting all the attention, Lady Carrolton became more demanding, making it difficult for Yvette to chaperone Lilith or leave the house much. The countess insisted on Yvette's company and began asking for things out of the red case again.

"You must tell her she doesn't need them," she appealed to Gregory when he came to visit his mother the second day after they had returned from the wedding.

He obligingly sat on the chair and set the case in his lap, but if the countess thought he would protect her precious pills, she was doomed to disappointment.

"Purgative," he read on one bottle of liquid. "Why would you need to purge yourself, Mother? Cook is very skilled." Likewise, he dismissed the pills to put her to sleep and wake her up.

"Exercise and fresh air will do more for both, madam," he informed her.

He left her with her vinaigrette box and handkerchiefs.

"Villain," his mother muttered as he carried off the rest.

"I will see what I can do," Yvette said, hurrying after him.

She caught up with him in the corridor. "Your mother relies too much on her medicines, but are you sure it is wise to take away so many?"

His arms cradling an assortment of pills, potions, and products, he shook his head. "I can't be sure of any of this, Yvette. Until I know they are safe for her, I'm keeping them out of her reach." He offered her a contrite smile. "I'm sorry. I know that will likely make your job harder. I'll stop by more often."

And he did. Twice every morning, tea in the afternoon, and after dinner. He read books to his mother, shared information from the *London Times* that had been delivered, and reminisced about her younger days. The last Yvette found particularly interesting.

"Do you remember when we used to go up to the Clarendon Square house with your father for the opening of Parliament?" she asked one day as they were gathered around the tea cart. Lilith and Villers were out riding, with an armed groom as attendant. If Lilith wondered at the precaution, she hadn't mentioned the fact to Yvette.

The earl leaned back in the chair, which squeaked in protest. He hastily straightened, balancing the delicate china cup in his large hand. "I remember when Father took me to see the King review the troops. Very stirring."

His mother sighed, glancing down into her tea. "Yes, your father always thought you shouldn't be overly influenced by the ladies of the house. I had Lilith, of course, but I wished I had more time with you."

He set aside his tea. "I'm here now, Mother. What would you like to know?"

Her eyes turned misty. "Why haven't you wed? Surely you don't want the estate to go to some distant cousin."

The chair squeaked again as he shifted, gaze darting to Yvette and back to his mother. "No, Mother. But I've been busy setting things to rights after Father's death."

She frowned. "For five years? He can't have left the estate in such a poor state as that."

"Your son has been devoted to your care as well," Yvette pointed out.

"Bah," the countess said. "High time you wed. A nice English girl of good family with a fortune. Surely you can find one."

None of those characteristics applied to her. She was aware of a distinct lowering in her spirits.

Not that she intended to marry Gregory. How could she reconcile the two images of him, hers and his family's?

There was the brute his mother and sister feared to cross.

The quiet gardener who grew them flowers in secret, never seeking their approval or thanks.

The commanding peer who refused to allow his sister to marry the man she loved.

The valiant protector who risked his own life to keep Yvette safe.

Who was this man?

But with all her questions, she could not question why she feared the truth. She had been hiding her heart for years. She could not feel safe revealing it now.

Her tensions rose as they prepared for church that Sunday. Claude must know she would be there. Would he find some way to strike? Gregory must have feared as much, for he stayed by her side while Villers pasted himself to the other.

"Just who are you escorting, sir?" Lady Lilith complained as they reached the door of the church.

"You, dear lady, always," Mr. Villers promised. He glanced at Gregory. "Only…"

"Only he wishes to make sure I do you credit," Yvette said. "I am not so used to fine company."

"Exactly," Villers said, straightening and frowning at her. "I will not have my beloved's reputation besmirched by improper behavior."

Lady Lilith patted his hand. "That is very kind of you, Beau, but I have the utmost faith in French. She has done wonders for Mother and helped me as well. Now, come along."

Gregory looked surprised. Yvette could only smile.

Safely surrounded in the pew, her head lower than any around her, she was able to relax and enter into the spirit of the service. She was still alive. Lady Lilith had complimented her. Friends surrounded her. She had much to be thankful for.

She glanced at Gregory. His gaze was intent on the vicar, but, every once in a while, his lips twitched, as if he were speaking to someone in private. Praying? She hadn't managed a prayer since the last time she'd entered this place. Would God listen to her? She'd broken so many of His commandments.

"Do you think God understands about the war?" she asked Gregory as they walked back to the carriage after service through a bright spring day. Villers was just ahead, Lady Carrolton on one arm and Lady Lilith on the other. She could hope he was scouting ahead, but she doubted it.

Besides, he had little need. Gregory's gaze roamed the churchyard as if attempting to see behind each gravestone, around every tree. His thunderous frown kept anyone from seeking conversation with them. "God knows everything," he said. "So He must."

Such a simple faith. A shame hers had been lost with her family. She glanced at the sheltered church, surrounded by its green hedge, the villagers so purposeful and polite. The man beside her, so strong, so open. If she could find peace anywhere, it would be here.

The countess was feeling well enough that they passed the afternoon in company. Yvette thought Gregory might allow them to venture outdoors at Villers's suggestion, but he insisted on ensconcing them in the south withdrawing room instead, where sunlight streamed through the windows. Surrounded by the crimson and blue tapestries, the carved-back furnishings, Villers offered to regale the ladies with stories of the *ton*. It was gossip. She had heard its type too many times in Paris. Besides, she was more interested in Gregory's reaction. Rather than join them near the hearth, he had gone to the window and kept glancing out. She got up from her seat and went to join him.

"Do you see danger in the bluebells?" she teased, nodding to the carpet under the trees. "Or are you considering them the next flower to plant?"

He turned from the view with a smile. "I have no need to cultivate them. They grow in profusion each year." He lowered his voice. "But I would like to see this done."

"Me as well. Yet you missed the opportunity to parade me on the lawn."

"And I will again. Julian should have been here by now. Until I know why he's late, you're staying where I can keep you safe."

She didn't know whether to thank him or protest yet again.

Just then Lady Lilith laughed at something Villers had said, and Gregory glanced her way with a frown.

"She is happy," Yvette murmured. "Be glad."

"I am more concerned with her happiness over the long term," he replied. With a nod to her, he strode back to the group.

"Mr. Villers, a word." It was not a request. Villers scrambled to his feet and followed the earl from the room.

Lilith collapsed against the back of the sofa as Yvette returned to her side. "You see. Gregory is still against him."

"And why would that be?" Yvette asked, hoping to soothe her fears. "The earl is a reasonable man."

"Sometimes," his sister muttered before biting her lip.

"You cannot blame Gregory this time," her mother said. "Mr. Villers has a ready address and a witty tongue. But he has no income and a questionable family. I might almost think him a fortune hunter."

Lilith burst into tears, jumped to her feet, and ran from the room.

Lady Carrolton tsked. "I didn't say I disliked him, but one must face facts. Besides, it might be interesting to have a fortune hunter in the family."

"You are incorrigible," Yvette said.

She smiled, straightening on the high-backed chair. "I am, aren't I? Well, French, the others have fled. It's up to you to be entertaining. What can you do?"

If she only knew.

Yvette spread her hands. "As you have seen, I listen well."

Lady Carrolton sucked her teeth a moment. "That's something. But I tire of talking."

"Recently?"

The lady frowned as if she wasn't sure whether Yvette was teasing. "Why not play the spinet for me?"

"My fingers are tired," Yvette replied.

"Do you perhaps sing?"

"Not on key."

"Perform recitation?"

"Only of dire predictions of the future."

Lady Carrolton clapped her hands. "Excellent. Let's hear

some."

"You want more gossip," Yvette accused her.

"That would suffice as well."

Yvette laughed. "Very well. I know little of your aristocracy, but I recall a thing or two about France." She told her a few stories from her time at court, and the countess gasped in delighted shock or railed at the vanity, as she felt was appropriate.

Neither Gregory nor Villers returned before dinner, and Marbury reported that Lady Lilith remained in her room. The countess decided on a tray in her room rather than eat with the others. Yvette had resigned herself to a quiet evening when Lilith came in. She wore a subdued wool gown Yvette had thought she had donated to the staff, and her hair was once more sleeked back from her face. Pale, eyes clear and watery, she went straight to the bed, bent over her mother, and kissed her on the forehead.

"Good night, Mother. Always remember I love you."

Something poked at Yvette, and she put herself between the lady and the door. "What are you doing?"

Lady Lilith drew herself up with her usual hauteur. "This is none of your affair."

"Perhaps not," Yvette allowed. "But is it your brother's?"

Her eyes widened. "No! You will be silent, or I will..."

"What?" Yvette asked. "Strike me? Careful, my lady. I strike back."

Lilith took a step away from her. "Mother, tell your companion that she must say nothing to Gregory."

"I will do no such thing," her mother replied. "She's right. You're acting oddly, and I want to know why."

She sagged, then hurried back to the bed. Her voice came out low and breathless. "Gregory will never give Beau permission to marry me. We're eloping to Gretna Green, tonight."

"What!" Yvette cried as the countess stared at her daughter.

Lady Lilith nodded. "You ought to be pleased, French. You encouraged me to take matters into my own hands. Well, now I have."

Gregory couldn't settle for the evening. A French agent prowled his estate, a French lady with silky red-gold hair prowled his thoughts. And Beau Villers was a spineless weasel.

"Fine, fine," he'd said when Gregory had taken him to the north withdrawing room to ask him again about his intentions. "You are right to question me. Every day I fall more in love with Lilith. She is everything I could want in a wife. However, much as I admire your sister, I find I cannot bring myself to offer for her. I'd be hard pressed to keep her in her usual style." His look had turned cunning. "Unless, of course, you were inclined to be accommodating."

He could not mean what it seemed. "Accommodating?" Gregory asked, hearing the growl in his voice.

For once, Villers wasn't deterred by it. He leaned forward. "Yes. She has a small inheritance from your father, I understand. A pittance, really. As her beloved brother, you would want to be more generous."

Cold and heat rushed up him in turn. "You want a bribe to marry my sister?"

He held up his hands as he straightened. "No! Never. I merely wish to ensure her happiness. I would be delighted to accept a small estate near London on her behalf, perhaps a townhouse, with its own mews, of course."

His smile made Gregory ill.

"You," he spat, "will get nothing from me. I want you out of my house by morning."

He washed white. "But the mission. Yvette's safety."

"I will see to Yvette and my sister's future. Goodbye, Mr. Villers."

He rose. "Are you so selfish you can see no one else happy?"

Gregory surged to his feet. "Out!"

Villers ran.

Gregory hadn't sat since.

Selfish. He had never thought to have the term applied to him. Was it selfish to want more for his sister than to marry a conniving scoundrel? She would be hurt by Villers's defection, but better that than life married to such a creature. Or should he have let Lilith make that decision?

Was it selfish to keep Yvette from the light, to protect her from her cousin? That was his duty, yet it was also his need. Thinking of her being harmed made it difficult to draw breath. But Yvette could take care of herself. Was he smothering her? Prolonging the danger to her by refusing to allow her to meet it head on?

He paced the withdrawing room for a long time, until the candles were gutting in the brass. He went and snuffed them out. A shame he could not shut off the sound of his thoughts so easily.

He was coming into the entry hall when he heard a noise on the stair. Odd. He should be the only one up at this time of the night. He'd sent Marbury to bed hours ago. The sound came again, a stealthy footfall. His muscles tensed, ready for a fight.

Someone was in his house.

Keeping his back as close to the wall as possible, he edged along, then ducked behind the statue of Apollo. A dark shadow darted across the tiles for the front door. Leaving? Was Gregory already too late? Had the Claude de Maupassant entered the house, harmed Yvette?

With a yell, he leaped across the space and seized the fellow, lifting him off the floor.

"Gregory!"

His sister's voice barely penetrated the red haze. Someone lit a lamp, and he became aware of Beau Villers's face, turning a horrid shade of purple, as one of Gregory's hands clamped around his windpipe.

He released the fellow, and Villers fell, coughing, onto the Blue John tiles. Lilith's shoes clattered on the purple-blue stone as she ran to his side.

"Beau, darling, are you all right?"

Villers rubbed his throat. "Yes, no thanks to him. I should see you up on charges of battery, sir."

The threat was its own form of battery, topped only by the look in his sister's eyes.

"What are you doing?" Gregory asked, feeling suddenly heavy.

"Eloping," his mother said.

Turning, he saw her at the foot of the stairs, leaning on Yvette's arm. Yvette's face was twisting, as if she alone knew what this betrayal would mean to him.

Lilith rose, head high. "Yes, I'm eloping. With the man I love. The man you refused to accept."

"Because he's only after money," Gregory protested.

Lilith held her ground.

"She knows he's after her fortune," his mother put in helpfully. "She doesn't care."

"No," Lilith said. "I don't. Beau treats me with respect. He listens."

"How long will he listen when your dowry is spent?" Gregory challenged.

"Longer than you," she sneered. "You are a bully and a tyrant, and I don't know why I've tolerated you as long as I have." She sucked in a breath, eyes widening, and her hand reached out to him. "Oh, Gregory, I'm so sorry. I didn't mean that. Oh, I'm no better than Father!"

His mother hobbled forward with Yvette at her side. "Yes, you are. You both are. You must be."

Had everyone gone mad? "What are you talking about?"

Lilith sucked in a sob as she bent to help Villers to his feet. "Stop acting as if you didn't know."

"Didn't know what?" he demanded, his voice echoing off the statues. Deeper in the house, doors shut, and footsteps sounded. He'd even woken the servants.

No one around him seemed to care they would shortly have an audience. His mother avoided his gaze. Lilith kept her head bowed. Villers looked from Lilith to him, clearly perplexed.

"I will tell you," Yvette said in the silence. "Your father treated your mother and sister cruelly, and they fear you will do the same."

CHAPTER SEVENTEEN

He stared at her, eyes wide, body stiff, and she knew the truth. He would never have treated them so poorly. He wasn't capable of it.

"That's not possible," he said. "Father was a good man. He would never hurt Mother or Lilith."

"He did." Lilith's voice was low and controlled. "More Mother than me, especially after I could look him in the eye. He said it was for our own good, that it would develop our characters to hear our faults clearly laid out. We were flawed you see, and in need of his correction and guidance."

Yvette felt sick. A similar revulsion marked Gregory's face.

"I never knew, never suspected." His hands rubbed at his trousers as if he could make them clean.

"Didn't you?" Lilith accused him. "Or perhaps you agree with him. Men like seeing a woman weakened."

"No," he insisted, shaking his head as if to clear it.

"It wasn't just us," Lady Carrolton put in. "I know he criticized you, Gregory. I heard him."

"Rarely," he said, "and I generally agreed with his assessment."

He would. He was too humble, and she rather thought that would have been his nature no matter his father.

Lilith shuddered. "I didn't. Or at least I didn't want to. But after hearing yourself belittled enough times, you began to wonder."

"We can learn from pain," Yvette murmured, "but I always thought love a better teacher."

Villers slipped his arm around Lilith's waist. "I am so sorry such indignities were forced upon you, darling. Rest assured I would never reveal your shame." He glanced at the earl.

Gregory was breathing hard, as if he'd run a race. She could not see him put through more, especially if Beau Villers was up to his usual tricks.

"No, you will not, Monsieur Villers," she said. "You know how distressed I become when my friends are threatened. You and I have discussed this before. Pointedly."

He rubbed his throat again with his free hand. When he'd attempted to blackmail her friend Harry over helping Yvette, she had pulled her dagger on him.

"Yes, of course," he said. "I would never do anything to distress any of you."

"So, you are determined to marry?" Gregory asked, gaze on his sister. "Despite my misgivings?"

Villers raised his chin. So did Lilith. "Yes," she said, and her voice echoed in the entry hall.

He nodded. "Very well. Villers, ride to London for a special license. You can be married here. No need to subject Lilith to the scandal of a Gretna Green match."

With a glad cry, Lilith turned and buried her head in Villers's shoulder. He nodded to Gregory over her head.

"We'll start on the preparations tomorrow," the countess said. "Come, French. It's time I was in bed."

She almost didn't go. He looked lost, so alone standing in his beautiful entry hall. She wanted to hold him close, tell him she believed in him, that she knew the truth even if his sister and mother might doubt.

But she had to play her part. A companion would never wrap her arms around her employer and hold him tight, whispering comfort against his breast. If dozens of people would be arriving shortly for a wedding, Lady Carrolton and Lady Lilith must not suspect her true identity.

Still, she could not leave him with nothing. "Thank you, my lord," she said. "*You* are a good man."

The look he cast her said he no longer believed that.

She did not see him the next morning. He wasn't at breakfast when the countess came down with Yvette, though Lilith and Villers were there, billing and cooing as if making the most of every moment before Villers traveled to London for the special license. Gregory didn't come visit his mother that morning or for tea in the afternoon. His absence made the countess more fractious.

"Let me see that paper," she demanded more than once, going on to mark out several names she had told Yvette to add to the growing list of people to be invited to the wedding. A moment later, she'd order Yvette to put the names back on.

"*Fini*," Yvette declared, setting the cross-hatched paper aside. "We will work on this tomorrow."

The countess pouted. "That is not your decision to make."

"As I am doing the writing, I think it is. And you are not attending. Admit it, Countess: you miss your son."

She hitched herself higher on the chair by the fire. "Of course I miss my son. I always did when he was away at school or traveling."

"He is not away now," Yvette pointed out. "I could find him for you."

The countess brightened. "I have a better idea." She reached for her bell on the table at her elbow and began ringing. The resounding clang filled the room.

Yvette put her hands over her ears. "I am here! Cease!"

"Not until I see Gregory," the countess insisted.

Ada appeared first. She scampered into the room, trembling. "Did you need me, your ladyship?"

"No," the countess said. "I want my son."

With a curtsey, Ada fled.

She must not have been successful in locating Gregory, for the next to respond to the countess' din was Mr. Marbury. He pulled up short when he saw Yvette seated next to her. Yvette spread her hands.

"Find me my son," the countess demanded.

"At once, your ladyship." With a bow, the butler saw himself out.

As the countess lifted the bell for another swing, Yvette grabbed it and wrestled it from her grip.

"That's mine," she protested. "I need it."

"What will your son think that you ring for him like a servant?" Yvette countered, rising to take the bell to the dressing table on the other side of the room.

"He'll know to come sooner next time," the countess said.

Yvette shook her head as she tucked the bell into a drawer. "Did you ring for your husband as well?" she asked, returning to Lady Carrolton's side.

The countess put her nose in the air, reminding Yvette of her daughter. "Certainly not. He would never have answered, and I didn't have a bell then."

Yvette managed to interest her in discussing the flowers for the wedding, but she was glad when Mr. Marbury returned a short while later. Unfortunately, his words did not soothe the countess.

"I regret that his lordship is busy with estate matters," he said. "He wishes me to assure you he has only the fondest thoughts for you."

Had the servants heard what had happened the previous night? It had been late, and they slept high above the back of the house. She had thought she'd heard footsteps approaching, but she'd left with the countess before seeing anyone else. Did Marbury know the sort of message he brought?

Only the fondest thoughts.

I would never harm you, Mother, but I don't trust myself with you just now.

Yvette rose. "I will speak to him, your ladyship. Excuse me."

She thought either the countess or the butler would argue with her, but neither spoke as Marbury led her from the room. Ada was waiting just outside, and Marbury nodded for her to go in and stay with the countess while Yvette was gone.

"Thank you, Miss French," he said as they started down the corridor. "I have never seen his lordship so troubled."

"Did you know his father?" Yvette asked.

"I did. I was head footman before the current earl elevated me to this position."

"And what did you think of the previous Lord Carrolton?" she asked as they came out into the entry hall.

"May I only say that the previous earl's death did not occasion much mourning."

His face remained impassive, but his tone was heavy with judgment. Perhaps none of the servants had approved of their master. If Marbury had known his employer's tendencies, what could he have done? If he had protested, the former Lord Carrolton would only have discharged him. And if he quit instead, he risked never finding another position because he lacked a reference. In a sense, they were as trapped as the countess and her daughter.

She thought Marbury would lead her to a study or one of the withdrawing rooms, but he ushered her out the rear door and pointed toward the greenhouses, gleaming in the sunlight. "His lordship asked not to be disturbed. I'm sure he didn't mean you."

She glanced at the butler with a frown. His face committed to nothing, but she thought there was a glint in those dark eyes. "What do you know, Mr. Marbury?"

"Only what I observe, Miss French. Good luck."

Gregory lifted the damaged *tulipa* bulb and set it in the soil he'd prepared. His under gardener had been spading up a section of ground and had accidentally cut a few of the naturalized bulbs into pieces. Gregory was trying to save them. They were a pale pink and looked well in Lilith's room.

Of course, it wouldn't be Lilith's room much longer, would it?

He drew in a breath and tried to focus. The work generally calmed him, made worries disappear for a while. Now images kept repeating in his mind.

His mother flinching away from him.

Lilith's defiant gaze.

Villers's knowing smirk.

Yvette staring at him as if she'd never seen him until now.

His hands were covered in soil, but his soul felt dirty.

His father had treated his mother and sister abominably. How many times had he drummed into Gregory a gentleman's role? He was to protect and support those entrusted to him—family, friends, tenants, even the citizens of the nation through his work in Parliament. How could his father have forsaken that by mistreating his own family?

Did he have the same capacity?

He heard the click of the door opening and shutting, then the whisper of fabric against the tiles.

"Not now, Lilith," he said, forcing himself to focus on scooping the dirt around the damaged bulb.

"But now is important," Yvette said.

Had they sent her because they somehow knew she was the one person he would never lash out at? He kept working. "Is everything all right with my mother?"

"Of course. With me as well. It is you who has us all concerned."

The bulb was safe, positioned to grow. Would that he felt the same. "No need for concern. I'll finish here shortly."

"Perhaps." She edged closer, until he saw the navy of her sleeve, the sweep of her fingers brushing the table. "But I think what troubles you is not so easily finished as repotting a plant."

He sighed, hands falling. "You made the accusation yesterday, and it appears to be true. The man I admired as father took advantage of weakness."

"I would say was weak himself," she murmured. "And he weakened your mother and sister by his actions."

His stomach cramped when he tried to picture it. He raised his head. "If I'd known…"

"You would have intervened." She was right next to him, gaze turned up and light reflecting in her curls. "I know you would."

"I'd like to think so." He glanced down at his hands, crusted with the black soil. "But am I so different from him? Could cruelty come from inside at the right provocation?"

She took one of his hands in both of hers. "There is darkness inside each of us. When my parents were killed, I wanted revenge. That man who pulled the lever to release the blade with no more emotion than if he was slicing carrots. The crowd roaring for more. I wanted them all dead. I wanted the men who led to suffer. It was a long time before I could forgive, could turn anger into determination to help my country. To fight to see honor and right restored."

He drew in a breath. "I don't have time. My mother and sister, my tenants, the Prime Minister and Prince expect me to make decisions, to take action. I must master these emotions."

"Or turn them to good," she insisted. "You are not your

father. I would stake my life on it." She offered him a
smile. "I *have* staked my life on it. I put myself under your
protection, and you have never failed me."

The knowledge washed over him, cleansing him. "It is
my duty."

"And you take duty more seriously than your father ever
did, it seems. You have chosen a different path. Stay on it,
mon coeur."

Twice now she'd used that term with him. He felt a
smile tugging at his lips. "*Mon coeur.* I was never good at
French, but if I remember the meaning correctly as *my
heart*, you honor me."

"And you honor me with your friendship." Her gaze
tilted up, warm. With her so close, friendship seemed as
lifeless as the bulbs he planted. Like them, might it blossom
into something more?

The hope lifted his head, his heart. But once more
doubts moved in. What if she was wrong? What if he hurt
her as his father had hurt his mother, not with a careless
gesture as he'd once feared but with a calculated word? He
had that power. How could he ensure he never wielded it?

He stepped back from her. "Thank you for coming to
make sure of me. I promise to return to the house in time
for dinner."

"*Bon.*" She stepped back as well. "But if you retreat here
after dinner, I will come for you again."

He could only hope.

CHAPTER EIGHTEEN

L ilith was with her mother when Yvette returned. She was in such sufficiently good spirits that she didn't even berate Yvette for not being on duty. Of course, it wasn't as if the countess had been alone. Yvette could see Ada peering from the safety of the dressing room.

"What do you think, French?" Lilith asked, holding out a fashion magazine as Yvette came up to where the countess was seated by the fire, her daughter beside her. "Puffed sleeves or long for my wedding gown?"

Yvette glanced at the hand-tinted pictures. "With your height, long sleeves."

Lilith nodded, pulling back the page. "Yes, of course." She turned to her mother. "But I want to go up to London to shop for material and be fitted, Mother. The fabric and skills in Chessington are so lackluster."

The millinery shop had seemed top notch, but perhaps the other establishments were of lesser quality.

The countess fanned herself with one hand. "London, fah! Too busy. Not enough attention from the shopkeepers. We'll ask the duchess who did the governess' gown."

Lilith stared at her. "I will not use a seamstress who sews for governesses."

"Why not?" Yvette asked. "She is likely the best. I doubt a duke would allow anyone less for the woman he loved."

She cocked her head as if she had not considered that.

Her mother turned to Yvette. "You were supposed to bring Gregory back with you. Where is he?"

"Busy, alas," Yvette told her. "But he promises to see you at dinner."

Lilith straightened to regard Yvette. "So, you left my mother to talk to the earl, alone?"

"As your mother requested," Yvette said with a dutiful smile to the countess.

Lady Carrolton did not return her smile. "Where's my bell?"

"Put away for safekeeping," Yvette assured her. "You have no need of it now. Your devoted daughter is at your side, and so am I. Ada is in the dressing room if you need her."

"And Gregory is apparently where only you can find him," the countess complained. She sniffed. "I know what you're up to, and I won't have it."

Yvette kept her smile in place. The countess had an odd canniness, but she could not have guessed Yvette's true reason for being in her home. "I live only to serve, my lady. Surely I have shown you as much."

"She is occasionally devoted," Lilith allowed.

Lady Carrolton shook her head. "I won't have it, I tell you. Lilith may marry a fortune hunter—"

"Mother!" Lilith protested.

"—but I won't have my son marry a foreigner and a companion at that. You need to remember your place, French."

Heat rushed through her. Oh, the countess did not know who she was baiting. Yvette had told Gregory about darkness. It stole over her now.

"Your son will not marry at all if you continue carrying on this way," she informed the countess. "What lady would want such a mother-in-law?"

Lady Carrolton collapsed against the back of the chair, hand fluttering to her chest.

Lilith gasped. "How dare you!"

"How dare *you*?" Yvette rounded on her, skewering her in place with her gaze. "Your brother manages your holdings, leads the government, and you? How do you help? You vex him with complaints, ignore his well-meaning advice. You snipe at his friends, berate his choices, and break him down little by little until he questions his own worth."

Lilith sank back against the chair. "I'm sure I never…"

Yvette didn't wait for her to finish. She turned to the countess. "And you. You claim illness, weakness, anything to force him to remain at your side. Do you ever think of his needs before your own?"

"You cannot speak to us this way," the countess said, lips trembling. "Marbury will discharge you."

"He will not," Yvette said. "I quit. I wash my hands of the pair of you." She dusted her palms together, spun on her heel, and stalked from the room.

Gregory returned to the house feeling surer of himself. It might have been his work with the bulbs, all safely potted with bone meal and limestone to nourish them. But he suspected it had more to do with Yvette. She had a logic, a wisdom about her that was hard to refute. And her smile never failed to warm him.

The moment he entered the rear corridor, his pleasant thoughts wilted under the noise. The clang of his mother's bell echoed through the house, again and again, until he thought even the statues in the entry hall shuddered. Why was no one answering?

Had something happened to Yvette?

He took the stairs two at a time, pelted down the north wing corridor, and crashed through his mother's door without knocking.

In her chair by the fire, she halted with the bell upraised. "Gregory. What's wrong?"

He drew himself up short. "Exactly my question. Where's Yvette?"

His mother lowered the bell with a sniff. "She quit."

He blinked. "She what?"

She set the bell on the table beside her and beckoned him closer. Bemused, he moved to her side.

"Lilith was unpleasant," his mother murmured as if afraid his sister would hear from wherever she was in the house. "Miss French refused to admit defeat. I like that about her. She stands her ground."

More than his mother knew. "Where is she now?"

"In her room, I expect, probably packing." She caught his hand as if she suspected he meant to go check right then. "Don't let her leave, Gregory. It hurts me every time one of these ladies abandons me. First Ramsey, and now Miss French. I don't know if I can bear another."

He hadn't considered that when he'd reluctantly agreed to let Yvette pose as his mother's companion. His mother had once traveled to Harry's home in Essex to beg Miss Ramsey to return, but he'd thought that had more to do with pride than desperation on his mother's part. How would she react when Yvette left for good?

How would he react?

He shook the thought aside, brought his mother's hand to his lips, and kissed the back. "Miss French likely won't stay as long as you'd want, Mother, even if I talk to her now. But if you and Lilith cannot find a way to be kinder to your companions, I fear you will never keep one worth having."

She nodded, and he released her to go find Yvette.

She answered his knock readily enough, and he could breathe again. Her smile was rueful as she opened the door.

"I have behaved badly," she said. "I cannot be as patient as Patience Ramsey. When your mother and sister speak nonsense, I correct them."

"As well you should," he said, careful to remain in the

corridor and not her room. "Though perhaps sweeten vinegar with honey?"

"I do not cook," she said, wrinkling her nose, "but that sounds vile."

He smiled. "But within your abilities, I believe. You have placated an emperor and his wife, the fawning members of their court. Surely humoring my mother is child's play."

She sighed. "I suppose so. But I begin to weary of subterfuge. For ten years, I have had to be what people believed me to be. I would like to be myself. We know my cousin is near and realizes I am under your protection. Must we continue the pretense?"

He spread his hands. "I never wanted to pretend in the first place."

She chewed her lower lip a moment, then shook her head. "*Non*, we must continue the game a while longer, until we see what Lord Hastings advises. Mr. Mayes will return to us any day. If not, Monsieur Villers will let us know when he returns from London with the marriage license. Besides, Yvette the companion still has a task or two to complete."

He wasn't sure what she meant, but across the corridor came the clang of a bell.

"You never found her a small, silver one," Yvette pointed out.

"She insists on this one," Gregory said, stepping aside to allow her to exit the room.

"She would." She moved out into the corridor and paused, glancing his way. "Does she wish me to stay?"

"Very much," Gregory assured her. *And so do I.* He was only glad the last words did not come out of his mouth.

"*Bon*," Yvette said, starting for the door to his mother's room. "Come with me."

He followed.

His mother brightened as they entered, then immediately schooled her face, fingers gripping the bell's handle.

"I'm glad to see you've come to your senses, French," she said.

Yvette bobbed a curtsey. "Oh, *oui*, madam. I will stay for an apology." She glanced to Gregory. "To your son."

"My son?" his mother asked with a frown. "Why must you apologize to my son?"

Yvette smiled. "You mistake me, Lady Carrolton. It is you who must apologize. You are not ill. You never have been. You pretend to gain his attention."

Gregory stared at his mother. He had taken her overly complicated medical devices and pills away, but in his mind there had been no doubt she had some sort of illness. The other doctors had assured him it was so. She'd always looked frail. Had it all been an act?

Now her hands trembled, and the bell fell with a rattle. "How can you say such a thing to an old woman?" she asked, voice trembling as well.

Yvette made a sad face. "Ah, I forget. You are approaching your eightieth year, *non*?"

His mother stiffened, eyes flashing and voice coming out sure and sharp. "I'm one and sixty, I'll have you know."

"Oh, so aged," Yvette said with a tsk. "And such maladies to have afflicted you. Leprosy, cholera, dysentery. We must keep the staff and family away for their own protection."

"I'm perfectly fine, and you know it," his mother declared. Then she blinked. "Why, you minx."

Yvette's smile deepened, but Gregory shook his head, more to clear it than to disagree. "So, you have been pretending all this time, Mother?"

She sighed, dropping her gaze to the bedclothes and plucking at them. "Pretend is a hard word. At times, I did wonder whether I might be ill, but I suppose it started with your father. If I was strong, he must be stronger, showing me my place beneath him. But if I were weak or sick, he was all solicitation. It was easier to be sick."

Another sin laid at his father's door.

"And to your son you say?" Yvette prompted.

His mother nodded, drawing in a breath as if gathering strength. "Forgive me, Gregory, if my behavior troubled you. I will do better."

"So will I, Mother," Gregory promised, going to take her hand.

She raised her head and smiled at him.

"Excellent," Yvette said. "We will call for Ada and get you dressed. I'm sure you feel up to coming down to dinner."

His mother's smile faltered, but she inclined her head. "Yes, of course."

They left her to Ada's care and stepped out into the corridor.

"And now your sister, I think," Yvette said, marching for the door to Lilith's suite.

Gregory was too interested in the results to protest.

But Lilith wasn't in her room. They located her in the south withdrawing room, reclining on the crimson sofa with a compress on her forehead and a maid and footman hovering nearby.

"*Non*," Yvette said, striding forward. "You will not go down that path."

Lilith sat up, compress plopping into her lap. "You! I thought you were leaving."

Gregory joined them. "Miss French has agreed to stay. She and Mother have made up. I suggest you do the same, Lilith."

Lilith's chin hardened.

Yvette spoke before she could. "Alas, my lord, it is not so simple. Your sister has repeatedly accused me of neglecting your mother. She slanders my good name. I demand satisfaction."

Gregory stared at her. So did Lilith.

"Satisfaction?" she asked, glancing between Gregory and Yvette. "Is she challenging me to a duel?"

"No," Gregory said before Yvette agreed to as much.

"Dueling is illegal in England, and gentlewomen do not indulge in the sport."

"Pity," Yvette said, eyeing Lilith. "Then I will accept an apology to your brother."

"My brother?" Lilith met Gregory's gaze, then dropped her own. Dampness was spreading from the compress in her lap. She picked up the cloth and held it out. Her maid hurried forward to accept it.

Lilith straightened. "Yes, Gregory, I suppose I owe you an apology. I thought you'd be as bad as Father, but you have been kinder and more supportive than I had any right to expect. I will try harder to return the favor."

"Thank you, Lilith," Gregory replied. "And I must apologize for refusing to honor your choices. I will try harder as well."

Her smile was hopeful.

Yvette stepped back. "*Bon*. I must return to my duties. Carry on." With a wave of her hand, she sailed from the room.

"Gregory, wait," his sister said before he could follow. "I wasn't the only one unpleasant to her. You said she and Mother made up. Did Mother apologize for accusing her of trying to ensnare you?"

Was there no end to the surprises this afternoon? "Mother accused her of what?"

"Trying to marry you. You aren't considering marrying her, are you, Gregory? I don't think the family would ever survive the scandal."

Him, married to Yvette. The image was all too easy to imagine. Discussing politics, opportunities. Working together in the greenhouse. Walking among the woods. Taking her in his arms and...

"You have your own wedding to plan," Gregory said, cheeks heating. "Let's focus on that for now." He excused himself and hurried after Yvette.

He caught up with her at the foot of the great stairs. "I

wanted to thank you for what you did just now. I can't imagine how you managed to convince them both to apologize."

Her blue eyes sparkled with laughter. "They wished to apologize. They just needed the excuse. Now, we must encourage them to continue to reform."

"How?" Gregory asked. "I've been trying for years."

She wiggled her mouth. "I will think. Will you work in the greenhouse later?"

"After everyone has retired for the evening, yes."

"*Bon.* I will meet you there, and we will strategize."

CHAPTER NINETEEN

Yvette was satisfied with her performance as she slipped out of the house that night. The countess had come down to dinner and stayed to play whist in the withdrawing room afterward. Lilith had been pleasant all around, even with her love off to London. There had been laughter, camaraderie. And Gregory had gazed at Yvette often as if he couldn't believe the changes she'd wrought. It felt good to be part of a family again.

She stopped in the middle of the lawn, moonlight brightening the path toward the greenhouse and a cool spring breeze brushing her cheeks. A family? Lady Carrolton, Lilith, and Gregory weren't her family. She was only playing a part and not for much longer. When Claude had been captured, she would leave Carrolton Park and her demanding, mercurial, amusing countess; the worrisome, wistful Lilith; and the kind, gentle giant of an earl, a man who tended his plants as lovingly as her father had tended his paintings. She would miss him most of all.

Funny. Before she had come to Carrolton Park, she had been plagued with bouts of melancholy. Here they came rarely, if at all. Here she had a purpose, a place. Here she felt safe.

But not at the moment. She heard the crunch of gravel behind her, felt the unwelcome presence. She threw herself to one side just as something hissed passed, flashing in the moonlight before it thudded into the ground. A dagger, much like the one she wore on her wrist.

Then she was up and running, skirts bunched in her fists. Footsteps echoed behind her. If she shouted, Marbury and the footman would come, and her cousin would escape again. Her best chance was to flee to the greenhouse and Gregory, hope Claude would follow. Surely Gregory would not let him get away.

She allowed the door to bang shut behind her, then darted in among the orange trees and crouched down to watch for her attacker. The lamps overhead made it easy to see the table with its little pots, the larger pots lining the walls. Where was Gregory?

The door eased open, and Claude entered. He wore rough clothing, as if he was no more than an itinerant worker, looking for his next position. His hair was still brown as it had been at the wedding. He must not have stopped to retrieve the dagger, for a longer blade gleamed in his grip.

"You cannot escape me, Yvette," he called in French. "Josephine and her friends can no longer shield you. You have betrayed France."

She said nothing, hunkering lower. Where was Gregory? Surely he had not left the lamps burning, or was that how the greenhouse worked? She had never bothered to look whether it remained bright inside when he wasn't working. Now the warmth sent sweat trickling down her back.

"Come out, little one," Claude crooned, moving deeper into the building. "I promise not to kill you. You will return home with me, to stand trial. Everyone must know your shame."

Stand trial, like her parents and brothers. She would be condemned as easily. She knew what waited at the end. Despite her determination, she was shaking.

She never saw him coming. Neither did Claude. One moment, her cousin was advancing along the table. The next he was grappling in the embrace of a man far taller and more muscular. The blade clattered as it hit the ground. Gregory grunted as her cousin must have lashed out, but he did not let go.

"Give up," he gritted out. "You will not escape this time."

Claude went slack in his grip, and, for a moment, Yvette thought they had won. But her limp-boned cousin merely slid to the ground, righted himself, and ran for the door. Gregory thundered after. Yvette ducked out of hiding, pulled up the blade, and followed.

She found Gregory at the edge of the yard in the moonlight, scanning the wall of darkness that was the wood.

"Get Marbury," he instructed. "Tell him to muster the footmen, the grooms, and the gardening staff." He started forward, and fear lanced her. She grabbed his arm with her free hand.

"Gregory, wait! You cannot go in there. He may have hidden a gun. He could have set up traps. I would not see you harmed."

"He threatened to return you to France," he countered. "My French may be rusty, but I understood that much. I won't allow it. This ends now."

Yvette clung to his arm, cold driving through her heart like an arrow. "*Non!* Let us find help first—more men, light, weapons. Anything else risks your life."

She felt him draw a breath. "Very well. I want you safely in the house, regardless."

He took the sword from her hand, turned, and escorted her back to the kitchen door, keeping himself positioned between her and the trees.

Mr. Marbury and Mrs. Clarke looked up in surprise as they entered.

"A man attempted to accost Miss French," Gregory informed the butler and the cook. "Gather every able-bodied man and lanterns, and open the armory. You have five minutes."

Marbury stood. "At once, my lord."

Mrs. Clarke clucked over Yvette, urging her to sit and have a cup of tea. Thanking her, Yvette turned to Gregory. "Let me go with you."

"No," he said. "My men know the area. And I will be more effective if I'm sure you are safe."

His logic was unassailable and utterly frustrating. At night, with no knowledge of the area, she would only be a liability. Claude must have been stalking the woods for days. Even he knew more than she did of the layout. She agreed to wait in the kitchen and watched as his staff hurried after him out the door.

Marbury and one footman stayed behind in case their quarry returned. Both were armed with pistols, though she thought Marbury's size and fierce demeanor at the moment might be enough to deter her cousin. The footman went to guard the front door. The butler locked the kitchen door behind the others, then closed the shutters on the windows, a pistol clutched in one hand.

"Most disturbing," he said, directing the cook and Yvette back to the table. "I assure you this is unusual, Miss French."

Mrs. Clarke hitched her apron up. "Never had such doings here at Carrolton Park. But you can be sure the earl won't stand for it. He takes care of his own. Unlike his father." She paled as Marbury frowned at her.

"You can retire, Mavis," he said. "I'll stand guard."

With a trusting nod, the cook bid them both good night and left.

"I don't stand for gossip," the butler told Yvette.

Yvette sat on the chair the cook had vacated. "Will you sit for it?"

That won a smile from him. "No. What's done is done. It's the present and future that should concern us." He affixed her with his best butler's look. "Is there some reason a gentleman would attempt to accost you, Miss French?"

Yvette spread her hands. "Why should there be? I am meek as a mouse."

"I seem to recall a story about a mouse subduing a lion," Marbury countered. "However, I will remind you that I can best do my duty to this household if I am kept informed."

Yvette nodded. The urge to confess was strong. Perhaps it was the craggy brow over deep-set eyes. Perhaps the fatherly smile that encouraged confidences. Yet Gregory hadn't seen fit to explain to the man. Should she?

A noise at the door saved her from a decision. Marbury raised the pistol at the portal. "Who's there?"

"Your master," came Gregory's voice, and Marbury rushed to open the door.

Gregory strode in as Yvette hopped to her feet. In his hands was a wool scarf, the sort men wore to stave off the cold.

"Do you recognize this?" he asked Yvette.

She shook her head. "I never saw him wear it, but it's possible he stole it, as part of his disguise."

"I'll take that chance." He turned for the door, and she darted in front of him.

"What will you do?"

His gaze was dark and determined. "Loose the hounds. They'll follow the scent."

"You have hounds?" She could not see him tormenting foxes or other small animals.

"My father had hounds," he corrected her. "I saw no need to turn the dogs out after he died."

He wouldn't.

She stood on tiptoe and pressed a kiss to his cheek. "Take care, *mon coeur.*"

His eyes were bright as he nodded and left.

Yvette turned to find Marbury frowning at her. She met his gaze.

"I am the daughter of a French count, who lost his life in the Revolution. I have been helping the British War

Office to uncover secrets in France that could end this war. When my French comrades discovered my betrayal, they incarcerated me. Sir Harold Orwell and Mr. Mayes rescued me, but the French vowed revenge. Lord Carrolton offered to assist the War Office by hiding me here. I have been discovered."

"I see," he said. Then he offered her a bow. "How might I be of assistance, your ladyship?"

It was a long, fruitless night. The hounds nearly ran the Frenchman to ground, but the trail ended at a stream. Try as they might, the dogs could not pick up the scent again upstream or down. Claude de Maupassant could be anywhere.

But not at the house. Gregory made sure of that as he and his staff returned. After assuring Yvette she was safe, he joined his men in searching each room, locking those that could be locked behind him. He checked each window on the ground floor and stationed a man at every entrance. He had never designed the house as a fortress, but he was rather pleased how well it served that purpose now.

Marbury put his finger to his lips as Gregory entered the kitchen. Yvette had her head on the work table, cushioned on her arms, tousled curls gleaming in the lamplight. The butler motioned Gregory back into the corridor.

"She couldn't stay awake another moment," he said with a proud smile. "But I must protest my lord. It is unseemly for the daughter of the French aristocracy to live in this house as a servant."

Gregory sagged. "She told you."

"Reluctantly," Marbury admitted. "I understand the need for secrecy, my lord, but surely now Lady Carrolton and Lady Lilith must be told, for their own protection."

"Of course," Gregory agreed. "If they are aware, they can

be vigilant. A shame Mr. Villers has already taken himself off or he could be of use."

"Is he part of this?" Marbury asked.

It seemed Gregory wasn't the only one who had a hard time seeing Villers as an intelligence agent once he was better acquainted with the fellow.

"He was stationed here by the War Office to protect the lady," Gregory told him, "for all the good it's done us. But then, I'm the one who sent him away."

"For good reason, I understand," Marbury said. "The staff offers your sister our congratulations on her upcoming marriage."

Entirely proper, but Gregory still thought he heard sarcasm under the polite tone.

"For now, we wait," Gregory said. "Try to get some rest. I'll take care of Yvette, and I'll speak to my mother and Lilith in the morning."

Marbury nodded and strode off, pistol still in one gloved hand.

Gregory ventured into the kitchen. She looked so innocent, as unacquainted with danger as her parents must have intended before fate had taken them from her. Those curls whispered to him. He allowed himself the luxury of touching one. Such silk, such strength.

Yvette twitched in her sleep, and he drew back his hand. She straightened, blinking. "You have secured the house, then."

"Yes. I'm so sorry he escaped, Yvette."

She covered her mouth with one hand as she yawned. "That one has nine lives. Perhaps we should set Fortune after him."

He smiled imagining the little cat taking down her cunning cousin.

"We will catch him," she insisted as if trying to convince herself. "Next time, I will help."

He didn't want there to be a next time. He wanted her

safe, happy. He bent and scooped her up in his arms.

"What are you doing?" she demanded as he started out of the kitchen.

"Escorting you to your room." He navigated to the main stair. The footman at the door stared a moment before averting his gaze.

"An escort, he calls it." She swung her feet, flipping her skirts about her ankles. "Gentlemen who escort ladies this way are not received in fine houses. If your mother saw you, you would be in trouble."

"No trouble at all," he said, reaching the top of the stair. Indeed, he was surprised now nicely she fit against him. He strode down the corridor for her door. The latch baffled him for a moment. As if she knew, she laughed.

"Put me down, dear heart," she said. "You should go no further."

Dear heart. Though he knew it was the English version of what she had been calling him, the sound of it was sweeter. He set her on her feet, and she raised her gaze, eyes bright and smile soft. He couldn't stop himself. He lowered his head and kissed her.

Sensations bloomed inside him, around him—joy, delight, a desire for more. He wrapped his arms around her, held her close. He never wanted to let her go. This was why he'd been made so big and strong—to love and protect her all the days of his life.

He wanted to tell her. He wanted to shout it down the corridors, cry it from the roof. He was in love with Yvette de Maupassant, the beautiful, the strong, the wise, the clever.

But how did he tell a lady who needed no one that he needed her most of all?

CHAPTER TWENTY

She could not think, only feel, and what wondrous feelings! A joy she had nearly forgotten, a delight she could not recall. She clung to him, this man who had won her heart.

Yet how could she give a heart so tarnished? She was darkness to his light.

She pulled back. His tender look was nearly her undoing. "You will regret that."

Even now, color climbed into those firm cheeks. "I beg your pardon. I don't know what came over me."

Yvette reached out to touch his shoulder, trying to ignore the pain building inside her. "It was the excitement of the night, *mon ami*. Think nothing of it."

Across the corridor came the clang of a bell. For once she was glad of it. "I must go. Try to sleep before you start the day."

His smile was polite, but it said he doubted sleep was possible. She went to tend to the countess.

Lady Carrolton remained on her best behavior, which was just as well, as Yvette was not at her best. She had gone with little sleep before, but she thought her weariness this time had more to do with that kiss.

So sweet, so fiery—promising a future of love she had never dreamed possible. Was it possible? Could she have a husband, a home, a family again?

Not until her cousin was vanquished. Not until she closed that chapter of her life. Only then would she feel as if she could start anew.

She wanted to go out, keep searching, but she knew the danger and the futility. Claude had darted away. They would have to bide their time until he ventured closer again. She could only hope it would be soon. She wanted this over.

In the meantime, she escorted the countess to breakfast. No one else had come down yet, and she could only hope that meant Gregory was getting some much-deserved sleep. Marbury could not have slept much either, yet he remained his polished self as he stood beside the sideboard, awaiting their requests.

"We must speak with Lilith," the countess told Yvette as they waited for their plates to be brought from the kitchen. "We have much to plan. I want to go over that invitation list."

Again. Yvette tried not to sigh. "Are there not other things to do?"

"Of course! I've been waiting for years for Lilith to reach this day. I know exactly what must be done—items for her trousseau, the wedding ensemble, flowers, the wedding breakfast." She sniffed. "You can be sure we'll do better than those starchy pastries Wey served."

Yvette had enjoyed the sweets. "And if your daughter should sleep late this morning?"

The countess shook her head. "I'll simply begin making arrangements myself."

She saw a fight coming. "Perhaps we should think of other pastimes. What did you do before you retreated to your bed?"

She frowned as if thinking. "I held teas for the local aristocracy, arranged flowers for each of the rooms, and assisted in raising funds for the Society for the Literacy of the Young."

"*Bon*," Yvette said. "You can write to the society today and see how you can help now. We will consider tea in the future, but flowers we can arrange now." She glanced to Marbury, who nodded his understanding.

No one else joined them for breakfast. Yvette wasn't sure whether to be disappointed or relieved. She longed to see Gregory yet couldn't help wondering how he would react to her. That kiss would make it hard for her to remember her role, but his face would betray any feelings.

Lilith appeared when Yvette and the countess were ensconced in a small, cozy sitting room in the north wing. The Tapestry Room, Lady Carrolton called it. Woven scenes from Biblical stories were framed and hung like paintings from the high ceiling, and similar scenes graced the upholstery on the settee and chairs grouped around the hearth. Marbury had had the footmen deliver a profusion of blooms as well as various vases and shears, and Lady Carrolton was creating arrangements.

"You're working?" Lilith asked with a frown to Yvette, as if she should be the one clipping the flowers.

Her mother snipped the end off an amaryllis, the purple rich against the reds and tans of the tapestries around them. "I'm beautifying the house. It's a suitable role for a lady of breeding."

Lilith did not look convinced.

"Perhaps you should discuss flowers for the wedding," Yvette suggested, handing the countess another blossom.

"What a delightful idea." Lilith seated herself near her mother. "I was considering roses, but they are so common."

"Lilies, perhaps," her mother mused. "We seem to have a number of them. The gardener would know."

So would Lady Carrolton's son. Gregory would probably be delighted to deliver flowers for his sister's wedding.

As if summoned by her thoughts, he came through the doorway and paused. He must have deemed his tweed coat too battered from the previous day, for he wore the requisite navy coat and fawn trousers of a gentleman, his cravat elegantly tied at his throat. Her breath caught.

"It's good to see you up and engaged, Mother," he said, coming to join them and bending to press a kiss against her cheek. Though it was a fraternal act, Yvette couldn't help remembering another kiss, the feel of those lips against her own. She busied herself with the blossoms.

"We were discussing flowers for the wedding," Lilith told him as if to prove she was industrious too. "Mother thought lilies."

Gregory stuck out his lower lip as he straightened. Though he could only have slept for a few hours, Yvette detected no weariness on his face, no bags under his eyes.

"Lovely thought," he mused, "but they are difficult to keep more than a day or two. What about *Campanula*, Canterbury Bells? We could grow them in tubs and place them around the church."

As his mother and sister debated the possibilities, he bent closer to Yvette, breath brushing her ear. "With your permission, I'd like to take my mother and sister into our confidence."

She nodded, feeling his cheek against her curls. She was blushing as he straightened.

"Not Canterbury Bells, then," his mother decreed. "The vicar will want to use the tall silver vases your father donated. We must have something with long stems, Gregory."

He inclined his head. "I'll consider the matter. But I had another reason for seeking you. There is something you should know."

Lady Carrolton looked up, wide-eyed. "You're going to marry Miss French. I knew it."

Yvette held back a gasp, gaze rushing to his. His cheeks flamed.

"I am not so fortunate," he told his mother, gaze darting away from Yvette's.

Lilith rose slowly to her feet, paling. "You're going to

challenge Beau to a duel."

He frowned. "No, unless you tell me there's some reason I must defend your honor."

She sank back onto the chair. "No, of course not."

Yvette found her voice. "Perhaps we should let him speak." She gave him an encouraging nod.

His mother set down her shears as if to give him all her attention. Lilith looked up expectantly.

"A few weeks ago," he told them, "the War Office approached me for a secret mission."

Lady Carrolton brightened. "Secret?"

"Yes. I was told to shelter a French aristocrat who had been serving the British. Because of her help, her life was now in danger from a Frenchman bent on revenge."

"How thrilling," his mother said. "What became of her?"

Lilith was staring at Yvette. "You."

Her mother waved a hand. "Don't be ridiculous, Lilith."

Yvette smiled. "But she guessed correctly, your ladyship. My real name is Yvette de Maupassant, and my father was the *Compte* de Maupassant."

"Making her rank equal to Lilith's," Gregory informed them.

Lilith leaned back in her chair.

His mother smiled. "Excellent. A French lady as my companion. Very clever of you, Gregory."

She was taking it far better than Yvette had expected. Lilith, however, was not.

"Why are you telling us now?" she asked her brother, eyes narrowing.

Gregory squared his shoulders. "Because we have reason to believe the villain seeking Miss de Maupassant's life has discovered her."

"He's here?" Lady Carrolton demanded, look more eager than fearful.

"I'm afraid so," Gregory said. "But don't worry. I've taken precautions to protect the house."

Lilith sighed. "If only Beau were here. He'd protect us."

Did she think her brother lacking? Yvette bristled on his behalf. "Mr. Villers has not been as helpful as he should."

Lilith stiffened. "He knows?"

"He was sent here by the War Office to protect Miss de Maupassant," Gregory explained.

Her face fell. "So that's why you protested our betrothal. His courtship was all a ruse, to give him a reason for staying at Carrolton Park. I suppose I'll never see him again."

She could not watch Lilith suffer, despite her annoying behavior in the past. "*Non, non,*" Yvette assured her. "He wished to court you. In fact, at times, he forgot his true duty, so enamored was he of you."

Her lips trembled. "Truly?"

Gregory nodded. "Quite true. He'll be back any day with that marriage license, I have no doubt."

She clasped her hands together. "Oh, I can hardly wait! Mother, we must hurry our plans."

"Yes, yes," the countess said. "Miss de Maupassant, fetch me that list."

Gregory eyed his mother.

She frowned. "What? Am I to lose my companion merely because you brought her into the house under false pretenses?"

Now, that was the countess she knew. Yvette rose. "I will fetch the list. It is no trouble."

Gregory looked to the butler. "Marbury, if you'd be so kind."

She thought a smile hovered on the butler's mouth. "At once, my lord." He strode from the room.

Yvette turned to find Gregory watching her. His regard made her cheeks heat once more.

He had shared her secret with the others. Now, if only she could convince herself to share her secret love with him.

How lovely she was. The sparkle in her eyes, the bloom in her cheeks, the curve of her lips.

The way her lips felt against his.

Gregory tore his gaze away from Yvette to find Lilith regarding him thoughtfully. He shifted on his feet. "If we could get back to the matter at hand. I need you both to understand the situation. I have men protecting the house, but I cannot say the same for the rest of the estate. There's simply too much territory, too many hiding places. Mother, Lilith, it is imperative that you remain inside for the time being."

His mother nodded. Lilith did not look convinced.

"For how long?" she asked. "I must go to London to arrange for my trousseau."

He wasn't sure what that entailed, but he knew she could not go now. "Mr. Mayes is aware of Miss de Maupassant's identity and is seeking direction from the War Office. I expect him any day with further instructions. Depending on the answer, you could leave for London immediately afterward."

She nodded. "Very well."

His mother picked up her shears. "Might as well finish the flowers. We can then turn our attentions to wedding planning."

"And perhaps your charming son would find us some more interesting blooms," Yvette said with a smile.

He returned her smile. "*Mais oui.*"

She beamed at him.

Lilith rose. "Gregory, may I have a word with you? Excuse me a moment, Mother." She swept for the door as if assuming he would follow. With a frown, he did.

She led him down the corridor, through the entry hall, and to his study, looking both ways before closing the door behind him.

"Is there another state secret of which I should be aware?" Gregory teased as she hurried to the windows to draw the drapes as well. The sliver of light that remained stabbed past the tall bookcases to make a stripe on the polished wood floor. He went to stand in the glow, and she joined him.

"How do you know she's telling the truth?" she asked.

So that was the issue. Gregory straightened. "The request came from the War Office, not Miss de Maupassant."

"And she was their spy," his sister pointed out. "They would likely say anything to protect her. They could very well play on your sensibilities. Do you know whether she's truly descended from a count?"

Was she jealous Yvette was her equal after all? "What does it matter, Lilith? She served England well, and now we must prevent her from paying the price."

"At our expense?" She worried her hands before the black of her gown. "I have waited all my life to fall in love, to find a man who returns my love. I won't have him harmed because of some Frenchwoman."

"That is beneath you," Gregory informed her. "Yvette didn't wish herself in this position."

"Neither did I. Yet here we are."

Gregory sighed. "When Julian returns, I will request that Villers be excused from this duty. Will that resolve your concerns?"

"Some of them," she admitted. "But there is more, Gregory. Perhaps it is because I am in love that I notice the emotions in others. You care about her."

His friends, his family had remarked on his open face often enough for him to doubt it or try subterfuge now. He settled for a lesser truth. "She is under my protection."

Lilith shook her head. "No, it's more than that. You're falling in love with her."

Gregory raised his chin. "If I am, I doubt it is reciprocated."

"I don't."

Hope surged. Lilith must have seen it, for she sighed. "Careful, Gregory. You know nothing about her. Do you wish your children to have a French criminal for a mother?"

Anger poked at him. He fought it down. "If I am blessed with children, I would expect they have an intelligent, loving woman for a mother."

She had the good sense to drop her gaze. "I am only thinking of you. You saw how people reacted when the Duke of Wey married the governess."

"I saw how *you* reacted," Gregory countered. "Wey's friends stood by him. His Jane is smart, warm natured, and a loving mother to his daughters. They will do well together."

"Oh, Gregory," she said, starting for the door. "Always the romantic."

"What's that supposed to mean?" he asked, following her.

"It means you see you see only the best in people— Mother, me." She paused. "Father."

He cringed.

She stopped and put a hand on his arm. "Just don't idealize Yvette de Maupassant. She must have endured impossible horrors, and she risked her life for England. But that doesn't mean she'd make you a good countess."

She released him and left the room before he could tell her she was wrong. Yvette would make an excellent countess. She was resourceful, clever, able to soothe with word or gesture, able to inspire with a look. She was everything he could have asked for in a wife.

He just wasn't sure he had what it took to be a good husband.

CHAPTER TWENTY-ONE

Julian Mayes returned the next day. Meredith and Fortune came with him. Though Yvette wondered why the solicitor had taken so long to bring them word from London, she could only be relieved at the sight of her friend and the sweet little cat. Lilith remained cool to the employment agency owner, but Lady Carrolton unbent sufficiently to pet Fortune, who allowed the familiarity. The countess sneezed.

After Julian and Meredith had settled, they all regrouped in the golden withdrawing room, with Marbury on duty beside the door. Lilith seated herself next to her mother on the sofa. Yvette and Meredith took chairs across from them, while Gregory stood nearby, and Julian leaned against the marble hearth. With the door safely shut, Fortune could prowl around the furniture. She still took exception to the tall brass lampstands, circling them as if watching for their treachery.

Yvette wasn't sure what Julian and Gregory had been able to share in the only quick, private conversation they'd been afforded, but Julian glanced around at the assembled group now with a polite smile. The bruises Claude had given him at the duke's wedding had faded, and he looked his usual confident self in his bottle green coat and tan trousers.

"I take it you are concerned about Miss French's safety,"

he said.

Lady Carrolton sniffed. "Miss French. Was that ridiculous appellation your idea, sir? I would rather have known a lady was under my roof."

"Indeed, Mr. Mayes," Lilith said, nose in the air. "I think it highly presumptuous of the War Office to keep my mother and me in ignorance."

"It was for your own safety, I assure you," Julian replied with an elegant bow.

Always so smooth, that one. With his red-gold hair and winsome smile, he accomplished what Beau Villers so often failed to do, convince his audience of his intentions. Lady Carrolton relaxed, and Lilith suffered her nose to come down.

Meredith was not so easily swayed. She leaned forward, lavender skirts brushing the carpet. "And what of Miss de Maupassant's safety?"

"Yes, Julian," Gregory put in, his tone considerably less pleasant. "We had an attack the other night. Miss de Maupassant was fortunate to escape with her life."

As Meredith reached out and grasped Yvette's hand protectively, Julian straightened away from the hearth, eyes lighting. "He was seen? Have you captured him?"

"No," Gregory said, and Yvette could almost hear his teeth grinding.

"Not for lack of trying," she assured the solicitor. "Men searched far and wide, and his lordship called out the hounds. My cousin escaped."

"Your cousin?" Lilith asked. "We were told it was a Frenchman bent on revenge." She looked accusingly at Gregory.

He shifted on his feet. "Miss de Maupassant's cousin is that man. He is the same fellow we chased at the wedding."

Lilith started. "The pickpocket? But of course. He wasn't a pickpocket, was he?"

Yvette shook her head.

"Well," the countess said with a look to Yvette as if finding her of even more interest now.

"I'm sorry to hear he escaped us again," Julian said, "But I think you will be glad to hear my news. After much discussion, the War Office believes you would be safer in London, Miss de Maupassant. I have been given leave to escort you there."

Gregory stiffened, but Lilith nodded as she sat taller.

"Good," she said. "We'll be joining you in London in a few days regardless. I must be fitted for my wedding gown. Surely Mr. Villers will have told you we are engaged."

"I regret that I have not had the opportunity to speak with Mr. Villers recently," Julian said. "But I suppose, with Miss de Maupassant elsewhere, our quarry could care less what you do."

Lilith regarded him as if she wasn't sure whether that was a blessing or an insult, but his words sent a tremor through Yvette. He meant for her to be taken from the family?

Gregory was regarding him more fixedly. "What do you mean, elsewhere?"

Julian gave him a friendly nod. "You have done your duty, Carrolton, and right manfully too. Now it's our turn."

His eyes narrowed. "Who do you include in this group protecting her?"

Julian shook his head. "Alas, I am not at liberty to say, but rest assured they are fine examples of English gentlemen. The important thing, as I'm sure we all agree, is to keep our fair ladies safe." He aimed his gaze at each of the ladies in turn. Yvette wasn't the only one returning his look with malice.

"Butter sauce," Lady Carrolton declared. "You may think yourself clever, sir, but I see through you. You'd shove my companion into a forgotten corner of London, hold her there until her enemy discovers her, then capture him with no thought to her concerns or convenience. You, sir, are no gentleman." She thumped her cane on the floor for emphasis.

Yvette hid a smile, but Julian inclined his head. "You are entitled to your opinion, Lady Carrolton. However, I fear my orders are specific. Yvette de Maupassant will be coming with me."

Gregory stepped into the path to the doorway. "Care to wager on that?"

The solicitor gazed up at him with a frown. "I don't wager, and neither did you last time I heard."

"Good, because you'd lose in this instance. Miss de Maupassant will stay with us. If she must go to London, she will travel under our escort and stay in our townhouse."

Lady Carrolton clapped her hands. "Excellent. I'll have Ada start packing."

Yvette could not take her eyes off him. He stood tall, noble, determination and purpose written on his stubborn jaw. She rose and went to put a hand on his arm.

"But, my lord, you put your family at risk for me. You put yourself at risk."

His gaze met hers. "Would you ask me to do less?"

"I would," Lilith put in. "How can you ask Mother and me to share the danger, Gregory?"

"Oh, be silent, Lilith," the countess ordered. "We are not cowards, and Gregory and your beau will be there to protect us."

Gregory nodded.

Julian shook his head. "I cannot allow this."

Meredith spoke up. "You don't seem to have a choice. I don't suppose the War Office put the request in writing."

"Hardly," he drawled.

She smiled. "Then you have nothing to prove your case, and you are overruled. I trust you understand, Solicitor."

He shook his head with a chuckle. "Madam, you continue to astound me."

"My goal in life," she assured him. She turned to Gregory. "There is an alternative, however. Your townhouse is on

Clarendon Square, is it not, my lord?"

"It is," Gregory acknowledged.

"So is mine," she informed him. "Yvette could stay with me. Julian is already a known caller—his visits would go unremarked. And she would be close enough for you to keep an eye on her."

He didn't like it. Concern flickered across his face, and his arm tensed under hers. But Julian spoke first.

"Out of the question. You have no part in this."

"No part?" Meredith's smile was sweet, but Fortune stopped her prowling and scampered under the settee as if she heard the danger in it. "I suggested this assignment, if you recall. I accompanied Yvette here. She is my friend, and I will not abandon her."

Lady Carrolton rose and hobbled to Yvette's side. "Neither will I."

"You need not ask where I stand," Gregory said.

Julian glanced around at them all, then appealed to the one woman most likely to support him. "Lady Lilith, surely you can convince them to see reason."

She rose, all majestic grace in her mulberry-colored silk gown, dark head high. "I have never been able to convince my family of anything, Mr. Mayes." She glided over to stand by her mother. "However, as they clearly feel strongly about the matter, I will support them."

Yvette leaned around Gregory to stare at her. Lilith offered a smile.

"There you have it," Gregory said to his friend. "We all go to London, or we all stay here. Which would you prefer, Julian?"

Meredith waited. She could feel Julian's indecision. He had his orders, and from a high source by the sound of it. Yet how could he fail to admire his friend's loyalty and courage?

Make the right decision. Please!

Ever since they had become reacquainted, she'd feared his reaction when he learned she had inherited her money from Lady Winhaven. She had confessed all after the wedding, waited for his condemnation. Instead, he had lamented the fact that, had he known more of the case, he might have found her again sooner. His reaction had melted her heart.

Since returning to London, he had been even more attentive, calling daily, bringing her flowers, offering Fortune treats. She'd begun to hope. When he'd invited her to Carrolton Park to visit Yvette, she'd been happy to accommodate. But, once again, he seemed determined to put her friends in danger. Was everything he did so calculated? How could she be sure of him?

"Very well," he said now, jaw tight. "Come to London. But I cannot promise the War Office will agree to your plan."

"Let them try to take her," Lady Carrolton said, and Meredith pitied the fool who challenged her.

They all agreed to be ready in a day's time. Meredith scooped up Fortune to keep her out of everyone's way as they parted. The butler hurried off to alert the staff. Lady Lilith and her mother made for the stairs to begin packing. Lord Carrolton and Yvette had their heads together, requiring considerable bending on his part. Meredith couldn't help remembering how he'd shielded Yvette at Jane's wedding.

"A romance, do you think?" she murmured to Fortune.

Fortune's tail swished lazily from side to side as if she was considering the possibility.

As the earl raised his head, Julian beckoned him over. She didn't like the two of them in discussion. Who knew what daft plan they'd hatch next? She moved closer to Yvette.

"Have you any concerns about all this?" she asked.

"Many," Yvette told her, gaze on the men across the

NEVER ENVY AN EARL 207

room. "Will he be safe?"

Definitely a romance. The wistfulness in her eyes spoke as loudly as the worried tone of her question.

"Lord Carrolton strikes me as a man who can take care of himself," Meredith told her, holding Fortune close.

"*Non*," Yvette murmured. "He trusts too much, expects the best of people. And I have known the worst."

"You are an unlikely couple," Meredith acknowledged. "But I have seen successful matches with greater differences."

She shook her head. "*Non, non*, you mistake me. The earl has no feelings for me."

"Does he not? How inconvenient when you clearly have feelings for him."

"I admire him, nothing more," she insisted. She lowered her gaze to Fortune, who looked back unblinking, and put her hand on the cat's fur. "And how is my *chat mignon* today?"

"Your sweet little cat is as unconvinced as I am," Meredith said as Fortune closed her eyes and arched her neck to direct Yvette's touch to the top of her head.

"You are one to talk," Yvette retorted. "You left Foulness Manor and Harry's ill-fated house party in charity with Mr. Mayes. You do not appear as enamored now."

Meredith kept her gaze on Fortune. "Frankly, I don't know what to make of him. One moment he is all charm, the next all cunning."

"That is every man I have ever known," Yvette said, "except two: my father and the earl."

"I don't remember my father," Meredith said. "He died when I was a baby. Most of the gentlemen in my life have been disappointing. But the Duke of Wey proved intelligent."

Yvette smiled. "You say that because he married your Jane."

"Proving my point about his intelligence. And Sir Harry

has a certain dash. Patience clearly adores him."

Yvette's smile grew. "Do all your clients end up marrying into the families they serve?"

"So far, thanks to Fortune." Meredith looked at Yvette pointedly.

Yvette threw up her hands, startling the cat, who gazed at her with wounded dignity

"Do not look at me," Yvette told Fortune. "I do not intend to further your record."

"We'll see," Meredith said, and Yvette laughed.

The men broke up their conversation. The earl came to Yvette and requested a private word. As they stepped away, Julian took Yvette's place at Meredith's side. Fortune eyed him. He reached out his hand, and she drew back against Meredith.

"Vexed with me, are you?" he murmured, gaze on the cat. "What can I do to earn your approval?"

"Stop threatening our friends," Meredith said.

He glanced up. "The safety of England outweighs other concerns."

"What of loyalty, sir, compassion?" Meredith challenged. "Are you willing to sacrifice all you hold dear?"

"If it saves the lives of thousands," he argued.

Meredith raised her chin. "I cannot think of thousands. I am focused on one."

"As am I."

She met his gaze and nearly gasped at the tenderness in it. He reached out a hand again, fingers brushing her cheek.

"You are who I think about when I see England in danger," he murmured. "This war, these intrigues, mean nothing if you are harmed in the process. Am I not allowed to keep you safe?"

"Don't do this for me," Meredith murmured back. "I cannot be responsible for putting those I care about in danger."

"Yet you would ask me to put you in danger."

Why was it so hard to think when he touched her? She wanted to lean into him, allow his lips to meet hers, feel herself embraced, cherished. But too much was at stake.

"I would ask you to remember there are other people with hopes, dreams of a future. I would ask you to use all your cleverness and cunning to find a solution that keeps Yvette and Lord Carrolton, his mother and sister, and yes, even Beau Villers, safe while still safeguarding England."

"You ask a great deal." He lowered his hand, and she caught it with her free one.

"I ask that you think beyond yourself, Julian. I suspect that need to further one's own goals is what truly separated us in the first place."

"Perhaps on both sides."

She could not take umbrage at the thought. She had been so young, so idealistic, so sure she knew more than anyone else. She was wiser now.

"I am no longer that girl, nor you the young man I loved," she told him. "If you are honest in your pursuit of me, we must both do better this time."

He nodded. "Very well, madam. I will do all I can. I lost you once, Meredith. I don't intend to lose you again, even if I have to save every man, woman, child, and cat in England."

CHAPTER TWENTY-TWO

Gregory insisted on Yvette staying with him in London. She regarded him with shining eyes as if he'd done something noble. He could have told her the act was entirely self-serving. He'd go mad with worry if she were anywhere else.

As it was, he'd watched every wooded copse they'd passed on the way to the Hampton Court bridge over the Thames. What had possessed his forebears to plant so many trees? His beautiful estate held too many hiding places.

Likewise, he couldn't trust any of the conveyances they passed on the long road to London. What if Yvette's cousin had stolen one and used it to force them off the road? Of course, few were as large as his mother's traveling coach. Built for her comfort with heavy springs and plush seats and pulled by six horses, the great landau could move at a surprisingly quick pace. They left Carrolton Park early morning and were in London by late afternoon.

He glanced around as he ushered Yvette from the coach to the house. Clarendon Square was a newer establishment north of Hyde Park, with larger houses at either end and row houses flanking the sides and surrounding a park in the center. He'd thought the area neat, tidy, orderly when he'd purchased the property. Now he couldn't help noting the shadows under the trees in the park, the wrought-iron fences blocking off the stairs to the kitchens. In the back were higher stone fences hiding the sight of the alleyways to the mews. Why had he never realized how easily a fellow bent on mischief could sneak up on the place?

At least his home was compact enough that he could easily patrol it. His was one of the wider of the row houses, with two rooms front and back on three floors. Yvette would take the guest room on the chamber story, next to his mother, who was nettled with him.

"I still don't see why I had to leave my bell at home," she complained as she climbed the stairs, clutching the rosewood banister. "What if I need you?"

Yvette, at his side behind her, gazed up at the Adams's ceiling with its frescoed medallion in green and white. "This house is much smaller than Carrolton Park. You have only to call."

He didn't like the smile on his mother's face as they left her in her room.

Marbury, Ada, and their cook, Mrs. Clarke, had come up from home with them and soon had the remaining staff ready for service. Gregory made sure a footman would be on duty at the front and back door day and night. Julian had brought word that the War Office was supplying men to watch the house from the outside as well. Gregory might have been more comfortable if he actually saw them.

"What would be the point in having them visible, *mon cher*?" Yvette asked when she caught him looking out the window for the third time the evening they first arrived. "The War Office wishes to capture my cousin. If Claude thought I was surrounded and he had no chance, he would not pounce."

But capturing her cousin continued to prove difficult. Claude de Maupassant did not show his face the first two days they were in London, though it seemed to Gregory that everyone else appeared at his door, from acquaintances and friends to the new doctor his mother had apparently engaged, who scurried up the stairs as if fearing Gregory would accost him.

The first to visit were Miss Thorn and Fortune, arriving before the evening was out to make sure everything was to Yvette's liking. The lady allowed her pet to stroll through each room, from the Wedgewood blue withdrawing room to Gregory's wood-paneled study, from the cream and gold dining room a quarter of the size of the one at Carrolton Park to the pink and green guest room.

Just as at Carrolton Park, he had spared no expense in furnishing the rooms for his family's comfort. Unfortunately, no matter what he had done to decorate the spaces, the place always made him feel as if he'd wandered into a dollhouse. Nothing quite fit his frame.

Still, Fortune approved. She seemed to be smiling as she passed his mother's room, tail in the air. He wasn't sure why, but he breathed a little easier.

The next to visit were Gussie Orwell and Lydia Villers. They arrived frightfully early the next morning, according to his sister. Ada hadn't even finished dressing his mother for the day. Gregory, Yvette, and Lilith met them in the withdrawing room.

"News of our return certainly traveled quickly," Lilith commented as they seated themselves on the blue damask sofa and matching chairs near the carved wood hearth. They made a pretty picture, his sister in Pomona green, Yvette in a navy that brought out the blue of her eyes, the blond-haired Lydia in frilly white muslin that suited her buoyant personality, and the iron-haired Gussie in a sky-blue gown trimmed in white. Feeling a bit dowdy in his tweed coat, Gregory stationed himself between them and the gauze-draped windows and tried not to look out yet again.

"Beau told us the good news," Lydia explained with a ready smile. "I'm utterly delighted, Lilith. I couldn't wait to welcome you to the family."

Now, there was a woman with character. Lydia Villers

had been dangled as marriage bait by her brother for years without success, yet she could smile and be happy for his sister's upcoming nuptials. He couldn't help remembering Lilith's darker reaction when she'd learned Patience Ramsey was to wed.

His sister returned Lydia's smile more shyly now. "Thank you. I always wanted a sister. And I will do my duty. Once Beau and I are married, we must double our efforts to see you as happy."

Yvette raised her brows.

Lydia glanced at Gussie. "But I am happy."

Gussie nodded approval. "Not every woman needs to marry, Lady Lilith. Some of us get on quite well without a man in our lives."

Lilith's smile cooled. "Yes, spinsterhood becomes some women."

"Others enjoy daring adventure," Yvette put in, twinkle in her eyes, "and great scientific feats. Tell me, how comes the formulation?"

Trust Yvette to find a way to turn the conversation away from a controversial subject. Gregory listened with interest as Gussie explained the plants she had been using to create her healing balm. They had been debating the properties of eucalyptus when Marbury announced another visitor.

Gregory straightened as Charlotte Worthington glided into the room. She was as lovely as he had remembered, all elegance and grace. Her thick auburn hair was confined behind her head, but her grey eyes crinkled at the corners with her smile. His smile rose to meet it.

"Lady Lilith," she said, moving forward with a whisper of dove grey silk, "how lovely to see you again."

"Charlotte." Lilith reached out to take her hand and draw her closer.

"Miss Worthington," Gregory said with all propriety even though the lady had long ago given him leave to use her first name. "I believe you know Miss Orwell and Miss

Villers. This is Miss de Maupassant, who is visiting us while she is in England."

Yvette nodded. Gussie shifted to make room on the sofa, but Lydia popped to her feet.

"Where has the time gone?" she cried. "Come, Gussie. We have work waiting."

Charlotte spread her skirts to sit beside his sister. "Please don't leave on my account, Miss Villers. I don't hold a grudge."

Lydia paled but demurred, and Gussie stood with a frown to offer her goodbyes. Yvette frowned after them.

As soon as they were out the door, Lilith turned to her friend. "What grudge should you hold against Lydia Villers, Charlotte?"

Charlotte patted her hand. "Nothing that need concern you. I had a more important reason for visiting. I came to wish you happy. Worth saw Beauford Villers at White's. It seems you are to be wed."

Lilith acknowledged her congratulations with a happy smile, and the conversation turned to wedding plans. The two seemed to forget there was anyone else in the room. Trapped in her chair, Yvette offered Gregory a smile. She did not deserve to be ignored, yet he didn't like taking attention away from his sister. She had been left out of it often enough.

Charlotte realized the issue sooner. "But where are my manners?" she asked, turning to Yvette. "Forgive me, Miss de Maupassant. I haven't seen my friend for an age, but that's no excuse to monopolize the conversation."

"Miss de Maupassant is used to being ignored," Lilith said. "She recently served as Mother's companion."

There came the venom. Gregory nearly sighed aloud. Charlotte glanced between Yvette, who remained smiling, and Lilith, who was darkening, then focused on Yvette. "How interesting. I admire a woman who can make her own way in the world despite circumstances. I don't think I could work as a companion, alas. I'm much too opinionated."

Yvette inclined her head. "As am I. Ask Lady Carrolton. She did not know what to make of me. And poor Lady Lilith felt it necessary to be forever showing me my place."

Lilith dropped her gaze. "Habit. Please forgive me, Yvette."

Gregory blinked. Yvette's smile widened, and Charlotte looked insufferably pleased about the whole thing.

She requested that Gregory walk her to the door when the visit ended.

"I did not wish to spread gossip," she said, pausing in the entry hall with its black and white marble tiled floor, the space feeling cramped after his grand entry hall at Carrolton Park. "I am not the one who bears a grudge against Lydia Villers and her brother. She broke Worth's heart last year. He blames her. I blame him. I just thought you should know since you'll shortly have a Villers in the family."

Of their set, Frederick Worthington—Worth to friends and family—was the prickliest. Fiercely independent, with an artist's sensibilities and a scholar's intellect, he had devoted himself to the furtherance of chemical knowledge. Gregory could see him falling in love with such intensity that he frightened the lady away.

Still, Lydia Villers, with all her engaging energy, didn't seem the sort to run. Her brother would have counted her alliance with the wealthy and titled Worth a coup. Why refuse, if he had been ready to lay his heart at her feet? She hadn't discovered her interest in science yet, and he would likely have encouraged it if she had.

"Thank you for the warning," he told Charlotte now, taking her hand and bowing over it. As he straightened, he found her regarding him, head cocked. When he raised a brow, she laughed.

"Sorry. I was trying to imagine you courting Miss de

Maupassant."

He took a step back, bumping against the half-moon table under the gilt-framed mirror. "I am not courting Yvette de Maupassant."

She smiled. "Certainly not. Those looks flashing between the two of you were merely because Lilith and I were so boring. Come now, Carrolton. You and I have known each other since we were children. You were never good at dissembling."

He almost wished he was. Those grey eyes were too knowing.

"I greatly admire the lady and am honored by her friendship, as I am by yours," he told her.

"Very prettily said, sir. Have your way, then. But if you care about the lady, don't be a fool like Worth and convince yourself anything is more important." She straightened. "I hope shortly to be wishing you happy as well, Carrolton. Good day."

He saw her out, closing the door behind her. The walls were far too close. Perhaps he should buy the house next door, expand the space. Then there was the bill the Prime Minister had sent him to consider sponsoring. And would he require a new coat for Lilith's wedding? She would hardly allow him to escort her down the aisle in tweed.

He stopped the frantic circling of his mind, recognizing the cause. Charlotte was right. It was easy to think of a dozen things to fill his time, when what was most important to him was the lovely French lady sitting in the withdrawing room, yet far away.

Yvette smiled at another young lady who had come to congratulate Lady Lilith, allowing the conversation to wash over her. She had thought attending these visits would take her mind off the danger, but they were no help.

Lilith would say she was here to shop for a trousseau, and it would be large and expensive, and if Yvette had to listen to it again she would scream. Was this all English ladies did? Small wonder Lady Carrolton pretended the vapors.

Her former employer had had trouble rebounding from the rigors of travel and had spent the previous day abed. The physician had sequestered himself with her for a time, then reported to Marbury that she required undisturbed rest. It was almost as if they were back at Carrolton Park, for Yvette had helped Ada entertain her, reading and sharing news from Lilith's many visitors. At least the countess had recovered sufficiently today to go out calling herself.

Yvette had declined to accompany her. If she left the house, Gregory would insist on escorting her, and he had enough to do watching each visitor who came in the house as if he suspected her cousin was hiding behind the muslin skirts. He enjoyed the visits even less than she did. She knew, because sooner or later his gaze would go unfocused, and she was certain he was back in the greenhouse with his beloved plants.

She would have preferred to be there as well. Indeed, she was surprised how much she missed Carrolton Park. She had always preferred the city to the country, the excitement of Paris to the quiet of the Picardy countryside on the way to Calais. But she could not argue the peace of Gregory's wooded home.

Or the comfort of his company.

They had had little time for conversation since arriving. The size of the house meant that everyone was together far more often than usual. However, Lilith had retired early the previous night. With Marbury standing by the open door to the withdrawing room, Yvette and Gregory had talked long into the night. How delightful to listen to the stories of his time at school, the many friends he'd made, their antics, what he'd learned while traveling. Some of his friends she had met—Harry and Julian Mayes and the

Duke of Wey. Some she looked forward to meeting, like this Viscount Worthington with the beautiful, clever sister who looked at Gregory as if he should live in her pocket.

Non, non, she would not be jealous. He was not hers. He would never be until Claude was vanquished.

Now she forced herself to focus on the latest visitor, a Miss Pence. Dressed in a beribboned pelisse of serpentine satin, the pinched-nosed brunette had insisted on keeping her bonnet, as if she only intended to stay a moment instead of the half hour she had rattled on. The white wicker frame was festooned with large yellow silk flowers and a reddish-brown ribbon that teased her pale cheek.

Yvette leaned closer to Gregory and nodded toward the bonnet. "*Helianthus, non?*"

"Too small to be a sunflower," he murmured. "More likely *Bellis Perennis*, or at least someone's idea of what a daisy should be."

Lilith glanced their way with a frown. Her friend's look was equally quelling.

"We were admiring your bonnet," Yvette explained.

She inclined her head, setting the bright yellow flowers to bobbing. "Thank you. I thought the ribbons particularly fetching. The latest color, I'm told."

"I considered it for the sofa at Carrolton Park," Gregory said. "Dead salmon, I believe."

Yvette bit her lips as the lady's smile froze. "I beg your pardon?"

"The color," Gregory elaborated with all earnestness. "It's called dead salmon. It suits you very well."

Yvette burst out laughing. She regretted it immediately, for Gregory began to look a bit like a dead fish himself as Lilith's friend took herself off in a huff.

"Really, Gregory," his sister scolded him. "Have you no sensibilities?"

"It is my fault," Yvette intervened. "I should not have laughed."

"No, you should not," Lilith agreed, nose in the air. "Imagine naming a color dead salmon." Her nose came down, her lips twisted a moment, and then the sweetest giggle escaped. "Oh, Gregory. You couldn't have made that up. What was the designer thinking?"

Smiling, Gregory inclined his head. "I didn't make it up, but I should have considered how your friend might react. Forgive me, Lilith."

She waved a hand. "I suspect we'll have a few more of those moments while we're in London. Everyone wants to call on me. Too many considered me on the shelf, you see. Now that I'm to wed, I'm a seven-day wonder. There will only be more comments when I go shopping for fabric for a wedding gown."

"And not in dead salmon," Yvette suggested.

Lilith laughed again as she rose. "No, certainly not. Someone very clever taught me that I look better in more intense colors, regardless."

"Perhaps silver or white," Yvette suggested, rising as well. "In long lines to emphasize your height and grace."

Lilith took her hand and gave it a squeeze. "You must come with me. What would I do without your fashion sense?"

Gregory looked so pleased with the situation Yvette thought he might pop a button off his blue waistcoat.

"You are comfortable with me going shopping?" she asked him.

His smile turned determined. "Of course. I'll come with you."

She knew it was a risk, but she couldn't stop the feeling of relief at the idea of leaving the house.

They were coming out of the withdrawing room when Marbury appeared on the stair.

"Your ladyship, my lord, Miss de Maupassant," he said, dipping his head respectfully. "Lady Carrolton returned from her outing looking peaked. She is in her room and asking for you."

Yvette made a face. "We have neglected her. I will go."

"We'll all go," Lilith said with a look to Gregory.

He nodded and motioned them to proceed him up the stairs.

Ada was laying a compress on the countess' head as they entered the pretty blue room she used while in town. Lady Carrolton lay on the counterpane, fully dressed in one of her black gowns. A shame she hadn't done more to heed Yvette's advice. The dark fabric sapped the color from her cheeks, made her eyes look sunken.

"Is that my family?" she asked in a wheezy voice. "I didn't mean to interrupt. I was having a perfectly lovely coz with Lady Agnes when I simply couldn't keep my eyes open another minute. Where's my red case?"

Yvette moved closer. Though Ada had turned down the lamp, Lady Carrolton's pupils were tiny pinpricks, and sweat beaded her brow. A chill went through Yvette.

"Mother," Lilith scolded. "You promised to behave."

Yvette straightened and met their gazes. "It is no act this time. She is ill. Send for the physician."

CHAPTER TWENTY-THREE

Gregory paced the upstairs corridor. It was far from satisfactory, a mere ten paces from one side of the house to the other. He wanted to be at his mother's side, but Lilith had been adamant.

"We don't know whether she's contagious," his sister had said, pushing him out into the corridor. "You are the earl, Gregory. Your heir is a distant cousin who cares nothing for us. You cannot take ill and die."

"We will stay with your mother," Yvette had promised, face sagging with sorrow. "And I will come for you if there is any change."

It had been an hour, and she hadn't come out of the room.

He looked up as Marbury ascended the stairs, towing the new physician. Gregory had met and interviewed him after his first visit, finding him singularly self-effacing for a man of medicine. The fellow had a carefully trimmed beard and mustache, and his hair was the same shade of brown. Clutching his black valise, he peered at Gregory through thick-lensed glasses as Marbury brought him to the bedchamber door.

"Dr. Smythe, my lord."

Gregory nodded. "Doctor. I trust Marbury explained the situation?"

"Yes, my lord," he said, voice calm and quiet, with a hint

of an accent Gregory guessed was Scottish. The man had
been trained in the famed school in Edinburgh, according
to what he had told Gregory.

Gregory stepped aside to let them pass and followed
them to the door.

The physician paused before entering, glancing at
Gregory as if he suspected Gregory intended to come
with him. "If it pleases your lordship, I prefer to see the
patient alone."

"My sister will insist on being present," Gregory said.
"And I must insist on her attendance as well. Marbury, ask
Miss de Maupassant to come out."

The physician's smile of thanks looked far too bright in
the dim corridor.

Yvette came out shortly, and the physician hurried past
her into the room. Yvette's gaze was all for Gregory. She
grasped his hand and held it tight in both of hers. "Do not
fear. She is stronger than she pretends. She will fight this."

"But how did this happen?" Gregory asked, warmed by
her touch. "She seemed to be recovering."

Yvette shrugged. "Who can say? These diseases do as
they please, make this one sick and another not at all. We
will not let it take her."

He felt a smile coming. "Able to fight death, are you?"

She paled. "I could wish as much, for those I love."

He focused on their joined hands. Hers had always
looked so small in his. Yet her fingers had a strength to hold
him, to thrill him, to wipe away concerns, to celebrate joys.
He had debated whether she could care, whether he cared
enough. Now none of that mattered. His mother's illness
and his sister's worries about the line of succession drove
home the point. His life was finite. Why waste another
minute?

"Dare I hope you include me among those you love?"
he murmured.

"Oh, *mon coeur*." She reached up one hand to touch his

cheek, eyes misty. "You most of all. I did not believe there were men like you still on this earth—true and honest and loyal."

Those qualities were far from what he wanted her to feel for him. He snorted. "I sound like your pet."

She smiled. "My tame lion. Majestic as the King of Beasts."

He sighed, defeat creeping closer. "So, I am a beast."

Her hand fell. "You mistake me. I have nothing but admiration for you."

"Admiration is a start," he acknowledged. "But what if I want more?"

In answer, she stood on her tiptoes and kissed him.

Once more, the world collapsed into sensation, emotion. He pulled her close, answered her kiss with another. In her touch, he felt alive, the man he was meant to be.

At length she pulled back, and he released her. She stared up at him.

"What do you wish from me?" she whispered. "Ask it, and it is yours. I could refuse you nothing."

"In that case." Gregory went down on one knee, putting his head below hers. "Yvette de Maupassant, would you do me the honor of becoming my wife?"

Joy bubbled up inside her, and she bent to take his face in her hands and kiss him again. "*Oui, mon coeur. Mais oui. Je suis honoré.*"

"English, if you would?" he asked, gazing up at her with hope shining in his eyes. "I don't want to mistake you."

"Yes," she said, taking his hands to encourage him to rise. "Yes, yes, yes. Only kiss me again."

He was rather thoroughly obliging her when someone coughed.

Yvette broke away, but Gregory caught her and held her

against his side. Standing in the corridor was the footman and Beau Villers. The former was trying not to smile. The latter was staring dumbstruck.

"Villers," Gregory acknowledged as if it were every day he was caught kissing his mother's former companion. "I've been expecting you for several days."

Villers shook himself and sketched a bow. "I found myself in your neighborhood but never had an opportunity to present myself at a decent hour."

So, he must have been one of the men Lord Hastings had assigned to watch the house. The dark circles under his eyes attested to a few sleepless nights.

"I was hoping to speak to Lilith," he continued, glancing from Gregory to Yvette.

"She is with the countess," Yvette offered. "It seems Lady Carrolton is truly ill this time."

Villers made a sad face. "How tragic. Of course Lilith would wish to be at her side. I admire her devotion. But I must protest. What if she too should contract the disease? You cannot put her life in such danger, my lord."

Yvette peered closer. His color had fled; his shoulders had risen. For once, it seemed Beau Villers was more concerned about another than himself.

Just then the door opened, and Mr. Marbury stepped into the corridor. The footman hurried back to his post at the door as the butler joined Yvette, Gregory, and Villers.

"Dr. Smythe would like a word with you, my lord, in the sickroom," Mr. Marbury said. "I regret that he asked the invitation to be extended to family only."

"Then I will be admitted," Villers said. "My place is at my beloved's side."

Gregory gazed down at Yvette tenderly. "Yvette will be welcome as well. She has agreed to be my bride."

Villers gaped once more.

Marbury's smile appeared. "May I be the first of many to congratulate you. However, given the countess' illness, perhaps it would be wise for fewer people to be in attendance."

Yvette nudged Gregory. "It is my turn to wait. You will tell me all, I know."

He took her hand and kissed the back. "Everything. I'll return shortly." He frowned at Villers, who reluctantly stepped back.

Marbury escorted Gregory to the door.

"Married, eh?" Villers asked in the quiet. "I suppose I should congratulate you as well."

Yvette nodded, feeling as if the joy would explode out of her if she spoke. Gregory, Earl of Carrolton, wanted to marry her. She would be his partner, his wife, a countess. It was everything her parents had wanted for her, everything she had been taught to believe was hers.

Yet was it? She would be an English countess, bound to the land most in France considered the enemy. She would not be able to return, to fight Napoleon, to see her country restored to sanity. Was that truly what she wanted now? Where had her impetuous heart led her?

Inside his mother's room, Gregory inched closer to the bed. His mother's eyes were closed, her breath stuttering, the sound like a knife in his chest. Lilith clasped his arm and held it tight, eyes haunted.

"Villers is here," he murmured, and he thought he heard her catch her breath.

"A challenging case," Dr. Smythe mused, turning from the countess to eye Gregory. "But not without hope. I fear your mother requires immediate treatment, my lord. I have heard of a medicine, a tincture found to have miraculous results, but the ingredients may prove difficult to procure."

Gregory straightened. "I'll find them."

The doctor nodded. "I'll write a receipt then. Lady

Lilith, I suggest you accompany him. Women have a better affinity for such things."

An interesting supposition. Yvette would likely agree.

Yvette, who was going to marry him. He must have spouted a grin, for Lilith was staring at him as if he'd lost his mind.

She turned to the physician. "I would prefer to stay with my mother."

"Quite understandable," he said in his soothing voice. "But you can do her the most good by bringing her what she needs to survive."

Lilith paled.

"Has she a maid, a companion who could be trusted to watch over her?" he continued, glancing from Lilith to Gregory and back.

Gregory met Lilith's gaze. "Yvette."

She nodded. "Of course. I'll speak to her." She hurried out.

The physician shut his medical case as if there was nothing more he could do. The sound was final, cutting off hope. He looked up with a polite smile. "Would you have a room where I could mix the tincture? One with water on hand would be best."

"The kitchen, then," Gregory said.

"I will need to work uninterrupted," he advised, lifting the case. "Some of the ingredients lose their efficacy if not infused in a timely manner."

"I'll ask the servants to remain in their rooms until you've finished," Gregory told him.

"Excellent. Shall we?"

Yvette and Lilith entered then, and the physician strode out the door. Villers frowned at him as the fellow passed.

Gregory closed the distance between himself and Yvette. "Did Lilith explain?"

Yvette nodded. "I am to watch the countess while you procure medicine. Is there anything I can to do help her while we wait?"

Lilith shook her head. "The physician said she is beyond our help." She choked and bowed her head.

Gregory put an arm around his sister, and Yvette touched her hand.

"We will not fail her," Yvette murmured. "Go. She and I will be waiting when you return."

By the fierce way she looked to the bed, he could almost believe it.

He led Lilith from the room. Villers immediately enfolded her in his arms. "What can I do, beloved? How can I help?"

Lilith rested her head on his shoulder. "We must find ingredients to make a tincture that might cure her. Will you accompany us?"

"Of course, darling." Murmuring words of encouragement, he started for the stairs, Gregory right behind. At least the fellow was being helpful. Gregory would have expected him to run at the least sign of trouble. Maybe Yvette was right, and this marriage to Lilith would be the making of him.

Marbury met them at the front door. As the footman offered Lilith her bonnet, Marbury handed Gregory a list.

"The ingredients Dr. Smythe requested, my lord," he said. "I must say I haven't heard of half of them."

Gregory scanned down the list, and despair gathered closer. "Neither have I."

Villers released Lilith long enough to glance at the list as well.

"Is that Greek?" he asked with a frown.

"What are we to do?" Lilith murmured, face bunching.

Villers straightened. "Never fear, darling. These may look difficult to procure, but I know just who to ask to locate them. Come with me."

The room was silent after Gregory and Lilith left. Just as at Carrolton Park, a chair sat waiting for Yvette beside the bed. She would rather have paced, but the bed hangings could block her view of the countess. So, she sat on the chair and watched the ragged rise and fall of Lady Carrolton's chest.

"We have not always agreed, you and I," she murmured. "Our wills are too strong. So, I ask you now to rely on that will. Fight this!"

Lady Carrolton gasped in a long breath. Yvette leaned closer, but the lady's eyes remained closed.

"Can you hear me?"

She waited but saw no change. She leaned back.

"I will pretend you can. I am good at pretending. I pretended to support the New Order in France, pretended to serve my cousin, pretended I enjoyed the Emperor's company, and pretended I was your companion. A short while ago I agreed to marry your son. I cannot decide whether what I feel is real or whether I simply became caught up in the role."

Lady Carrolton sighed.

"I feel the same. He is a fine man, your son, despite his father. He is good and kind. Perhaps he would do better with an English rose than a French lily." She laughed. "See? He even has me thinking about flowers."

The silence pressed the laughter from her. She stood and went to the wash basin to wring out another compress. The physician had apparently told Lilith nothing would help, but kindness could not hurt.

She returned to the bed to find the countess watching her. The compress fell from her fingers, and she dropped to her knees beside the bed. "Lady Carrolton, do you know me?"

"Miss French," she murmured, eyes over bright. "I dreamed you were going to marry my son."

Yvette smiled at her. "And did this trouble you?"

"Yes," she said with some of her usual spirit.

Yvette's smile faded.

"He isn't good enough for you," the countess complained.

Yvette took her hand. "*Non, ma chère comtesse.* He is far too good. And you wouldn't like a French daughter-in-law."

"It is tolerable," she said. "Do you love him?"

She had not told him, had barely admitted it to herself, but the answer was easy. "Yes."

Lady Carrolton smiled. "Then welcome to the family, my dear."

The door opened behind her. Yvette turned to see the physician framed in the opening. He stepped inside and shut the door. She had never looked closely at him until now, but, even before he pulled off those ridiculous spectacles, she knew.

Cold washed over her. Releasing the countess' hand, she climbed to her feet. "Claude."

"Dr. Smythe," he corrected her, smiling as he moved closer. "Ah, I see our patient has not awakened. Pity."

Yvette glanced to the bed. Lady Carrolton's eyes were closed, her cheeks pale. Had Yvette been the one dreaming? Was that why the woman had given her blessing to the marriage, because Yvette wanted it so badly? Was this her answer as to whether she should marry Gregory?

Before she could marry him, she had to survive. She returned her gaze to her cousin. "Leave now, or I'll scream."

"Scream, then. No one will hear you. The earl, his sister, and her beau are racing about London looking for unicorns. The staff is in their rooms high above us. I have taken care of the butler."

Marbury! She moved closer. "If you have harmed him..."

He laughed. "You even fight for a servant? You embrace the Revolution's notion of equality more than I do." He sobered. "But that will not stop me from returning you to France to stand trial. A ship will stop tomorrow night near the home of your accomplice. We will meet it."

Yvette reached for her dagger, held it out in front of her. "*Mais non*, cousin. I will go nowhere with you."

"You will," he said. "Because you care for these English, that old lady on the bed. You always cared too much, for all you tried to hide it. But you will follow me now. I know why she is ill. Surrender, and I will leave a note on how to cure her. Kill me, and she dies too."

Her hand was shaking. She may never have truly been the countess' companion, but she could not see her harmed now. If there was a chance to save her, she must take it. Time enough once they were away from Gregory and his family to escape her cousin.

She handed her cousin the dagger and followed him from the room.

CHAPTER TWENTY-FOUR

"**O**f course we'll help," Gussie Orwell said when Gregory, Lilith, and Villers called at the Orwell townhouse not far from Clarendon Square.

"Whatever you need," Lydia promised with a comforting smile to Lilith as they all sat in the cozy withdrawing room.

Gregory drew in a breath. His muscles had been tight since the moment he'd heard of his mother's illness. Now he was glad to surrender the physician's list to the amateur apothecary.

Lydia crowded close on the camel-backed sofa to read the ingredients as Gussie's gaze scanned the page.

"Aconite," Gussie said. "Lady Agnes should have that. She swears by it for curing a headache. We can send someone to ask her."

"We might be able to find some bitter vetch growing in the hedgerows on the way to Kew Gardens," Lydia suggested.

Gussie nodded. "I have several of the other ingredients here in London. In large enough quantities, I believe."

Villers smiled. "I knew it. Thank you."

"You cannot know the hope you've given me," Lilith said, dabbing at her eyes with a handkerchief.

Lydia was frowning. As Gussie continued to study the list, the little blonde glanced up at Gregory.

"I don't understand. We've tried many of these ingredients

in Gussie's formulation and found them to be ineffective for any healing purpose. Under the wrong circumstances, some might be considered poisons."

"Poison?" Lilith gasped, hand going to her throat.

That made no sense. "Perhaps it's the combination," Gregory said, "or the portion of the plant used in the tincture."

"No," Lydia insisted. "Look." She took the paper from Gussie with one hand and pointed out the oddities with the other. "The acidity of the orange oil would counteract the nature of the hazelnut. I don't know what your physician intends to make, but I doubt it would have much effect against any illness."

Heat flushed up him. "Another charlatan!"

Gussie raised her head. "I beg your pardon!"

"Not you, Gussie," Lilith assured her. "Mother's physician in Chessington proved unreliable. We had higher hopes for this one, especially since this time Mother is truly ill."

"Is she?" Lydia asked.

"Now, see here, Lydia," her brother put in. "Just because you dabble in science doesn't mean you know anything about medicine. You aren't a physician."

"I never claimed to be," Lydia replied, her gentle smile turning harder. "But I've studied enough about plants and minerals with Gussie and by reading the scientific literature to know what they cure and what they don't." She turned to Lilith. "Can you describe your mother's symptoms?"

Lilith frowned at Gregory but went on to explain the situation, while Villers crossed his arms over his chest.

Gregory shifted in his seat. If chasing after all these ingredients was a useless gesture, he had to return to the house, find someone who could help his mother, if such a person existed.

"It very much sounds like an overdose of laudanum to me," Lydia said, her usual sunny smile returning. "I'd give her syrup of ipecac. I have some in my room. It's been useful as we experiment."

Gregory stared at her. Lilith and Villers were doing the same.

"Laudanum?" Gregory asked.

"Are you mad?" Lilith demanded. "My mother doesn't dose herself with the stuff."

Lydia's smile finally evaporated, but Gussie held up a hand. "She's right, Lady Lilith. The symptoms could well have been brought on by the sedative. You said your last physician was a charlatan. Could he have prescribed it without your knowledge?"

"It seems he prescribed a great many things," Gregory said. "I removed all such medications from her personally."

"Then perhaps a servant intent on revenge slipped it into her tea," Gussie suggested.

Gregory shook himself. "No. Our family has no enemies."

Lilith grabbed his arm. "Of course we do. The person who spread rumors about my reputation."

Villers started. "Now, darling, I doubt she would go so far."

Lilith stiffened. "*She?*" She glared at Lydia.

Villers's sister threw up her hands. "I most certainly never said a word about anything to anyone. I'm not even sure what you're talking about."

Villers shook his head. "It doesn't matter. Dearest, think. You have someone far deadlier interested in your house. The Frenchman after Miss de Maupassant."

Gussie and Lydia hopped to their feet. "Of course!" Gussie cried.

"It's exactly the sort of thing a French agent would try," Lydia agreed.

Lilith scowled at Gregory. "Does anyone not know this secret?"

Determination pushed him to his feet. "Ladies, thank you," he said with a nod in their direction. "Villers, stay here with Lilith. I must return home. Yvette is in danger."

Villers nodded, but Gussie started for the door, skirts flapping. "Don't be ridiculous. If Yvette is in danger, we intend to help. Cuddlestone!"

A well-dressed little man with a head ringed by a fringe of white hair scurried to answer. "I'll have your redingote down in a twinkle, madam. The carriage is being brought around. I only wish I'd thought to bring Sir Harry's sword from the manor. How else might I be of assistance?"

It seemed her butler listened at keyholes and was ready to serve. Gregory strode toward him. "Send word to Julian Mayes."

"Tell him to send as many men as possible," Villers added, standing at Lilith's side. "Trevithan and Laughton are on duty watching the house this morning, Carrolton. If you shout, they should come running."

"I don't understand," Lilith said. "Who are these men? Why are they watching our home?"

Villers put an arm around her waist. "I'll explain all, darling, but we must let your brother go."

"To do what?" Lilith begged.

Gregory glanced back at her. "I intend to capture Claude de Maupassant before he does any more harm."

They all urged him to wait for the carriage, but nothing could have kept him away from Yvette another minute. He galloped out the door, leaving the Orwell butler with his mouth hanging open. Gregory's legs ate up the pavement the short distance between the Orwell townhouse and his own. Ladies stared, and gentlemen dodged out of his way with cries of protest. Every moment he kept imagining the worst—his mother dead, Yvette taken beyond his reach to meet her own fate. She'd been alone so long, fighting the danger around her. How did she bear it? He could hardly think straight.

But he must, if he was to save her.

He paused on the front steps and shouted. "Trevithan, Laughton, if you can hear me, send for reinforcements."

He didn't wait for a response. He burst into the house.

And was struck by the awful silence.

"Marbury!"

No tall form moved to answer.

Gregory scaled the stairs. He had no sword or pistol in the house, had never felt the need. At least his fists would suffice. For once, he was glad for his size; it meant he might be able to keep her safe.

He ripped open the door to his mother's room and skittered to a stop. His mother was sitting on the edge of the bed, swaying and obviously trying to catch her breath. She aimed her glare at him.

"I told you I needed that bell. I've been shouting for hours it seems. Where is everyone? That villain took Yvette."

Fear stabbed at him, but he made himself move to her side. "Mother, you aren't well."

"I'm likely dying," she informed him. "But I refuse to stay abed. He's taking Yvette back to France to stand trial. You must stop him."

A sound in the corridor set them both turning. Marbury staggered into the room, one hand holding his head. "Forgive me, your ladyship. Someone struck me, and I only now woke to your calls. What's happened?"

"The Frenchman we've been expecting took Yvette," Gregory told him.

Marbury sucked in a breath.

"He played the physician, the despicable cur," his mother said. "I played dead." She cackled. "And I heard everything. There's to be a ship tomorrow night, at a cove near Foulness Manor. He's taking her to meet it."

He bent and kissed the top of her head. "Thank you, Mother."

Marbury took another step into the room, lowering his hand. Gregory could not like his pallor. "How can I help, my lord?"

"Tend to my mother," Gregory said. "We believe she's been dosed with laudanum. Miss Villers suggested syrup of ipecac."

His mother waved her hand. "The villain left a note saying something similar. I have any number of emetics about somewhere. We will contrive. Now, don't just stand there. Go rescue my future daughter-in-law."

Hours later, Yvette lay on the bench of a coach as it rattled its way out toward the coast. She'd tried to scream for help earlier, even attempted to hurl herself out of the coach. Now her hands and feet were tied, and her mouth gagged. Her cousin thought of everything.

"You never knew how to be a lady," he jeered across from her. Blood dripped from his nose where she'd slammed into it attempting to escape, and he muttered a curse as he sopped it up with his handkerchief.

She only wished he hadn't gagged her so she could tell him what she thought of him. Her anger must have flashed from her eyes, for he rounded on her.

"Don't look at me that way. This is your fault. You chose to leave my employ to work for the Emperor. You decided to feed information to the rapacious English. You brought this on yourself."

Perhaps all this was a consequence of her actions, but she could not regret her efforts. The information she had sent to England had routed armies, prevented more deaths at the guillotine. Her only regret was that Gregory would never know what had happened to her. He might guess that the physician was involved when he returned home and found the man gone as well. But he would not know where she had been taken or how to save her.

Worse, she had never told him she loved him.

Fool! She'd once counseled Patience Ramsey that life

was too uncertain to leave important things undone. What could be more important than telling the man she loved her feelings? Who would have thought she, who had been so fearless, would hesitate to take a risk on love?

"I hope you try escaping again," Claude said with a sniff to keep the blood from falling. "I promised myself I would return you to the Emperor, but you would save me some trouble if you break your neck falling from the coach."

He glanced at the door as if wondering whether he should throw her out himself, and she chilled. So long as she lived, there was a chance for escape, a chance for rescue. She could not let him take that from her. She made her eyes as soulful as possible, allowed her limbs to tremble, and gazed up at him with no evidence of her true feelings. Prayer was as easy as breathing. She counted off the seconds, hoping.

Her cousin laughed. "How frightened you look. Good. Give me no trouble, and you will live to see France. But once I have returned you to the Emperor, I make no promises for your future."

She could. Somehow, she would return to Gregory. She had to believe that.

A long night and day later, Gregory crouched in the darkness, the marsh grasses sighing around him. Dressed in dark clothing like him, Sir Harry Orwell reached out and tugged him lower. Gregory smiled in thanks, though he doubted his friend could see his expression in the fitful moonlight. He wasn't even sure he was in the right place. A cove near Foulness Manor, Harry's home in Essex, Gregory's mother had said. Thanks to Julian's quick response to Gregory's request, Lord Hastings's men were stationed in every cove within ten miles of Harry's ancestral pile. Claude de Maupassant could be heading for any of them.

Harry nudged his shoulder, and Gregory's gaze went out across the sand to the Channel waters beyond. Something flashed. A lantern, quickly hooded? Who did the sailor think would answer?

Harry rose and returned the sign with his own lantern, then sank back down.

"Ours, then?" Gregory murmured.

"Doubtful," Harry answered. "But most of the smugglers along the coast follow a similar pattern. I may have told him all was clear or called his mother a tortoise. Either should bring him ashore soon enough."

That was Harry—always the wit. His reputation for charm made many believe he was carrying on illicit affairs with any number of women. The rumors made excellent excuses for being out at night in the wrong places as he spied for England. His men were hidden about the cove now, standing vigil for a French spy who might never materialize.

Gregory shook the thought away. Somewhere tonight, Yvette would be rescued. The reverse was too much to contemplate.

His legs were cramping, his toes numb inside his boots, when he heard the crunch of wood on sand. A dark shape bobbed on the edge of the tide, shadows spilling from it to pull it higher.

He started to rise, and Harry tugged him down again.

"Wait," he whispered, voice no louder than the sigh of the grass.

He didn't want to wait. He wanted to act, to rush down the sand and seize a Frenchman, demanding that he be taken to Yvette's side. But they likely didn't know where Yvette was either. If they had put ashore for her cousin, they must wait too.

But not for long.

A call came from the hill to their right. Lit by the lantern he carried, a man descended, rope in the other hand. Behind him stumbled a figure, the rope disappearing into the hooded cloak. He'd tied the noose around her neck. If she fell, if he pushed her, she'd strangle before Gregory could reach her.

Anger shoved him to his feet, and this time not even Harry's iron grip could stop him. He hurled himself from their hiding place, barreled up the path, and slammed his fist into Claude de Maupassant's startled face. The lantern tumbled to the grass, and flames leaped up. With a cry, Claude rolled away.

As Harry's men converged on the boat and the man beside Gregory, he grasped the hooded figure in one hand and tore back the hood with the other. Eyes shadowed, Yvette stared at him over a gag. He was vaguely aware of shouts, shots below him as he pulled the sodden material away.

"Good evening, my lord," she said, voice raspy. "Thank you for coming for me and forgive me for putting you to such trouble. You were right. It is not easy to be a companion."

CHAPTER TWENTY-FIVE

Yvette sat in the elegant blue and white withdrawing room of Foulness Manor, a cup of tea cradled in both hands. If those hands shook a little, no one would blame her. It had been a close-run thing.

"Drink it," Patience said kindly on her chair across from the sofa, pink skirts arranged about her slender form. "And try to eat a little."

The tray on the table before Yvette was loaded with delicacies—smoked salmon, pickled asparagus, strawberry tarts. The lumpy bun was probably the cook's attempt at a French pastry.

"*Merci*," Yvette murmured. "It seems I was expected."

"The moment Lord Carrolton alerted Mr. Mayes that you had been taken, riders went out to inform Lord Hastings's network," the pretty blonde assured her. "You have many friends in England, Yvette."

So it seemed. She could scarcely credit it.

"We weren't certain we'd be fortunate enough to find you," Patience continued, shifting the tray a little closer to her, "but we wanted to be prepared. I know Gussie and Lydia wanted to be here when you were found. Harry advised them to stay in London."

Yvette nodded. She raised the cup to her mouth and took a sip. The warm liquid soothed her throat.

The noose. Her cousin. France.

She shuddered and set down the cup. "Where is Lord Carrolton?"

"Here," he said from the doorway. There was something solid, something strong and right about those broad shoulders in the tweed coat. He strode to her side and only paused a moment before seating himself on Gussie's fine sofa, which protested just a little.

"Your cousin is on his way to prison," he reported. "He confessed he came on his own after his man failed to bring you back the first time. Of course, he hadn't been satisfied since his men allowed you to escape with Harry and Julian. I gather they have been dealt with. No one else in France is aware you spied for us. He was ashamed to let them know until he had dealt with the problem. Your old friend Lord Trevithan has put it about that you decided to join friends in England after Empress Josephine left court. You are safe, Yvette."

She drew in a breath. "*C'est fini.*"

He smiled. "Yes, it's finished. When you are ready, we can go home."

Home.

Light pushed back darkness, hope crowded out fear, love leaped up so strong she nearly swayed with it.

"Harry had hoped Yvette might stay with us for a while," Patience ventured, warm brown gaze moving from Gregory to Yvette. "You would be most welcome."

"*Non,*" Yvette said, gaze on Gregory. "I must be where my heart lies." She glanced at Patience. "Would you leave us a moment, Patience? Lord Carrolton and I are betrothed, so there should be no impropriety."

Patience's golden brows rose, but she climbed to her feet and slipped from the room.

"Another secret to confess?" Gregory teased.

"*Non, mon coeur.* I suspect anyone looking at me must see the truth. But I wished you to hear it first." She set down the cup and took one of his hands—so large, so strong, so capable—and gazed into his open face.

"*Je t'aime*. I love you. You who cannot, will not, lie; who raises his hand only to rescue. You are everything I could have dreamed of in a husband. Thank you for showing me what love could mean."

Were those tears in his eyes? Only her earl would be so strong as to share them.

"And I love you. *Je t'aime*." The French, mangled a bit, was still the most beautiful sound she'd ever heard. "You are everything I ever dreamed of in a wife."

Yvette laughed through her own tears. "*Oui*, opinionated…"

"Intelligent."

"Stubborn."

"Determined."

"Manipulative."

"Dedicated to those she loves. You cannot fool me, Yvette. I see you for who you are."

She did not correct him, but she knew he was wrong. He saw not who she was, but who she might be, the woman she hoped to become.

"Then let us go home," Yvette said, "to Carrolton Park. We will ask the vicar to read the banns."

"Forget the banns," Gregory said. "We'll ride to London, obtain a special license, and be married before the week is out."

Yvette laughed again. "My lord, how impetuous! I love it. *Vien!*"

He pulled her up, held her close a moment, and kissed her. To think she had envied him, then pitied him his life. Now she would share it with him—in sickness and in health, in tragedy and triumph. She could imagine nothing finer.

She truly was coming home.

In London, Meredith looked up as her butler, Mr. Cowls, made his way into the room. The silver-haired fellow always moved with stately grace, even though he was well beyond retirement. She felt far less graceful at the moment. She hadn't been able to settle since Gussie had sent word that Yvette had been captured three days ago. Worry for her friend was bad enough, but she couldn't help worrying for Julian as well, as he had gone out with the others to rescue her.

Fortune must have sensed Meredith's agitation, for she prowled around the room as if hoping to pounce on a fat mouse. Not that Meredith's competent staff would have allowed rodents to take up residence.

"News?" Meredith demanded.

"Miss de Maupassant has been rescued and will shortly be marrying Lord Carrolton," Cowls intoned, gaze on the distance as if he were peering into a crystal ball like a gypsy fortune teller at Bartholomew Fair. "Mr. Mayes is on his way back to London."

She did not ask how he knew. Her butler had an uncanny way of learning the truth, about any number of people. His connections were more impeccable than the prince's. He was quite the asset to her profession.

Still, Meredith leaned back on the sofa, sending thanksgiving heavenward. "Wonderful."

"And Miss Villers is here to see you."

She straightened. Come to provide more details, perhaps? It was now common knowledge that Lydia's brother was marrying the earl's sister. Surely she would be among those to know what Yvette and Lord Carrolton planned.

"Show her in," Meredith said, sitting higher and arranging her lavender skirts.

Lydia dashed in with her usual enthusiasm, pink velvet spencer topping her frilly white muslin gown. Fortune scampered to meet her. She scooped up the cat before

Fortune could do more than wind around her ankles and crooned nonsense as she came to sit next to Meredith. When her fawning attention did not appear to be ending soon, Meredith cleared her throat.

Lydia glanced up with a smile. "Thank you for seeing me. I came on business."

Disappointment was swiftly replaced by interest. "Business?"

"Yes," she said, hand continuing to stroke Fortune's soft grey fur. "I wondered if you would be willing to take me on as a client. I have some money put aside from my work with Gussie."

Meredith waved a hand. "The house into which I place my clients pays my fee. But I thought you were happy with Gussie. What happened?"

She drew back from Fortune, who promptly slipped to the floor. As if she had to do something with her hands, Lydia knit her fingers together in her lap.

"Gussie is a dear," she said with a fond smile. "I might never have discovered the depth of my affection for scientific endeavors if she hadn't encouraged me. And I've learned so much from her. But she's done."

Meredith frowned. "Done? Do you mean she gave up?"

"No," Lydia said, smile broadening until it lit her green eyes. "When that French agent was pretending to be Lady Carrolton's physician, he made up a list of ingredients for a potion he claimed would heal. Lord Carrolton shared the list with us. Gussie later realized that one of the ingredients— Aloe vera—was what she needed for her formulation. She has complete faith in this latest batch. She sold the recipe to an apothecary who will be distributing the ointment in London. She is trying to determine her next goal. And I am left with no greater purpose than to wait."

"And you refuse to be patient?" Meredith asked. "It has only been a day or so."

Lydia shrugged. "I have had enough time with Gussie to

know that, whatever she decides to pursue next, it will be with full enthusiasm and determination."

Not unlike the woman sitting across from her. "You are well matched," Meredith pointed out.

Lydia spread her hands. "We are indeed. I should be content. I'm well paid by a conscientious employer to do nothing. I find I want more." She dropped her hands. "I want to make a difference, develop something of import to others. Surely this knowledge was meant to be shared more widely than for skin cream."

Fortune hopped back up onto the sofa, put her paws on Meredith's thigh, and gazed up at her.

"So, you think I should take this commission, then?" Meredith asked.

Fortune rubbed against her arm.

From the first time Lydia had met Fortune at a house party a few weeks ago, the girl had always accepted Meredith and Fortune's unusual relationship. It was one thing in her favor. She brightened now, as if knowing Meredith would be swayed by her pet's optimism.

"Very well," Meredith said, and Lydia clapped her hands with glee.

Meredith shook her head. "You may not be so eager when you hear what I have in mind. It won't be easy to find a position where a woman can use her scientific skills. Our leading scientists are still remarkably medieval in their attitudes in some areas."

Lydia nodded as she lowered her hands. "I know the challenge I present. But surely with your connections, you know someone."

"I do," Meredith said. "But taking on the work will require you to find an inner strength, to hold your head high through adversity to win the prize."

Lydia raised her head as if ready. "I will do what I must to persevere at my craft."

"Even if it means you must work for the man who

refused you?"

Lydia's eager smile and color faded. "Him?"

As Fortune leaped across the space and transferred her affections to Lydia's skirts instead, Meredith made her look stern. "You know his reputation, the regard to which he is held among the other scientists in the Royal Society. He has in the last year built a team of talented women to share his work, led by his sister Charlotte. I understand she's looking to add another member. I can think of nowhere better to place you."

Lydia hung her head. "He'll never agree. He despises me."

"But he needs someone with your skills to achieve his goals. We have an opportunity. We must seize it."

Meredith rose, reaching out to take Fortune up into her arms. "Never fear, Lydia. Fortune will have to approve of Lord Worthington before I allow you to work for him. Now, gather your composure. We'll begin the opening discussions today, and, by tomorrow, you will be on your way to your future with the viscount."

D^{ear} Reader

Thank you for choosing Yvette and Gregory's story. When Yvette appeared in Harry's withdrawing room in *Never Borrow a Baronet*, I knew I had to tell her story. Hers was a tragic beginning, but a happy ending. If you missed how Gregory's friend the Duke of Wey met his Jane, look for *Never Doubt a Duke*.

If you enjoyed this book, there are several things you could do now:

Sign up for a free email alert at **http://eepurl.com/ baqwVT** with exclusive bonus content so you'll be the first to know whenever a new book is out or on sale.

Post a review on a bookseller or reader site to help others find the book.

Discover my many other books on my website at **www. reginascott.com.**

Turn the page for a sneak peek of the fourth book in the Fortune's Brides series, *Never Vie for a Viscount*, in which Lydia Villers finds herself facing her greatest challenge— contributing to science while battling the doubts of the scientific elite, the women who are angling to marry her viscount employer, and the longings of her own heart, which say that she and the viscount might just make the perfect chemistry.

Blessings!

Regina Scott

Sneak Peek:
NEVER VIE FOR A VISCOUNT
Book 4 in the Fortune's Brides Series by Regina Scott

London, England, late April, 1812

A townhouse had never looked so daunting.

Lydia Villers stood on the pavement looking up at the four-story white row house situated on fashionable Clarendon Square. Her muslin dress had seemed light and airy when she'd donned it that morning; her pink velvet Spencer hardly needed for the warm day. Now she felt perspiration trickled down her back.

"It is the best situation for your goals," Meredith Thorn reminded her.

Lydia glanced at her companion. Oh, for an ounce of that confidence! Meredith, owner of the Fortune Employment Agency, always looked in complete control of herself. Perhaps it was the sleek black hair, so unlike Lydia's pale ringlets. Or the depth of her lavender eyes, the color so much more compelling than Lydia's misty green.

Or maybe it was the grey cat in her arms, gazing serenely at Lydia as if she didn't doubt Lydia was capable of winning over anyone who stood against her.

Lydia drew in a breath. Her family and friends had consistently commented on her sunny smile, her optimism and enthusiasm. She should not allow the fear of one man to dim her light.

"You're right," she told Meredith. "Let's go."

Meredith nodded in satisfaction. Her cat Fortune's tail swung like a cavalry flag as they moved forward.

A man answered their knock on the green-lacquered door, and Lydia could only marvel at his size in his sturdy brown coat and breeches. He took the card Meredith held out in one massive ungloved fist.

"We'd like to call on Miss Worthington, if you please," Meredith said. "We've come about a position."

His brown-eyed gaze traveling over Meredith and Lydia and lit on Fortune in Meredith's arms. A smile tilted up, making him seem approachable. "Come in and wait. I'll see if Miss Worthington is receiving."

Rather direct for a footman. As he ambled off, Meredith and Lydia stepped into the entry hall. It was not the most remarkable place, for all the work in this house had the chance to change her life. The painting of a ship in full sail still graced one of the light blue walls. Like it, she felt the wind pushing her to new horizons. The gilt-framed mirror and half-moon table still stood opposite, the reflection in the oval glass showing her a bit paler than usual, her eyes luminous. The only thing to give her pause was the gentleman's tall hat and ebony walking stick laying across the polished wood surface. She swallowed.

She would not be working for him. Not directly. She had to remember that. If she never saw Frederick, Viscount Worthington, again, it would be too soon.

The footman returned and tipped his head to the corridor on the right of the stairs. "This way, if you please."

She knew the layout of the house. He was no doubt taking them to the withdrawing room at the back. It was a pleasant space, done in shades of rose and blue, with a settee in front of the wood-wrapped hearth and a few chairs scattered about. The Worthingtons entertained rarely. Far too busy with more important matters.

Charlotte Worthington was sitting at the walnut secretary along one silk-draped wall when they entered. Setting down her quill, she smiled at them. Lydia had always admired her. Like Meredith, she was cool, confident. She tended to speak her mind, even if she knew how to coat vinegar with honey. Only her auburn hair, coiled up in a bun at the back of her head with tendrils escaping along her sculpted cheeks, was at odds with her polished demeanor.

"That will be all, Bruiser," she said.

Bruiser? The footman didn't show any signs of resenting the rough name. He nodded and withdrew, leaving the door open behind him. Charlotte rose and swept toward them, grey lustring gown glinting in the sunlight coming through one velvet-draped window. Fortune sat taller in Meredith's arms as if ready to welcome her.

"Miss Thorn," she acknowledged. "And Miss Villers. What an unexpected pleasure."

Another time, in another situation, it might have been a pleasure to see Charlotte again. She'd been polite, even friendly, the one other time they had met since Lydia had returned from her sojourn in Essex. Why? Charlotte's brother could have made no good report of Lydia. He'd been the one to sever all acquaintance, as if she'd developed some dread disease.

She shook off the thought and dipped a curtsey. "Miss Worthington. Thank you for receiving us."

"Of course. I want you to know you are always welcome in this house."

She was? Straightening, she gazed at Charlotte in wonder, but those deep grey eyes did not suggest a lie. Still, Lydia could not embrace that truth.

"Please, have a seat," Charlotte said, going to sit on the settee. "Would your pet like a cushion?"

Meredith drew a hand along Fortune's back. "Fortune prefers to stay with me. But I appreciate the offer." She sat on the closest chair and nodded Lydia into another nearby. "I won't take much of your time. I understand you're looking to add a member to your team."

Charlotte glanced between the two of them as if she wasn't sure who was being offered. "I had just begun making inquiries. Did you know of someone?"

Meredith glanced at Lydia.

"Yes," Lydia said, pausing to take a deep breath. "Me."

Charlotte's russet brows rose. "I wasn't aware you were interested in scientific pursuits, Miss Villers."

Few knew. She'd always loved learning about discoveries. When she was little, she used to sit on her father's knee in his study as he read aloud from *Philosophical Transactions*, the journal of the Royal Society. After he'd died, she'd made sure the subscription continued, devouring the latest advances in science, medicine, and technology. How thrilling to read how scientists like Sir Humphry Davy, Sir Nicholas Rotherford, and William Herschel were pushing back the boundaries of chemistry, peering into the recesses of space. She'd begged her brother to take her to one of the Thursday lectures of the learned society, but he'd been appalled by the very suggestion.

"Never speak of this unseemly fascination outside this house," Beau had ordered, glaring down his long nose at her. "They'll think you a bluestocking."

A bluestocking. A far too educated woman. The term conjured up spinsters gathered over tea, clucking like hens, dreams of husband and family supplanted by second-hand accounts of scientific pursuits. That wasn't her. She was destined to marry well. Beau had promised her parents before they'd died that he'd make sure of it.

And so she'd tried. She'd danced and flirted, played the piano at far too many musicales, endured dozens of drives through the park. At Beau's insistence, she'd shoved herself at every titled gentleman on the *ton*. Several had shown interest. She knew how to dress and bat her lashes and appear suitably winsome, after all. She knew how to play the game, appear more interested in the color of their waistcoat than their discussions of politics and advancements. But no matter how much she flattered their consequences, none had felt compelled to offer.

Even the one she'd prayed would offer.

Now she squared her shoulders. "I am very interested in scientific pursuits, Miss Worthington. I've spent the last six weeks working closely with Augusta Orwell as she developed a formulation to heal skin conditions. I understand the properties of various substances—animal, plant, and mineral. I am fluent in the actions of various change agents like heat, light, water, and air."

"Miss Orwell would be delighted to provide a reference," Meredith put in.

Charlotte leaned back, gaze uncompromising. "We work long hours. There's little time to socialize."

Lydia smiled. "Excellent. I no longer need to socialize."

"So you are off the marriage mart?" Charlotte challenged.

That was the one question she was thoroughly confident in answering. "Absolutely. I plan to devote myself to the furtherance of science."

"Hogwash."

The male voice behind her sent a shiver from her, and her breath left with her confidence. Her head swiveled of its own volition. Hair as smoldering as his sister's, cut long enough to brush the collar of his coat. Eyes as grey but brighter, suggesting a spark of starlight within. Today he was dressed in a simply navy coat and fawn trousers.

Beau would have known the name for that fold in his cravat. The Mathematical? How suitable. Anyone looking at that slender physique, that high head, would think him no different than any other gentleman on the *ton*.

She knew better. She could not move, could not speak, as the viscount she'd once vied for moved into the room.

Frederick, Viscount Worthington—Worth to his friends and family—stared at the vision of loveliness seated on the chair across from his sister. That silky blond hair, those big green eyes, the curls outlined by her fashionable gown. Lydia Villers, in his home? He'd never thought to see it again.

But he couldn't believe the preposterous story any more than he'd believed she'd actually cared for him, not after he'd learned the truth about her.

"Worth," Charlotte said, an exasperated tone creeping into her voice. "I hadn't realized you were home. This is Miss Thorn, of the Fortune Employment Agency."

The other woman, a regal female with a stylish lavender-colored gown and raven hair, swiveled to meet his look. He inclined his head in greeting, and his gaze lit on the grey cat in her lap. A handsome creature. The blaze of white down its chest made it look as if it was wearing a cravat. He couldn't help his smile.

"Miss Thorn, a pleasure," he said. "And I'm delighted to meet your companion as well."

"Surely you remember Miss Villers," Charlotte chided.

"Of course I remember Miss Villers," Worth said, refusing to look at the woman who had broken his heart a year ago.

"I believe your brother is referring to my other companion," Miss Thorn said with a smile. "This is Fortune, my lord. Fortune, meet Viscount Worthington."

He bowed, straightening to find the cat regarding him with interest in her copper-colored eyes. Miss Thorn relaxed her hold, and her pet dropped to the carpet and padded up to him to twine herself around his boots.

"She likes you." Lydia sounded shocked.

No more shocked than he'd been to hear her proclaim a love for science. But then, that was part of her charm—her unbridled enthusiasm for everything.

And everyone.

He'd let it sway him before, convinced himself what she felt was real, unique to him alone. He knew better now. People tended to let you down. Animals were different.

He squatted and put out his hand, allowing Fortune to sniff at his gloved fingers. She arched her back, inviting his touch, and Worth ran his hand gently along the fur. "I see that Fortune is a highly discriminating creature."

"She is," Miss Thorn agreed. "She approves of you almost as much as she approves of Miss Villers."

Perhaps not so discriminating then. Or perhaps Lydia had taken in the gentle creature as well. He straightened. "Nevertheless, I believe we are fully staffed at present."

Charlotte was frowning at him. "We need one more to achieve your timetable, and you know it. Miss Villers has been working with Augusta Orwell. She has experience."

"I find it hard to equate puttering in the stillroom with scientific experience," he said, trying to keep his voice gentle and look kind.

Lydia swept to her feet and turned to face him fully, and he took a step back from the intensity blazing from her eyes.

"Our work," she said, moving toward him, "may look simple to a man of your letters, Lord Worthington, but it is hardly puttering. We follow the scientific method laid down by Bacon. We observe that certain elements appear to affect healing. We hypothesize that a particular ingredient may be beneficial to that process."

With each step in the process she described, she advanced, and Worth retreated.

"We devise experiments to test its efficacy both alone and in combination with other ingredients. We measure response, attempt to replicate the experiment, and see if we gain similar results. We document our findings. Our work may never be published in *Philosophical Transactions*, but the formula we recently developed has been evaluated by other apothecaries and found to have merit. It will shortly be sold on the market to help others. Can you say the same of your work?"

His back was to the wall, literally and figuratively. His best application, the result of years of painstaking experimentation and documentation, had been stolen by a colleague who had claimed all credit. That's when he'd first learned the pain of betrayal, even if hers had hurt more.

"Perhaps my brother questions your dedication rather than your credentials," Charlotte said. Over Lydia's head, he could see that a smirk had replaced her frown. She was enjoying this, the brat!

"Six weeks is a short time to be involved in scientific pursuits," she qualified when he shot a glare in her direction.

Lydia drew herself up, until her pert nose was pointing at his chin and he could see deep into her eyes. "Six weeks laboring from breakfast until long past dinner. I'm not afraid of hard work, when it has a purpose."

Miss Thorn rose and came to collect her pet, who had retreated with Worth to the wall near the hearth. Fortune gazed up at him as if she expected him to make the right decision. Would that he knew what that decision should be.

Charlotte was right—their timetable was tight. He had promised the Prince Regent to have something for review by the end of May. He was so close! Another pair of hands, another mind focused on the task, might make all the difference. And if he accomplished what he'd set out to do, he'd be able to hold his head up among his peers again.

"Miss Villers has already made significant sacrifices to

pursue a career in the sciences," Miss Thorn said, bending to pick up her pet. "She has left her position in Society, defied her brother."

Interesting. Beauford Villers had been instrumental in introducing Worth to Lydia. He had always thought the fellow would be over the moon had his sister and Worth married. Did he still insist that she wed?

"Most women of our class face persecution when stepping away from traditional roles," Charlotte acknowledged. She knew. She had suffered unkind comments from Society's reining belles, slights from former friends. He was thankful she had chosen to remain at his side, help him achieve. There wasn't much he wouldn't do for his sister.

Except perhaps hire Lydia Villers.

"I don't care," Lydia said, chin in the air. "I was ill-suited to the traditional role. I don't miss it."

Now, that he could not believe. Everything about Lydia Villers—from the artful ringlets framing her piquant face to her frilly muslin gowns and normal exuberance—was designed to appeal to a gentleman seeking a bride. She had certainly appealed to him. He was more than a little chagrined to find she still did.

"So, what do you want?" he asked.

She beamed up at him, the sun coming out after a storm, lifting his spirits despite his reservations.

"I want to learn more—how things work, why they function as they do." Her voice rang with determination. "I want to expand the boundaries of knowledge, discover great things that help others." She flung out her arms as if she would embrace the world. "I want to cure disease, double the food supply, soar beyond the stars."

She dropped her hands. "Surely that's not too much to ask."

Not in the slightest. The same longings pushed him. How had she known the one thing that might sway him? Was he that obvious? Was this a trick?

He glanced to his sister, unable to speak.

As always, Charlotte knew his mind better than he did. She rose, serene in her grey gown.

"Well said, Miss Villers. I believe you will get on famously with the rest of the team. When can you start?"

Learn more at
www.reginascott.com/nevervieforaviscount.html

OTHER BOOKS BY REGINA SCOTT

FORTUNE'S BRIDES SERIES
Never Doubt a Duke
Never Borrow a Baronet

UNCOMMON COURTSHIPS SERIES
The Unflappable Miss Fairchild
The Incomparable Miss Compton
The Irredeemable Miss Renfield
The Unwilling Miss Watkin
An Uncommon Christmas

LADY EMILY CAPERS
Secrets and Sensibilities
Art and Artifice
Ballrooms and Blackmail
Eloquence and Espionage
Love and Larceny

MARVELOUS MUNROES SERIES
My True Love Gave to Me
Catch of the Season
The Marquis' Kiss
Sweeter Than Candy

SPY MATCHMAKER SERIES
The Husband Mission
The June Bride Conspiracy
The Heiress Objective

Perfection

And other books for Love Inspired Historical.

ABOUT THE AUTHOR

Regina Scott started writing novels in the third grade. Thankfully for literature as we know it, she didn't sell her first novel until she learned a bit more about writing. Since her first book was published, her stories have traveled the globe, with translations in many languages including Dutch, German, Italian, and Portuguese. She now has more than forty published works of warm, witty romance.

She would never claim to have Yvette de Maupassant's skill at subterfuge. Her face, like Gregory's, tends to be more open, and you know what she's thinking. She's just glad her critique partner and dear friend Kristy J. Manhattan helped her come up with the idea for Fortune's Brides. Kristy is an avid fan of cats, supporting spay and neuter clinics and pet rescue groups. If Fortune resembles any cat you know, credit Kristy.

Regina Scott and her husband of 30 years reside in the Puget Sound area of Washington State. She has dressed as a Regency dandy, driven four-in-hand, learned to fence, and sailed on a tall ship, all in the name of research, of course. Learn more about her at her website at *www.reginascott.com.*

CPSIA information can be obtained
at www.ICGtesting.com
Printed in the USA
LVHW041449110619
620864LV00003B/544/P